Alan Bleasdale was born in 1946 and, apart from three years in the Gilbert and Ellice Islands, has always lived in Liverpool. He is married with three children.

Since leaving teaching in 1975, he has written not only the *Scully* novels but also numerous stage and television plays, notably the award-winning *Boys From The Blackstuff*, *The Music Market*, *Having a Ball* and *It's a Madhouse*.

His spare time interests lie in his family, football and a deep lifelong personal study of melancholy and hypochondria.

Also by Alan Bleasdale

SCULLY
BOYS FROM THE BLACKSTUFF

Scully and Mooey

ALAN BLEASDALE

CORGI BOOKS

SCULLY AND MOOEY

A CORGI BOOK 0 552 12526 1

Originally published in Great Britain by
Hutchinson & Co. (Publishers) Ltd.
Under the title *Who's Been Sleeping in My Bed?*

PRINTING HISTORY
Hutchinson edition published 1977
Corgi revised edition published 1984
Corgi edition reprinted 1984

This book is set in 10/11 Century Schoolbook

Corgi Books are published by Transworld Publishers Ltd.,
Century House, 61-63 Uxbridge Road, Ealing, London W5 5SA

Made and printed in Great Britain by
Hunt Barnard Printing Ltd., Aylesbury, Bucks.

TO JULIA, TIMOTHY, TAMANA, JAMIE
AND MY MOTHER AND FATHER

With thanks to Caroline Smith,
Jim Walker, Al Glynn, Tony Smith,
Barbara McDonald, Robert Cooper,
Sylvia Clayton, Willy Russell,
Bill Morrison, Pete Gore, Al Shell,
Geoff Cathey, Barry Vincent,
John Gilbert, and Alan Hilton.
(A chapter each.)

The author acknowledges
assistance from the Arts Council of
Great Britain.

1

I had to put Hovis to bed in the end. There was no
one else to do it. Our Arthur was at the Cubs, Gran
had a promise, Henry was in the cockloft playing
with his train set, my Mam was painting her face
and my dad had slipped down the Boundary for
half a dozen quick ones before they went out. I
wouldn't mind if they were going to Alcoholics
Anonymous or something, but they were only
going down town on the ale.

After I'd told Hovis 'Goldilocks and the Three
Bears' and threatened him a couple of times, he
seemed to go asleep and I came downstairs. My
Mam had followed after my dad, but she'd left
thirty pence on the mantelpiece for me. That
wouldn't get much these days, no more than a bag
of chips, but it'd still be twenty pence more than
the rest of the gang'd have when I saw them, now
that their old fellers were on the Social Security. At
least mine had still kept his job painting and
decorating on the Corporation.

Longest my dad has ever kept in work by all
accounts, but he had to after what happened last
year when my Mam threw him out and almost got
a fancy feller for herself. He's only back on
probation now and there's no sign of that ending.
My Mam makes sure of that. One word out of place
and she's asking him if his bags are packed. She's
alright though, my Mam. She's dead fair, she's got
no favourites – she's rotten to the lot of us.

Things are a lot better than they were though. I
think our Vera and Tony leaving home made the
difference. I was glad to see the back of both of

7

them, I know that much, even though our Vera left little Hovis for my Mam to look after and Tony only moved next door. You've got to laugh at our Tony; it's the only way to treat him. Liverpool's answer to Burt Reynolds, according to him and all his stories. The way he used to talk, every woman he ever met was supposed to have dropped her drawers at the very sight of him and pleaded for it. And what does he end up marrying? Out of all the millions of ravers, which stunning sex maniac does he put in the pudding club? Mrs Barrett next door, a forty-five-year-old widow with a liking for Communion wine, young priests, and a quick leg over on the way home from the Labour Club.

I put my Wrangler jacket on and combed my hair in the mirror by the picture of the Virgin Mary. It was gone eight o'clock and the others should have been here by now but I hate staying in doing nothing, so I opened the door and went down the path, past our Tony's broken moped tangled in the privets. When I got to the gate I saw Father O'Connell coming out of the house opposite. Friday night, collection night for window cleaners, milk-men and priests. He still had his back turned blessing their front door so I shot up the road before he could shame me out of my chip money. Sod that.

Halfway up the road I met Mooey Morgan coming down to meet me, wearing his usual happy grin and his eldest brother's cast-offs. Mooey's slow at the best of times and even his clothing's five years behind the times, but he's not bothered. If his grandad died he'd be wearing spats by the end of the week. The whole Morgan family were behind the door when the brains were given out, but Mooey wasn't even in the house. Do anything for anyone though. Walk under a bus for tuppence.

Cash on delivery.

'Alright, Moo,' I said. 'You're lookin' happy with y'self.'

'I know I am,' he said. 'We had a smart time in school t'day.'

He goes to the Simple Simon school at the other side of the park and it's murder getting him to skive off 'cos they do nothing all day long except enjoy themselves. The way he goes on about the place it sounds like being at Butlins forty weeks a year.

'What did y'do today then?' I said. 'Another hard slog playin' rounders an' five-a-side?'

'We had slides,' he said.

'Jeezus! Slides! Wha' is it? An adventure playground?'

'An' talks,' he said. 'A man came an' told us what we were goin' t'do when we left school. He give us a little book each as well.'

Teach Yourself Brain Surgery?

'No.'

'Wha' are y'goin' t'do, anyway, Moo?' I said. 'Won't be long now f'both of us. Another term.'

'I know,' he said. 'A lot of me mates at school're goin' on the bins if there's anythin' goin'. The man told us, they take us on down there.'

'I wondered why we kept on gettin' our bin emptied in the entry.'

'I fancy that though, y'know. Our Marie used t'be friends with a binman. He told her people give y'cups of tea f'nothin' an' a quid t'move their old pianos an' that.'

'All the liftin' an' carryin' as well 'ey, Moo. Build y'muscles up real hard that will.'

'I know,' he said. 'I'll be like rock.'

We met the others at the corner of their road. There's only four of us in my gang now: me, Mooey and the two Dog brothers, Mad Dog and Snotty

9

Dog. Until just before Christmas there used to be Half A Dog as well, but they took him into hospital then to try and give him a nose 'cos he was born all wrong and he's never had one; just two holes above his top lip. Anyway, he hasn't come back yet but he keeps running away and writing home saying he's fed up with them 'cos they won't stop messing about with him. Someone said in school that they nearly had him fixed up once but the Araldite wouldn't work. As for his brothers, well, Snotty Dog's complaint is the opposite to Half A Dog's. He's got an enormous nose and it never stops running not even in the middle of summer. It runs that fast, when he's getting chased by the law, he always get caught, but his nose gets away. Mad Dog's another one who lives up to his name and all. His Mam puts him by the front door for the rent collector every Thursday and the postman's terrified of him. He's calmed down a lot lately, but if he ever gets in a temper he's been known to kick his kennel to pieces.

They're not much to pose about, my gang, but I mean, who wants competition? I'm not soft. When I'm with them, there's only one star and that's me. It's the same with tarts when you go to the Disco. There's always one cracking bit of stuff there and you can guarantee her mate'll be in mourning for her living bra.

'All right there, Scully,' Snotty Dog said.

'All right there, Scully, wha're we goin' t'do t'night then?' Mad Dog said, the same as he does every single sodding night.

'That's what I like about you, Mad Dog,' I said. 'Y'haven't got an original thought in the whole of y'head, have yer?'

'Er, wha'd'y'mean, like?'

'Well, y'know, y'can be depended upon.'

'Wha' for?' he said.

'T'say the same friggin' thing over an' over again.'

'Yeah, but wha' I want t'know is, wha're we going' t'do t'night?' he said.

'We could er go the pictures,' Mooey said. 'I like the pictures.'

He didn't need to tell us that. Without him Hollywood'd be bankrupt. He saw *Jaws* that many times the manager of the ABC gave him two goldfish in a bowl when it finished. Mind you, he still thinks *Gone With the Wind*'s an advert for Alka Seltzer.

''Ey,' Snotty Dog said, 'I went down town with our Maureen last week, t'see that film, y'know, thingy, the one about the girl what's got the devil in her.'

'Sounds like our Marie,' Mooey said.

'Nah, softarse, it's a real devil. Y'know, it had a fork in its hand an' it was covered in smoke an' it made a lot of dirty noises.'

'Er, er, it still sounds like our Marie.'

'*The Exorcist*?' I said.

'That's right,' Snotty Dog said. 'It was ace.'

'It's an old one that,' I said. 'Me Mam seen it years ago.'

'But it was still ace. This tart, the devil got into her body, y'know ...'

'Disguised as a corned beef butty?' I asked him.

'No, she was got at in her sleep, I think.'

'Just like me Mam of a Saturday night.'

'Are you listenin' or wha'?' he said.

'Go on, Snotty Dog,' I said as I yawned, 'the way y'tellin' it's real scary.'

'Well, anyway, this kid, she has t'do everythin' the Devil wants her t'do, 'cos y'see she was repossessed by him, like, an' there's this really horrible bit where she's havin' a canary fit an' her head twists right around on her neck!'

11

'Wha', honest?' Mooey said as he got hold of my shoulder with one hand and kept tight hold of his neck with the other.

'Yeah, I heard about that,' I said. 'It is supposed t'be a bit frightenin'.'

'A bit?' Snotty Dog said. 'Christ, y'not kiddin' it was. Our Maureen threw up all over her double-decker hamburger an' this girl next to her dived under her seat an' then started screamin' her head off.'

'W . . . wh . . . why 'ey?' Mooey said. 'Wa . . . was the devil down there?'

'Nah, Mooey, she'd just burnt her knees on a ciggie stump.'

'An' what did you do then 'ey, Snotty Dog?' I said. 'You wettin' y'self an' all were yer?'

'Who me? Get out, I'm used t'things like that. I just closed me eyes an' got hold of me St Christopher's medal.'

We walked up through the estate towards the village. When we got to the main road shops there was only the off licence at the side of the Boundary open. All the other shops had big steel shutters over the windows, and some of the owners keep them shutters on all day you know. It's like going into an underground grotto just to get a packet of Brillo pads.

'We haven't been in the off licence f'a bit,' Mad Dog said as we crossed the road.

'Oh aye, yeah, great,' I said. 'I'm gettin' all excited already. Just think, we could inspect her wide range of bottled stout an' flavoured crisps, not t'mention the added attraction of the teeth marks we'll get all over us from her alsatian. Not that she'll let me in anyway, the old boot.'

'Well, it's startin' t'rain.'

'We could stand on the alehouse steps.'

'It's last, that is, Scully. Wha'd'y'wanna stand

outside an alehouse for?' Mad Dog said.

'Wha' about last Friday night?' I said. 'Y'must have heard about that. Jimmy Davidson came right through the bar-room window.'

'Must have been in a hurry,' Snotty Dog said. 'Was a bus comin'?'

'Not only that, he was still sat on his stool with a pint in his hand.'

'Arr, it's still last,' Mad Dog said. 'It's not the same as it used t'be around here. We can't even go the sports centre any more thanks t'you, Scully.'

'Just because we were playin' table tennis with the billiard balls,' I said.

'An' er head tennis too,' Mooey said.

'Only you played head tennis, Mooey,' I said. 'When they took you t'Casualty nobody else tried it.'

'I'm fed up,' Mad Dog said. 'There's nothin' t'do an' there never is anymore.'

'Well, now we're here,' Snotty Dog said, 'how about goin' in f'a pint?'

'Y'wha'?' I said. '*You* go in the Boundary?'

'I'm sixteen. Next month.'

'Aye, an' four foot two. Wha're y'goin t'be when y'leave school, Snotty Dog? A hod-carrier f'Leggo?'

'Very funny, I don't think,' he said. 'Just 'cos you've put a few inches on lately.'

'Near a foot, pal,' I said. I had too, just like that, all of a sudden. Everyone kept asking me if there was someone dead in our family with me walking around with my trousers at half mast for weeks, but my Mam couldn't afford to buy new ones and no-one else's in our family fitted me, which isn't surprising 'cos they're all midgets in our house.

'How much money y'got anyway?' I asked.

We just had enough for four bottles of brown ale between us, so we sneaked into the snug. The others sat behind the juke box out of the way while

13

I went up to the bar. We'd have been alright and all if it hadn't have been for all the flamin' halves and pennies I had in my hand. The others must have robbed their money boxes to come out. I was still trying to get all the money on the counter when the manager came up behind me. Big feller with a buckled belt and a scar right around one side of his face from where he'd stopped a broken glass one night.

'Who're y'buyin' them for, sunbeam?' he said.

'My grandson's just arrived back from Australia,' I said. 'We're out celebratin' as a matter of fact. I haven't seen him for all of twenty years.'

'Is that a fact?' he said. 'Married young did yer?'

'Well, y'know how it is, guv'nor, bit hot in the pants I was when I was a lad. Not as much freedom as this younger generation's got t'day like, but y'know . . . Here y'are barman, er keep the change, be seein' yer, Boss.'

'I'll give y'a hand with the glasses,' the manager said. 'Don't want an old cock like you fallin' down an' injurin' y'self now, do we, 'ey?'

'No, it's alright,' I said, but he leant over and took the bottles in one hand and I had to go back to join my grandson, all the way over from Australia after such a long time.

'An' which one of you lads is lucky enough t'have this fine specimen of manhood f'a grandad?' he said, really enjoying himself.

'Wha'?' Mooey said.

'Alright, boys,' the manager said, 'get back t'play-school, the game's up.'

'Wha'd'y'mean,' Mad Dog said, 'we've just got our pay packets.'

'Where d'y'work then?'

'Fords, Halewood,' Snotty Dog said. 'I'm on the assembly line.'

'An' I work in the offices,' Mooey said, catching

on real quick. Even we had to laugh.

'Well, they must pay y' in one-pence pieces then,' the manager said. 'Go on, get out, the four of yis. Not old enough t'work, never mind drink.'

'I help our breadman of a Saturday,' Mooey said.

'Y've got no chance of comin' in here an' orderin' ale unless y'eighteen.'

'We are eighteen though,' I said and then I saw him look down at me and the line of his scar go all purply coloured, and I realized that the joke was over as far as he was concerned. 'Er, between us anyway.'

'Can't we have our money back?' Mad Dog said, gettin' ready to throw a King Kong.

'Go on, get out before I throw yer out.'

'That's not fair,' Mad Dog said as we pulled him through the doorway.

'I know it's not, lads,' the manager said. 'It's brown an' I'm goin' t'drink it as soon as y've gone.'

'*Fuckin' scarface!*' Mad Dog shouted at the top of his voice. When we were about two hundred yards down the road.

'We used t'have a good time y'know, Scull,' Snotty Dog said as we sat on a bench in the park, smoking my last ciggy. 'We did. It's just not the same around here anymore.'

'What did we do?' I said. 'Y'know, when we was havin' this good time y'keep on talkin' about.'

'Well, we used . . . we used t' . . . we played games, like. Y'know.'

'Knock an' run,' Mad Dog said. 'Thunder an' lightnin'.'

Thunder and lightning's a game where you throw a massive big brick on top of the corrugated roof of one of the prefabs and it sounds like thunder and you run like lightning. And all the prefabs around our way were knocked down when we were in the Juniors.

15

'Christ Almighty, Mad Dog,' I said, 'y'goin' back in history a bit aren't yer? I was in short trousers when we last played that. We must have done somethin' else in the last eight years.'

'Well, I don't know what it is, but I'm fed up.'

'So am I,' Snotty Dog said.

'So am I,' Mooey said, smiling at the lot of us.

'Course, I could have told them why they were fed up, but they wouldn't have believed me. I felt just like them too, and I knew at least part of what was wrong. We were growing up. Not kids anymore, but not nothing yet. Almost grown, all of us. Well, apart from Mooey, like. Wanking away and nothing to show for it except ruined undies, whatever we all claimed.

'Come on,' I said, 'we may as well go home.'

'Y'wha'? Go home?' Mad Dog said. 'We can't go home yet. It's only a quarter t'ten, they'll all take the mickey out of me in our house if we go home now.'

'Y'know what I want,' Snotty Dog said. 'I want adventure. That's what I want.'

'Yeah, like Mickey Brown,' Mooey said. 'He tried t'join the Foreign Legion in the Sahara desert.'

'That's right,' I said, 'an' give himself up to an ice-cream man on Llandudno beach. Heard them all talkin' in Welsh an' thought he'd made it.'

'It's nice, Llandudno,' Mooey said, 'but Rhyl's better.'

'There's adventure for yer, Snotty Dog,' I said. 'But the kind of adventure I want doesn't get any further than the bushes in Chinsley Woods.'

'I haven't been bird watchin' f'ages.' Mooey said.

'That's all Scully'll be doin' an' all,' Mad Dog said. 'Watchin'.'

'We'll see,' I said. 'Y'might be in f'a few surprises now I don't need stilts t'chat a bit of skirt up.'

'Hey, did y'see Josie McKenna's tits in school

16

this morning'?' asked Snotty Dog, between sniffs and slobbers and a quick grab at his cock. 'Ugh, wha' a pair of tits they are.'

'It's a long long time since I've seen any tits,' Mooey said. 'Our cat ate the last one I seen.'

'I heard that when she does exercises in PE she can make them both swing separate ways,' gasped Snotty Dog, 'at the same time!'

'She fancies me y'know,' Mad Dog said. 'So the whisper goes anyway.'

'Fancy you?' I said. 'Josie McKenna? Y've gorra be kiddin'. She's goin' with that mechanic from Athertons Garage. Has been f'ages now. He's gorra car an' all.'

'That's all he will have as well,' Mad Dog said, spitting at the ground. 'The lucky get. Didn't fancy her anyway. Got breath like a postman's sock.'

'It'll all come to us when we get a job,' Snotty Dog said. 'Just you watch, this September, we'll pick them up then, no danger.'

'Where're you goin' t'get a job?'

'I'll get one,' he said. 'You see if I don't.'

'Let me know when y'do then,' I said. 'I'll borrow off you f'a change.'

'I think I will go home after all,' Mad Dog said. 'Anythin' 'd better than sittin' here listenin' t' you. Y'aren't half turnin' into a right misery hole, you are, Scully, I'm not kiddin'.'

'Even if there's nothin' goin' around here ...' Snotty Dog started.

'There won't be.'

'Well, even if there isn't, there's always jobs up in Scotland on the North Sea oil. Three hundred pounds a week, flat rate an' all.'

'Aye, if y'can dive.'

'I can dive,' Mooey said. 'Off the top board an' all. But I er can't swim yet.'

'That'd be the place,' Snotty Dog said, 'the baths

17

at the sports centre, if we weren't friggin' well banned. Pick a tart up easy there. An' y'get a free inspection of the goods an' all. I wouldn't go on the North Sea oil if I had a tart. There'd be somethin' t'do then, instead of just wanderin' around every night.'

We started off home as soon as it got dark, through the park gates past all the courting couples in the long grass where the tennis courts used to be, biting cobs out of each other's necks so they could pose about it in school, or at work the next day. Snotty Dog wanted to creep up and watch them at it, but I couldn't be bothered.

It was when we were going past the flats that it all started. We hadn't been near there for ages, and we were only pushing the lids off the bins, giving the cats a feed, when the caretaker of the flats came out at us.

'You four, go on clear off t'fuck out of it, I'm fed up with you lot comin' around here all the time causin' trouble, go on, gerrout of it,' he shouted as he came after us, his medals bouncing off his chest and his hat falling off his head. He ran us around the back of the flats and onto the waste land and we shouted 'Desert Rat' and 'Town Mouse' and things at him out of the dark till he got fed up and went in muttering about the Welfare State.

It was easy to get into the flats. All you had to do was go past the caretaker's window on your hands and knees and into the lift and we were away up to the fifteenth floor. It was a new block of flats and the lifts hadn't been set fire to. There weren't any names on the walls. I felt tempted to start them off but we don't do that anymore. 'It's not cool' as the niggers in school'd say. You can't get on a bus these days without the back seat being covered with 'Bootle Boot Boys Rule, OK' or 'The Clockwork Apple Murder Squad' or something like that,

18

and they're all done by little nine-year-old kids coming home from the Saturday matinée. I can remember when there was just my name all over our estate, 'Scully Rules, OK'. I was the first. That's good enough for me.

You could look all over the city from the fifteenth floor. Even guess where the river must be 'cos there was a line where there were no lights. Follow the cars down the roads into the estate, watch the gangs on the corners, the old women coming out of Bingo and running for the bus. You could see Speke airport all lit up low, and then a big pile of blackness in the distance where it's nothin' but countryside and where Wales starts, I expect.

The first door we knocked on, as soon as the light appeared in the hallway we nipped around the corner an' down a flight of stairs and tried again. We were on about the ninth floor before we finally knocked on a door and nothing happened. I looked through the letterbox but all the doors inside were shut and I couldn't see a thing.

'Wha'd'we do now?' Mad Dog said.

'I dunno,' I said. 'Get in the lift an' go home, as far as I can see.'

'But it's just gettin' excitin',' Snotty Dog said.

I felt inside the letterbox and almost wet myself on the doorstep when I pulled out the front-door key on a piece of string.

'Let's go home,' Snotty Dog said.

'But it's just gettin' excitin',' I said. 'Remember? An' anyway, you was the one what wanted adventure.'

'Well, it's, y'know, it's me probation, like,' he said. 'It's up next month. Be daft spoilin' it now. Er, tell y'wha', let's memorize the flat 'ey, an' come back then.'

I put the key in the lock and turned it and the door swung open. There was a smell of old clothes.

19

A crucifix on the wall.

'Come on,' I said, 'a quick bit of murder an' rape an' home f'the midnight movie. Wha'd'y'say 'ey, Snotty Dog?'

'Stop messin' about will yer, Scully, f'Jesus' sake.'

'Is that you, Mary?' a feller's voice shouted from behind one of the doors in the flat. 'You're home early.'

Mooey ran back up the stairs and the rest of us shot into the lift and pressed the button for the ground floor. Snotty Dog was so nervous he was running on the spot ready to shoot out of the lift at the bottom and leg it off home.

Only the lift never stopped at the bottom. Not quite anyway. Just as the floor of the lift came below the ceiling of the ground floor it came hissing to a stop, and there was this cackling laughter from down below us.

'Got you now, you little twats,' the caretaker shouted and hopped up and down like Rumpel-stiltskin. 'Trapped, that's what you are. Trapped!'

'I've just been t'me aunty's,' I said on me hands and knees. 'We've been playin' Monopoly all night, me an' these an' me Uncle Joey. I smashed them all.'

'"Go straight to jail, do not stop,"' he said and almost passed out with the fun of it all.

'I'll bring me Ma up t'you,' Mad Dog said, butting the lift door and then holding his head. 'You've had it then.'

'Don't bring her up t'me, sonny, bring her up to the police station. After all, that's where you lot're goin'.'

'Arrey, mister—'

'Arrey off, y'little bastard. The number of phone calls I've had from my residents in the last quarter of an hour, all about you four.'

'See,' I said, 'see, y've got it all wrong, there's only the three of us in here. I've solved it for yer, it wasn't us. Now press that button an' let us down, I'm frighterned of heights. The doctor won't even let me wear platform heels. Come on, please, I go all dizzy, honest.'

'I could have sworn...' he said, and then shuffled closer towards us. 'Are y'sure there's only three of yer in there?'

'Oh no,' Mad Dog said before I could stop him, 'me brother's small f'his age an' I carry him about in me pocket.'

'Don't give me cheek,' the caretaker said, taking two steps back, 'just don't give me cheek, or I'll have you up there all bleedin' night.'

'Y'won't,' I said, ''cos if y'do, me Mam'll be down t'every solicitor's in town t'morrow mornin'. You won't even get a job at Rent A Tent after all this, I'm tellin' yer. An' if I was t'have one of me blackouts now ...'

Another retreat, and he reached out for the controls to bring the lift down, and I thought to myself, 'Won again, Scully la',' but there was one thing I'd forgotten about completely. Something outside the control of man or beast. Mooey Morgan. Standing there by the emergency lift controls at the foot of the stairs, trying to work out what was going on.

'An' wha're you doin'?' the caretaker said as he started to bring the lift down.

'Oh, y'alright, don't worry about me, I'm with them,' Mooey said and the lift came to a stop again.

'An' what were you doin'?' Isaiah said to Mooey as we all sat in a row in the police station.

'I was with them,' Mooey said. 'I think.' He looked at us out of the corner of his eye. 'That's right, I recognize them.'

'I could throw the book at you f'this, y'know.'

'I can't read,' Mooey said, and we all carefully moved away from him and the danger of blood being spilt but Isaiah give up and turned instead to me. It would have to have been him that got called to the flats. Knows me well, Isaiah does. First time I ever got caught was by him. Stealing crab apples, six years old. The bastard made us sit there and eat them all. I was crapping little green ollies for about a fortnight after. He wasn't called Isaiah then though. He got that name on account of his face; you know, one eye's higher than the other. Ever since he got his face wrecked in a big fight with about two hundred Catholics on Orange Lodge Walking Day a couple of years ago. He wasn't on duty at the time. He was frigging well walking, the Protestant pig. Hates Catholics and all. Always raiding the Parish Club ten minutes after closing time to see if there's anyone having a stay behind. Father O'Connell's the only priest in Liverpool with a criminal record, 'cos the licence is made out in his name.

'An' what about you, Scully?' he said.

'I wasn't doin' nothin'.'

'You were in there with intent t'steal,' he said. 'A serious offence. An' with your record, a puttin' away offence, unless I'm very much mistaken.'

'Prove it,' I said and ducked, but not quite quick enough as he knocked me off the bench onto a wastepaper basket full of dog-ends and plastic coffee cups.

'I'll have you,' he said, 'all of y'. Good an' proper. Make no mistake. Your kind, y'all the same, seen one, y've seen them all. An' I have seen them all on this estate; whole families of them. I just have t'look into y'eyes, it's all there, that's where it is: trickery, lyin', deceit, slyness, plain thuggery an'

22

violence. Y'eyes tell me all that an' more. I can see y'future planned out right there. It's all ahead of yer, y'know, y'future, that's what it is—'

'Er, can y'read palms as well, mister?' Mooey said and got a quick clout across the ear.

'—An' I know as sure as I'm standin' here t'day, what lies ahead of you four; petty crimes, a little muggin', a few burglaries, Borstal, jail, in an' out of courtrooms an' prison yards all y'empty slimy little lives—'

'He's good, isn't he,' Mooey said to the rest of us, and we all winced and looked away. 'Just by lookin' in our eyes. Flippin' heck.' Isaiah was nose to nose with him, but Mooey thought he just wanted a closer look and opened his eyes wide. 'Can y'see anythin' else?' he said. 'A gypsy once told me Mam I was goin' t'be the next Prime—'

'You,' Isaiah said, prodding Mooey, spitting the words out all slow, 'you, your dad should have had his bollocks cut off at a very early age. Saved the State a lot of bother, he would.'

'That's not a very nice thing t'say,' Mooey said. 'My dad's got nothin' t'do with me.'

'An' I'll tell y'somethin' else f'free, softarse,' Isaiah carried on, 'if I ever so much as see yer in here again, I'll cut yours off f'you. Free of charge.' He got hold of Mooey by the armpits, up against the wall, two foot off the ground. 'D'y'hear?' He let go of him and turned to us three as Mooey slid slowly to the floor. 'Now all of you, I'm goin' t'let yer off with a warnin' this time, but just let me find you anywhere near trouble again, anywhere near, an' I'll run you in here so fast, y'feet won't touch the ground.'

We all moved towards the door at the same time, as fast as we could without actually doing a sprint start.

'An' where d'y'think you're goin'?' he said. 'Sit

23

down, I haven't finished with yis yet.' He looked at the clock above the desk and walked towards the door leading into the back room. 'Twenty-five t'eleven, just right, the alehouses'll be lettin' out, everyone'll see yer.'

'Two each,' he said when he came back, 'one between y'shoulder-blades an' the other on y'jacket fronts. Y'don't have t'lick them, they stick on themselves an' they shine in the dark.'

'Oooh smart!' Mooey said as he put on his big red cardboard sign with 'DANGER' written on it in capital letters, and got Mad Dog to put the other one on his back.

'Y'can't do that,' Snotty Dog said, and then Isaiah stood on his feet. 'Yes y'can, y'can do anythin' y'want. I just forgot f'a minute.'

'But they'll laugh at us,' Mad Dog said.

'That's the idea, son, the whole idea, an' just t'make sure y'don't take them off, I'll be followin' yer all the way home in my squad car.'

'Can I keep mine?' Mooey said. 'Can I? Do they really light up in the dark?'

Too right they did. All the frigging way home, near enough, past every pub on the way from the village; Isaiah's headlights picking us out just to make sure, all the drunks laughing their socks off, shouting pissed-up things like, 'Watch out, there's danger about,' as we walked along holding our heads in our heads, pretending to be Mickey Brown and his gang.

'I'm fed up with all this,' Mad Dog said as we ran through all the old biddies outside the Boundary. 'Nothin' but trouble wherever we go. Y'can't even walk down the street around here without bein' arrested f'loiterin' or somethin'. I feel like, y'know, I wanna make a fresh start in life. Begin again. From the beginnin', like.'

'I'v told yer,' Snotty Dog said, 'what we want is

somethin' else. What we want is a tart, that's what we want. An' I'm gonna get meself one.'

'Apple or gooseberry?'

'Shut it, Scully, I'll pull one dead easy. None of this crap would have happened if we'd had some meat with us. Keeps y'out of trouble a woman does.'

'An' gets yer into a whole load more,' Mad Dog said as we crossed the road and went past the youth club with coats over our heads, all except Mooey who was waving and shouting, 'Look, everyone, look, see, it's me!'

'What trouble can a tart get yer into?' Snotty Dog said. 'None of the tarts I know go on the rob.'

'Club trouble,' Mad Dog said. 'Up the shoot with no paddles. I want me end away as well, but they're all as fertile as fuck on our estate. Just look at some of them an' they get mornin' sickness.'

'I don't want that kind, I want a nice girl,' Snotty Dog said.

'No y'don't,' I said. 'What y'really want is a scrubber. Someone what's been at it since the Juniors.'

'I wanna marry a virgin,' Snotty Dog said, gettin' all upset. 'I don't wanna marry no scrubber.'

'Christ, y'only fifteen, no one's talkin' about gettin' married – just a quick hump in the back fields, that's all.'

'What's so smart about knockin' off a scrubber?' he said. 'Anyone can get that.'

'Yeah, an' that's what I mean,' I said. 'If she gets in the club, it could be anyone's kid. She can't blame you, can she?'

'But ... but I wanna be the first,' Snotty Dog said.

'Wha'd'y'think y'doin'?' I said. 'Climbin' Everest or fuckin' a tart? Listen, la', here's another thing an' all, y'don't want t'make y'mistakes with class

25

piece do yer? 'Ey? A decent tart might save herself for yer, I don't know, but none of them expect you t'do the same for them. What she expects is that you'll be a bit of an expert, show her how, like. She's not goin' t'think much of you if y'stick it in her bellybutton an' start gettin' excited, is she? Stands t'sense, Snotty Dog.'

'I dunno.'

'Look, imagine it's like woodwork – it's y'first go – y'don't get given a piece of best mahogany t'have a crack at do yer? Y'get somethin' lying around the workshop floor that nobody else wants. It's the same with everythin'. Y'don't think that apprentice surgeons in hospital get given real live people t'carve up when they start? They get bulls' eyes an' pigs' livers t'fuck up first.'

'Well, would you go out with a scrubber?'

'No, of course I wouldn't.'

'Well, there y'are then.'

'I wouldn't *go out* with her, Snotty Dog,' I said, 'not like y'go out with a proper tart, all chocolates an' holdin' hands an' lookin' in jewellery shop windows, an' all that, but I'd still have it off with one. On the quiet, in the woods, up a back alley, baby-sittin' of a Saturday night. It's not a romance, y'know. It's a leg over.'

'Y'all talk, you are,' Mad Dog said, 'an' y'gettin' worse. I bet y've never got t'first base with anyone yet, never mind all the way'

'That's right,' Snotty Dog said. 'I haven't even seen y' chat a bird up.'

'I've been bidin' me time, haven't I? Sussin' it all out. I don't jump in wavin' me dick about like a baseball bat just 'cos everyone else's got theirs hangin' out.'

'A baseball bat,' Snotty Dog said, 'listen t'him, lyin' again. More like a table-tennis handle from what I've seen.'

'A ciggie stump, if y'ask me,' Mad Dog said.

'But king size,' I answered as I ripped the 'DANGER' sign off my coat and stuck it over my flies. 'An' from now on, lads, they'll all better watch out f'the smoke risin' 'cos the time has come. An' 'ey, Isaiah's fucked off so let's dump these friggin' things before anyone else sees us.'

'Arrey,' Mooey said, 'do we have to?'

I practically had to peel my Gran and this feller away from the front door when I got home, and then when I got in, there was nothing to eat except some thin bread. I threw two slices together and made some toast for me and our Henry but even though I shouted him twice he never came down for his, so I ate that too.

He came back from sea last month, our Henry. First time he's been home for nearly a year. Been all over the world, he has, but still the same as ever. And his same's not the same as everyone else's. Always has been different in a quiet sort of way. Don't get me wrong now, I'm not saying there's anything the matter with him ... but to be honest, I think there is really. Not looney like, or even soft like Mooey. Just different.

My Mam fell down two flights of steps when she was carrying him, and then it didn't help matters when she came out of Mill Road Maternity after having him, and my dad was standing with her in a bus shelter, holding Henry and going, 'Coochie coochie coo' an' 'iggledy iggledy' and all that crap and throwing him up in the air. Just before the bus came he threw him too high and he came crashing down off the bus shelter roof. My Mam knocked my dad through the shelter window and Henry cried for two weeks solid.

I don't know what it is, but you can't seem to get near to Henry like you can everyone else. You can't even upset him. He'll just sit there in a corner on his own with his mind somewere else; on his train set I suppose, maybe one of his trips around the world. Or the times when he used to take us nesting when we were kids in Chinsley Woods.

In fact, his train set's the only thing in his life that seems to mean anything to him. It'd be alright if he was in the Infants and saving up for the latest *Beano Annual* and a new cowboy suit, good luck to him, but he must be at least twenty-five now. You know, we hardly ever see him when he is at home. If he's been out during the day, he comes back, belts down his tea, whips upstairs, puts his British Rail jacket on, and all we hear for the rest of the night is 'choo-choo, choo-choo-choo'.

Mind you, it's none of that made in Hong Kong plastic rubbish run off two torch batteries and a piece of elastic. Nothing like that at all. It's got everything, it has. A whole network of trains and tunnels and tracks and stations; Inter-Cities, stopping trains, buffet cars and communication cords and even a toilet that leaves a long line of piss on the tracks. It's ace, you've got to give it to him. If it's electrical and it goes on train tracks, he's got it.

I was just about to join him in the cockloft 'cos there was only cricket highlights on the telly, when my Mam came in with a long face on her, closely followed by my dad who just looked pissed like always on a Friday night.

'It's disgustin', that's what it is,' my Mam said. 'At her age—'

'But Berna—'

'An' on my bloody doorstep.'

'I know, but she is—'

'Old enough t'know bloody better, that's what she is. I thought our Vera was bad enough, but at least it was the first flushes of spring with her. Me Mam's on the last legs of soddin' winter an' she still can't keep away, make me a cup of tea will y',

28

Francis, did y'see how they had t'come away from the door t'let us in? Did yer? 'Ey, I'm talkin' t'you, Alfie.'

'Yes, love.'

'Sideways, stuck t'gether like crabs on heat, that's how they got off our doorstep, an' boil the bloody water this time, Francis.'

'*Nanna, Nanna, I fright, I fright, Nanna!*' Hovis at the top of the landing, crying and holding onto his teddy for dear life. My Mam didn't even have to tell me. I put the tea on the sideboard and went up the stairs to Hovis, stopping just for a bit to hear my Gran giggling outside, and her feller's heavy breathing. He either had bronchitis or a hard-on.

'I want "The Three Bears", I want "The Three Bears", I want "The Three Bears".'

'I'll feed yer t'them if y'don't get into that bed an' lie down, now shut up an' keep still.'

'I want "The Three Bears".'

Smack.

'I want my Nanna.'

'Y'can't have her, she's havin' a cup of tea.'

'I wanna cup tea, I wanna cup tea.'

'There's none left, now lie still an' I tell y'the story. Alright, are y'ready? Once upon a time there was this little girl ca—'

'Called Goldilocks an' she—'

'Friggin' hell, who's tellin' this story?' I asked him. 'You or me? Close y'eyes an' go asleep.'

'Tell bit 'bout bed, go on.'

'Y'not ready f'that bit yet.'

'Go on, go on, "Who's Been Sleepin' in My Bed?"'

'An' so this lovely golden-haired little girl called Goldilocks was lyin' there in the baby bear's bed fast asleep . . .'

Nearly three now, Hovis, and he's as bright as a button. A chocolate button. He came about as a

29

result of our Vera going with this big buck nigger from the Dindle, but he did a bunk when she got pregnant, and our Vera didn't even know his second name or anything, not even which street he lived in, and anyway they'd long broken up by the time Hovis saw the light of day. She ended up marrying fat and fearful Freddie Fletcher last year but he wouldn't have nothin' to do with Hovis 'cos of his shade, so he had to stay with us. He's alright really, except at half eleven at night when he wants frigging fairy stories.

We've all got used to his colour and all now, but I'm not much bothered about the blacks anyway. Not now that I know a few. We had no niggers in our school till the end of last year, and then all of a sudden we had ourselves a black Christmas. They're alright though – especially when they're on your side playing footie. Within a month of coming back to school in the January we were in the quarter finals of the knock-out trophy and third in the league and everyone called us the All Blacks 'cos only me and Brian Bignall could get in the team. But I don't care. I'd rather win with niggers than get battered with the knock-kneed lot that used to play for us.

Hovis was snoring away but I still sat on the end of his bed, thinking about the last coon family to move up our way, just before the spring half-term. They went into the house next door to Mooey Morgan's and it was a week before Mooey realized that they weren't delivering coal. Their names were Mr and Mrs Kew and they've got a son the same age as me who's an ace footballer and in a way my best mate though I'd never talk about him that way, not to the others. His name's Tommy Kew but we call him Dole to get him upset and he's got a twin sister, Joanna, and she's known as Fuckew and we all would and all, black or blue and

30

green stripes, no danger, but she doesn't flash it about. They never do around here, not like they're supposed to, if you listen to all the stories, and not like some of the white slag on the estate.

Hovis turned over and started mumbling about a cup of tea and baby bear so I slipped out of his room. My Mam was at the bottom of the stairs giving my Gran some stick about something she'd just heard and her feller was standing and shuffling about at the doorway, cap in hand, trying to get a word in edgeways. I left them to it and went into the room I share with our Arthur and Henry. Arthur had gone asleep with his cub's outfit on and a piece of rope in his hands so I put the eiderdown over him and went to the bathroom. Henry was getting the midnight express ready so I sneaked up to the cockloft and shouted through the door.

'Ey, Henry,' I said, 'without a word of a lie, there were two fellers at the front door t'night tryin' t'get platform tickets f'that junk of yours. Did y'hear that, our kid?'

'Fuck off,' he said, very very quietly and gently.

2

'So y'don't want t'come with us then?' my dad said
as he wiped his bread around the plate, chasing
the last of his gravy.

'Well, y'know, dad,' I said as I did the same,
'there'll be nothin' there f'me, will there?'

'Suit y'self,' he said, 'but it's the first holiday
we've had in years.'

'An' God alone knows when we'll have another
one, the way things're goin',' my Mam said.

'Y'mother's right as usual. Seems a pity f'you
t'miss it, especially with you growin' up now.'

'Not before bloody time an' all,' my Mam said as
she took the plates away.

'I'll be okay, dad—'

'Henry'll be away again by then,' my Mam said
at the doorway. 'There'll only be you in the house,
come t'think of it.'

'Must be courtin',' my Gran said, 'dirty little
bugger, wants the house t'himself.' She dunked a
digestive in her tea an' had a little laugh t'herself.
'It's the time of the year, Bernadette; hot weather
just startin', the grass dry enough t'lie down on,
an' little Francis finally dry behind the ears. Hair
under his arms, bit of bumfluff over his lips, thinks
he's a man. Heh heh heh.' Bits of digestive were
stuck to her chin.

'I hope that's not y'plan,' my Mam shouted in
from the back kitchen, ''cos if it is, y'll be in bloody
North Wales with us an' like it!'

That wasn't it at all, if you really want to know.
It was just that I didn't fancy being lined up as
baby sitter, looking after Hovis and our Arthur all

the time. That's what would have happened, you could have depended on it. My Mam and dad down the alehouse, Gran in the sand dunes with a horde of Welsh pensioners, and me in the boarding house bored out of my mind telling Hovis fairy stories and bursting our Arthur like I used to. No thanks. Mind you, now that my Gran'd mentioned it, being on my own in the house for a fortnight wasn't a bad opportunity for a bit on the sly. All I needed was the hardest part - finding someone soft enough to do it.

'It's alright, Mam,' I said, 'y'can trust me. I've got better things t'do than that.'

'I'm glad t'say I haven't,' my Gran said as she got her coat from under the stairs and went to sneak out the door.

'An' where d'y'think you're goin'?' my Mam said, catching her in the hallway.

'Er, quick game of Bingo,' my Gran said, 'down the Granada.'

'It's closed of a Monday.'

'Well, I'll go over t'Kensington then.'

'That's closed an' all.'

'Friggin' Jesus, Bernadette, wha' is this? A house or a soddin' nunnery?'

'Someone's got t'look after yer, Mam. Y'don't seem capable of doin' it y'self.'

'I'm over seventy y'know, I'm allowed out after dark.'

'Well, I hope that y'not seein' the last one y'turned up with.'

'George Daniels? What's wrong with him? He's got new teeth an' all now.'

'Sod his teeth, it was his flamin' eyes. Wouldn't look me straight in the face once.'

'I'm not bloody well surprised. Fancy draggin' me off the doorstep, y'own mother of all people.'

'The letterbox was open, I could hear every word

33

he was sayin', the dirty old sod, an' I'm buggered if I'm goin' t'have all the neighbours talkin' about us just because you're on heat.'

'Now that's a fine thing t'say t'me, I'm sure. Well, I'm not standin' f'that, I'm off.' And before my Mam could stop her, she was out and staggering down the path in her best stilettos. She's been in her second childhood so long, my Gran, she's a randy little teenager all over again. All the old fellers down the pensioners' club are after her, y'know. Until she met this Georgie Daniels feller, there was nothing but knocks on our door from these old codgers, standing on the step looking like spare parts out of a Fred Astaire film, asking my Gran to go down the Top Rank Over Seventies Night with them.

'I don't know,' my Mam said, coming in and sitting down with a plate in her hand, 'y'expect most things in this life; y've got a good idea of what's comin'; what lies ahead for yer. Y'know y'kids're goin' t'be at it sooner or later, but I never thought the day'd come when my biggest problem was my own mother.'

'Y've got t'see the funny side of it, though,' my dad said. 'When I was courtin' you, she used t'come everywhere with us. Sittin' in the pictures, watchin' George Raft, with her stuck in the middle; down the Grafton Rooms or the Locarno doin' a quickstep – the three of us.'

'Aye, if she hadn't have had that holiday in the Isle of Man, I doubt if we'd ever got married,' my Mam said and then looked at me. 'I think y'd better come t'Rhyl with us after all, Francis.'

'Flippin' 'eck, Mam, I'm only sixteen.'

'So was I, son, so was I.'

There was a knock on the door then and my Mam went to see who it was. If it had been another Fred Astaire he wouldn't have made the garden gate alive, but it was only Mooey.

'Er, er is your Francis comin' out t'play, Mrs Scully?' I don't know how many times I've hit him for saying that, but he always forgets. I went out into the hallway to see the state of him. He had a smart new plastic ball under his arm and he was wearing his football shorts and a Liverpool shirt that they must have worn in the Second Division in the fifties. I didn't like to give him the knock-back, especially as he'd just learnt to dress himself, and anyway I knew that if I went back in the front room I'd only get a lecture off my Mam about being careful. And it wasn't road safety neither.

So I slipped upstairs, put my old jeans on and changed into my training shoes and we went to the Dogs. It was getting dark and we walked up to the top of our road to have a kick about 'cos the lamppost up there is the only one with a light in it. 'Course, there had to be a catch, and there was: Mr an' Mrs Leigh.

Posh they are. Think they are anyway. Tuppence ha'penny toffs, that's all they are, really. You know the kind, fur coat and no knickers, only wash the parts people can see. They've got plate-glass windows and one of them imitation oak doors and two dwarfs in their garden. Mr Leigh works in an office in town, wears a suit and a tie and carries a briefcase. Tea lad probably. He must be daft, especially living around here 'cos the only other people I know in our road that work in an office are the cleaners. But it's his missus that's the real gobshite though. She works in the big biscuit factory in the village that my Mam used to work in until Hovis came to stay. We call her Crackers 'cos that's what she makes and that's what she is, and what's more, if your ball goes over their hedge, you've had it, no danger. I'm not kidding. They've got so many balls in their house, Slazengers made a takeover bid last week.

We weren't doing anything that night, y'know. Nothing at all, just the four of us kicking a ball about outside their house, and we'd have been alright if Mickey Brown hadn't come along in his big seven-leaguer slip-ons. He's another head case like our Tony. Well, he would be if he wasn't such a pain in the arse. He used to be a big mate of ours last year until we found out about him, and we only ever see him now if he's got nothing to do, or we haven't. He's a year or two older than us and since he finally got a job he's had more clothes than sense, but he never flashes his money in our direction. He reckons he smokes dope and all and takes pills and goes to these orgies in the posh houses in the village but if you ask me, the nearest he's ever been to all that is taking Anadin and delivering milk.

He hadn't been playing more than two minutes when he toe-bunged the ball right up in the air and straight into the Leighs' front garden. She must have been on sentry duty behind the lace curtains 'cos she ran out and caught the ball, second bounce, and legged it back in and locked the front door before we even had a chance to say, 'Arrey, Crackers, that takes the biscuit.'

'Me ball,' Mooey wailed, 'she's taken me ball.'

'An' she'll keep it an' all,' I said. 'Waste of time even goin' an' askin' for it.'

'But I've only had it since Friday,' Mooey said. 'It was almost brand new when I robbed it from school.'

'I know what we should do, boys,' Mickey Brown said in his best Clint Eastwood impersonation. 'We should go in there an' get our ball back, that's what we should do, gang.'

'Wha'?' I said. 'Break in? You, Mickey? Y'couldn't even get in y'own house over Christmas when y'Mam left her key at your Josie's.'

'Well,' he said, 'well, that wasn't my fault. How was I t'know the drainpipe came away from the wall?'

'He's right though,' Mad Dog said. 'We should screw them. It's only fair after what they've done t'us over the years. I mean, our Freddy's bein' married ten years now an' he used t'get his ball pinched by Crackers. She's been at it all her life.'

'She's never pinched any balls in our family,' Mooey said, but we didn't take any notice of him 'cos we were having a vote on what to do. Poor Mickey was terrified to death when we all agreed that his idea was the best and that we should go and get our ball back. I don't know about breaking into a house, Mickey even gets nervous if he breaks into a pound note.

'Er, well, I tell y'what, men, it's no use doin' it now is it? I mean, they're still in there aren't they? An' who knows when they'll come out t'night.'

'Half past seven, Mickey, regular as clockwork,' Mad Dog said. 'They go down the Boundary. Two straws an' a glass of shandy, accordin' t'me dad.'

'An' it's nearly that now,' I said.

'Is it?' Mickey said. 'Is it that late already. Who'd have thought it 'ey? Well, I've just remembered—'

'Don't tell us,' I said, 'we all know. Y've gorra go.'

'That's right,' he said, 'how did y'guess? Our Maureen's the usherette at the Jacey, y'see, an' I get in free. I'll just make the last film.'

'Can I come?' Mooey said. 'What's on?'

'Arr, you wouldn't like it, Mooey. *The Camp of Sex an' Sin.*'

'I think I've been there,' Mooey said.

'That's right,' I said. 'It's Pontins, Filey.'

'Nah,' Mickey said, 'this film has been banned in over seventeen countries. Seventeen!'

'How're we fixed then, Mickey?' I asked.

'Y'kiddin'? The lot of yer? I don't—'

'Alright then, suit y'self, it doesn't matter, we'll screw the Leighs without yer, despite Isaiah bein' on the warpath, but I mean, it's goin' t'look bad isn't it 'ey?'

'What'd'y'mean, like, Scull?'

'Look at it this way, Mickey. It was your idea, right, lads? You all heard him didn't yer? Fact that, isn't it? An' where will you be when we're doin' it? Bouncin' up an' down on y'seat, jerkin' off in the Jacey with two hundred old men in plastic macks.'

'I'm not payin' y'bus fares,' he said, 'an' if the manager's there, y'not with me.'

'Shall I get changed?' Mooey said.

'I think y'better had, Mooey,' Mickey said. 'They might just wonder how old y'are if y'turn up in y'football shorts. An' while we're at it, go home an' get some seven-inch high heels, Mad Dog.'

'I'll tell them I'm a jockey, home f'the day,' Mad Dog said.

I'd never seen a dirty film before, and after that one I'm not sure I'll ever bother again. They're a waste of time. You don't see anything that's going to be much help to you when the chance comes. Four sets of tits, a prick, two fannies and about a hundred bare arses, that's all we saw, and never at the same time neither. There was only one good bit in the whole show and that was no thanks to the film. It was where this tart and this feller were in the games room of some Swedish holiday camp, and he was trying to cop off with her and she wasn't having any. He was standing at one side of this billiard table and she was at the other side. He kept attempting to grab her and she was throwing the snooker balls at him until she had none left, and she was stood there in the knacker, except for a cushion, cos she'd just had one of those steam bath thingys, and then she climbs on the billiard table and he climbs on after her and he's tearing off his trousers and his undies and she's clutching this cushion tighter to her fanny, and then he jumps her and they're rolling about for what seemed like frigging half an hour or more on this billiard table with nothing happening, until someone in the audience shouted out, 'In off the cushion pal, f'fuck's sake, an' get it over with.'

'Look,' Mooey said when we were on the bus home, 'look what this nice man give me in the pictures.' He held up a Mars bar and a packet of Maltesers, melting away, and I remembered the feller sitting next to him for a bit at the end of the row.

'Wha' did he give y'them for, Mooey?' I asked.

'I don't know, honest. He just er give me them an' asked me if I'd do somethin' for him.'

'Y'didn't, did yer?' Snotty Dog said, moving away from him on the seat and crossing his legs.

''Course I didn't. He never told me what it was he wanted me t'do. I think he was a bit frightened though when they were on the billiard table. He kept tryin' t'get hold of me hand. Er ... er, wha' y'all laughin' at me for 'ey?'

'Oh, nothin',' Mickey said and give us all a big wink. 'Have y'ever had it 'ey, Mooey? Have yer?'

'Er, had wha'?'

'Y'know, a good juicy knee trembler down a back entry, a quick bash in the back kitchen when her mam was at the shops.'

'Oh aye, I know what y'mean now, Mickey.'

'Well, come on them, Moo, tell us.'

'It's a long story,' Mooey said and looked out of the window and then looked around at us as we tried to stop sniggering. 'Don't y'believe me?' he said. 'Don't yer? Arrey, I have y'know, I have had it, like. Honest.'

''Course y'have, Mooey,' I said. 'Here, have a ciggie as well.'

'Y'think I'm tellin' fibs, y'do don't yer? I can tell.'

'Don't get upset, Mooey,' I said. 'Y'not the only one here, if y'haven't.'

'Speak f'y'self, kidder,' Mickey said. 'I had it only last night.'

'That poor bloody cat of yours,' Mad Dog said. 'I don't know how it stands it.'

'Ha ha ha, very funny I don't think, but if y've got any doubts, ask him,' Mickey said, pointing t'Mooey. 'It was his sister.'

'Oh no, Mickey,' I said. 'Not Marie?'

'Yeah, why?'

'Marie Morgan. Mooey's sister?'

'That's right, I just told yer. In the cemetery.'

'Our Marie's not dead,' Mooey said.

'Oh fuckin' hell, Mick,' I said and shook my head as if it was the worst news I'd heard in years.'

'Why? 'Ey? What's the matter?' Mickey said, going all twitchy. 'They was all havin' a go, it wasn't just me. I only joined in. She can't blame me.'

'It's not that,' I said. 'I only wish it was. F'your sake.'

'Wha' is it then?'

'Y'really haven't heard?'

'No, no, I haven't.'

'How d'y'feel now, y'know, in y'self?' He looked as white as an advert for soap powder.

'Well, I felt alright, like,' he said, undoing his shirt collar. 'I don't know though, I feel a bit hot now—'

'Hot?' I sighed and shook me head.

'Arr come on, tell us.'

'Sorry, Mick. I don't wanna be the first t'tell yer—'

'Friggin' Jesus, Scull, *please*.'

40

'I've had sexual intercourse with a girl,' Mooey suddenly piped up in a loud voice as if it'd been on his mind for years, and half the bus looked around and I pointed to my head and pulled a face.

'But have y'ever fucked anyone?' Snotty Dog said. 'That's the thing.'

'I have. I've done that an' all.'

'Look, Scull, whatever it is, I can stand it, y've just got t'tell me, I can take it, I know I can.'

'Fancy you not knowin' that, Mickey,' I said. 'We all knew that didn't we?'

''Course we did,' Snotty Dog said and so Mad Dog said it then as well, but Mooey was lost in another world.

'Is . . . is it somethin' bad?' Mickey said. 'It is, isn't it?'

'Somethin' bad?' I said. 'He wants t'know if it's somethin' bad.' And I laughed and Mad Dog laughed and Snotty Dog laughed so much he had to wipe his nose and ruined another good shirt.

'Y've got t'listen t'me,' Mickey said. 'It wasn't my fault, they made me do it, y'know. They did. As God is my witness. I'd have been happy with a quick snog an' first base, but all the others were laughin' at me.'

'There'll be none of yis laughin' in about a fortnight,' I said.

'It was at the back of Conway Castle,' Mooey shouted, getting all carried away, 'with Harold Batten's sister from 4C. She asked me, Scull, she did. An' she charged everyone five pence a look an' kept all the money. It was her idea. She used me body an' told me a lot of dirty things.'

'Did she tell yer slowly?' I asked.

'Well, she had t'repeat some of them.'

'It's the crabs!' Mickey shouted out as soon as Mooey had stopped, but there was no need to worry about anyone turning around, 'cos the whole sodding bus was staring at us on the back seat. 'It is, I know it is, it's the crabs. I can feel them already, crawlin' around, all over me whatsits.'

'Sorry, Mick,' I said, 'it's not that. I'd like it t'be f'your—'

'Oh God, no,' Mickey cried out and buried his head in his lap and then realized what he was doing and took his head away again. 'It's not . . . I mean, there can only be one thing worse . . .' He looked at me like a condemned man in the old films, hoping against hope that a reprieve would come from the Governor and save him from being grilled for breakfast.

'Tough luck la',' I said and put my hand on his shoulder but took it away again dead quick and wiped it on Mooey's coat. 'I'm sorry, I really am.'

'I knew I should have gone the Conservative Club with me Mam,' he said. 'She's always tellin' me about knockin' about with that lot. If only I'd have listened.'

'Come on, Mick,' I said, 'cheer up, it's not the end of the world. 'Ey, I heard a smart joke in school the other day. Are y'ready? What's green an' eats nuts?'

'I dunno.'

'Syphilis.'

He got up and ran down the length of the bus, crying and screaming, 'Oh, no, oh no,' over and over again. Mooey opened a window and shouted down to him as he got off the bus.

'See, Mickey, I have had it,' he said. 'I told y' I had . . . er, it's not your stop yet, why've y'got off? Er, wha' the matter. Mick? Wha' y'bangin' y'head on the floor for 'ey?'

'What was it, Scully?' Snotty Dog said two stops later.

'Wha'?'

42

'Well, y'know, what Marie Morgan's got an' given t'Mickey?'

'Nothin' as far as I know.'

'But you said—'

'But I didn't, Snotty Dog. I never said anythin'. I just let him work it out f'himself.'

'An' hasn't she?' Mad Dog said.

'I hope not.'

'She must have made about three quid,' Mooey bellowed again. 'All our class give her five pence an' there was two charas full of pensioners as well. One old lady wanted me address.'

'It was probably me Gran.'

When we got off the bus at our stop Dole Kew was waiting at the corner for me, lighting the night up with his purple jeans, blue velvet jacket and yellow T-shirt. On any of us it would have been instant vomit but on him it looked great. But you know what they say – black goes with anything.

He plays goalie in our school team, Dole, and he's nothing short of brilliant. We'd all heard about him off the other coloured lads before he even got to our school, and although you don't believe everything you hear, me and Brian Bignall knew that all we needed was a goalie and we were made. Dole only came into school for the first time on the Friday afternoon and none of us actually saw him but we made sure he was picked to play on the Saturday. Me and Brian Bignall and the outside left, Geoff Long, pick the team 'cos the PE bloke, Samuels, doesn't give a monkey's about us, and none of the other teachers know their arse from a hole in the ground, except the science teacher, Steve, and he used to be a real footballer once upon a time, but he's been off sick with his bad leg most of this term.

43

I remember the first time I ever saw Dole. It was behind the changing huts on the Blessed Virgin's playing fields that Saturday. He was fast asleep on the ground in his football kit and sunglasses. So keen to play, he'd been there since about eight o'clock and the game wasn't supposed to kick off until quarter past ten. Me and Brian went and got changed and then Geoff Long brought him in with his clothes all wrapped up under his arm. He just stood there smiling with his sunglasses still on and his socks hanging out from under his arm. Close up, you could see that one of the lenses was cracked in his glasses. And he had shoulders like an old-time docker.

Geoff had known him down the town and so he went through all our names and Dole just stood there with a big wide grin on his face and then said, 'Hello, St Malachy's under-sixteen.'

Brian Bignall got up off the bench and walked over to Dole at the doorway. They stood facing each other while we all went quiet, and while the grin stayed put on Dole's face, you could see him flexing his muscles and moving his feet slightly apart in the sort of way that made you know he'd had his share of fights.

'Not another fuckin' nigger?' Brian said. 'I don't know, it's like the Black Hole of Calcutta in here already without another one.'

Brian's the cock of the school, has been ever since he started going to nursery, and when he looks at you all hard your first and only thought is to find somewhere safe to hide. Like Manchester. But the daft thing is that he wouldn't harm a fly, Brian, unless the fly sent the head in first and then there'd be murder alright. But Dole wasn't to know that and everyone watched and waited to see what he'd do.

He took his glasses off and squinted his eyes and

44

then opened them up like the nigger slaves in *Uncle Tom's Cabin* as he looked at Brian and then at me. 'Well, hallelujah, brothers,' he said, 'y'all looked nice an' sweet an' black from behind these glasses. I didn't know there was goin' t'be two white honky trash playin' in *my* team.'

'You'll do,' Brian said.

He did and all. The match that Saturday was against the Protestant school down the road from us, and we'd never beaten them in the five years that we'd been playing them, but we never had the team we've got now. It'd be kid's comic Roy of the Rovers stuff if I told you that Dole saved three penalties and put an eighty-yard header into their goal that Saturday, but I reckon we would have just about won without him. The big difference he made though was that he looked good. We all felt for the first time that if all else failed, we had a goalie on the line, not a Chivers jelly. Mad Dog was the last keeper we'd had and you could never really trust him to either catch the ball or even watch the game. We played this school over in Hunts Cross by the railway track at the start of the season, and Mad Dog was hanging from the crossbar waving to the London train when they got the winning goal.

The only trouble with Dole is his bastard of a dad. It didn't take us long to realize what a twat he was. Even Mooey noticed, especially with the walls in the houses around our way being like Kelloggs cornflakes boxes. You could hear him from out in the street some nights after the pubs were shut, shouting and screaming the odds and using his belt, and then you'd hear his Mam crying and Dole trying to fight back and Joanna attempting to stop everything. I got told from someone that'd known them a long time down the town that his dad was alright when he was sober, but no one'd ever seen him anything less than nine parts pissed since they'd come up here, so we wouldn't know.

Some Saturdays Dole'd turn up for a match looking like death warmed up on a cold stove, but somehow as soon as he got out on the pitch and put himself between those goalposts he'd find the rhythm and the life and he'd strut around his penalty area like Attila the Hun. It's true. Everything always seems to be under control when he's in goal. He never looks nervous or worried or awkward or nothing, not even with a dozen players in his six-yard box kicking lumps out of each other. And what's more, he always seems to be laughing. He'll fingertip a header over the crossbar or dive into the middle of blood and studs and come out with the ball in his hands and that big easy grin spread all over his face. Every team we play hates that grin more than anything.

'Alright, Tommy?' I said. 'Wha'd'y'want?'

'A tin of white paint,' Mad Dog said, all sulky 'cos he's never forgiven Dole for takin' his place in the team and being ten times better than him.

'Y'about as funny as a hole in a parachute, Mad Dog,' Dole said, giving him a friendly little push which knocked him through someone's privets. 'It's you I want t'see, Scull,' he carried on. 'Playin' tomorrer, big league match, an' seein' as y'were off school t'day, the word is that if you don't make it f'registration t'morrer mornin', you won't be makin' hot chocolate with the rest of us at four o'clock. An' that word comes from the arse's mouth itself, suckhole Samuels.'

'What's wrong with Saturdays?'

'The other team've gorra game.'

'I was bankin' on stayin' off till Friday afternoon an' all.'

'Look, y'd better be in school t'morrer, no shit.'

'Y've gorra laugh, haven't yer?' I said. 'Samuels

doesn't give a toss where we are an' who's playin' when we're losin' six-nil every week, but as soon as we start winnin', he suddenly turns up with all these friggin' rules an' regulations.'

'Man, I don't make the rules, I just break them.'

'On y'bike, Dole,' I said, 'you're a suckhole an' all, an' y'know it.' It wasn't exactly right, but he was in the top class and he had homework and what's more, he did it too. 'Next winter when we're queuein' f'soup, you'll be alright.'

'Yeah, I'll be queuein' f'black-eyed peas,' he said. 'Remember my shade, Scull. The dole queues in town're full of my colour.'

'The wha' queues?'

'The dole qu – ah sod off.'

'Yeah, well, I'll be in t'morrer.'

'In the mornin', an' on time.'

'F'break?'

'F'registration. I'll call for yer if y'want.'

'Bring y'sister,' I said. 'She can get me breakfast in bed.'

'She's hot f'you, man, she really is. Her pants, they're on fire, but I just won't allow it, no way. It's against nature, so I've been told. Soul brothers any day of the week, that's cool, but me an' you brothers-in-law? F'get it.'

'Why don't y'speak the Queen's English like the rest of us?' Mad Dog muttered as we left Dole at their gate and reminded Mooey that he lived next door. But if Mad Dog was expecting a reply he never got it 'cos Dole's door opened and his dad's voice roared across the front garden like a lion with an arrow up its arse. 'Where the hell have you been?' he asked Dole, and we shot off up the road in case Dole incriminated us.

'D'y'really think his sister fancies yer?' Snotty Dog said as we stood at their gate.

''Course she does.'

'She wants her head examined then,' Mad Dog said.

'I'm goin' t'examine her all over very shortly,' I said.

'Aye, aye, more talk,' Snotty Dog said and the pair of them nudged each other.

'It'a a fact,' I said. 'Every time she meets me she's near t'faintin'.'

'I've told you before about not changin' y'undies,' Mad Dog said and he had to hold onto the gate he thought it was so funny.

'She'd be alright with you though, wouldn't she, Mad Dog?' I said, ''cos you don't wear any.'

'Don't fancy her anyway. Can get better than her.'

''Ey,' Snotty Dog said, 'did Mickey tell y' about that party he'a goin' to next Saturday; the one in the village?'

'He was too busy itchin'.'

'An' I don't care what anyone says,' Mad Dog said, 'her brother isn't as good a goalie as me.'

'He told me durin' the interval,' Snotty Dog said.

'Couldn't hold a party, that Dole,' Mad Dog said. 'Did someone mention "party" just then?'

'Yeah,' I said. 'You did. Have y'ever had a nervous breakdown before, Mad Dog?'

'I haven't been t'a party f'ages,' he said.

'This is no jelly an' cakes get-t'gether,' Snotty Dog said. 'It's goin' t'be one of them hippy orgy things, y'know, with free love an' free ale an' Mickey reckons some real dopeheads're goin' t'be there as well.'

'Does Mooey know he's been invited?' I said.

'I could play as well as him behind that defence,' Mad Dog mumbled.

'I'd really like t'go,' Snotty Dog said. 'Those posh tarts, they're the ones what really give it out. They're all on the pill, so I've been told, it's their upbringin', like. They don't give a fuck. Well, they do give a fuck, that's the thing about them.'

'I don't give a fuck what colour the black bastard is, it's got nothin' t'do with that . . . .,' Mad Dog trailed off, talking away to his shoes.

'I thought you wanted a virgin, Snotty Dog,' I said.

'Arr, it's different though, isn't it?'

'Yeah, the difference bein' that she'll be a posh scrubber instead of a rough one.'

'There is a difference,' Mad Dog said. 'They can't help it but they're inferior t'us whites, that's what it is. Me dad said so.'

'Anyway, I don't care,' Snotty Dog said.

'I do,' Mad Dog said.

'I know where they're havin' it, in this rich kid's house. Mickey told me the address, an' I'm goin' t'bunk in.'

'Listen,' I said before Mad Dog could start again, 'bring a bottle of plonk an' y'Mam's nerve pills an' we'll make a bomb.'

'How're we gonna do that?'

'Never you mind, Snotty Dog, just bring them.'

'An' you tell him from me, he'd better not push me in no more privets neither,' Mad Dog said. He was still threatening to join the National Front when he knocked on their door and Snotty Dog asked me again about the nerve pills.

'Are y'sure?' he said.

''Course I am,' I said. No brain, that's what wrong with most people you know. No imagination, like. I'll never pass nothing at school when it comes to reading and writing and knowing what the capital of Rio de Janeiro is, but there's many a lad left our school with certificates and ace reports and all kinds of special awards, and I know as sure as anything that I've got more going for me than he'll ever have – even if he shits gold bricks all day

49

long. I wasn't interested in all that so-called hippy beef and free wank at this party 'cos I knew we'd get none of it. But I knew straight away how we could pull a fast one on them. You don't have to be clever to be smart.

I was coming down the brew back towards our house when I saw Marie Morgan walking along the road leading from the village and the cemetery. I couldn't help but laugh out loud when I thought of what I'd kidded Mickey Brown into believing. The sucker, he'd have probably surrendered himself at the nearest VD clinic already. Mind you, it was easy enough to kid him about Marie. She's had more rides than Bob Champion. Everyone used to know her as the Binmens' Moll 'cos she used to follow them about. Whenever she went missing, Isaiah and his crew used to drive around the estate searching all the bins. Poor bugger really, like, I mean, as Snotty Dog'd say, 'Who's goin' t'marry her when she grows up?'

'Alright there, Marie, y'lookin' well.'

'Wha'd'y'want, Scully?'

'Arrey, flippin' 'eck, can't a feller be polite anymore?'

'Yeah, but you never have been before.'

'Well, I'm gettin' older now, girl. Gorra learn sometime haven't I?'

'Oh aye?'

It was only then that I saw she was crying. Not a lot like, just a trickle. Two black lines coming down from her eyes.

'What's the matter, Marie?'

'Nothin'. Piss off.'

'Has someone hit yer?'

'Frig off, go on, get away from me, go home t'y'Action Man.'

'Don't take it out on me, Marie, I haven't done nothin'.'

50

She just sort of snorted down her nose and carried on walking and I went with her, even though I was now traipsing back up the road I'd just come down.

'Come on,' I said. 'It can't be that bad, I mean, it can't be; nothin's worth cryin' for, especially if it's some greaser on a motorbike.'

'You think y'know everythin', don't yer? 'Ey, Scully? Y'do, don't yer?' She stopped and looked at me. 'You an' our kid an' y'little mates. One smart gang, don't make me laugh. You know nothin'.'

She carried on walking. This wasn't the Marie Morgan I used to know and laugh at.

'An' anyway,' I said, blundering on and coming to the point which made me wait for her and walk with her and let her slang me out for the last fifty yards or more. 'I was just wonderin', I thought maybe if y'fancied goin' out with me one night. Y'know. T'gether, Just you an' me. Like.'

'Just you an' me?' she said. 'An' where will we go, just you an' me, on this night out, 'ey? Some alleyway or park or dark corner?'

By Christ, I hadn't half picked the wrong night to chat her up. Usually you don't even have to say 'Drop 'em' and she's jumping at your cock. So I've been told.

'Well, I thought, y'know, we might go down t'Otterspool like, an' walk along the Prom an' that, it's er nice there at this time of the year, an' then maybe get some chips after, that sort of thing.'

'Oh really?' she said. She wasn't crying no more anyway, but there was this look on her face that my Mam sometimes gets when I'm telling her a whole bunch of lies. And then she laughed and I could see her teeth and I almost told her to forget all about it. 'An' when were y'thinkin' of havin' this big night out? Y'know, just you an' me on Otterspool Promenade?'

51

'Well, like tomorrow, no, not t'morrer, we've got a match, I'll be knackered. How about the day after that? The Wednesday.'

'Make it the Thursday,' she said. 'Should be just about right that.'

'Great, thanks Marie,' I said.

'My pleasure, I'm sure.' She leaned on her gatepost and grinned at me.

'Er, I'll meet yer down there 'ey? I've gorra go over t'me aunty Jean's in Dingle anyway, y'know, an' it's near Otterspool, isn't it? Save me comin' all the way back here, like, wouldn't it? Wha'd'y'say?'

'Nothin' doin',' she said. 'I'm not goin' all the way over there on me own, just f'you an' a bag of friggin' chips.'

'Oh balls,' I thought, 'someone's bound t'see me with her!' 'Alright then,' I said, 'but I wouldn't do it f'anyone y'know. I'll see yer at your bus stop at half past seven. Don't be late.'

'If I'm late, I won't be comin',' she said and laughed so loud you couldn't hear the screaming and fighting coming from Dole's house.

I walked back home again, and I didn't bump into Bo Derek or Boy George or someone off page three in the *Sun*, so I reckoned it was me and Marie after all. I was just congratulating myself on being the first one on our gang to crack it when I remembered what Mooey had said about him and that girl behind Conway Castle. You could guarantee he hadn't been lying, but the question was, did he know what it was he was doing? If you ask me, he'll live to be a hundred years old and have a great time every day of his life. It was almost enough to hate him for, if you didn't know him.

3

History, first lesson in the afternoon, what a waste of bleeding time. What good is history going to be to us when we leave school, hey? Go on, you tell me, 'cos nobody else can. I even asked Mrs Faconfield, the woman who teaches us, last term but my only answer was a walk down to the headmaster's office for givin' cheek.

Right bag she is and all, this Mrs Faconfield. She takes us for music as well and that's another waste of time. I wouldn't mind if she was Winifred Atwell or someone but you want to hear her make us suffer when she plays the piano in assembly. Last year's school-leavers put grease on her keyboard and then on the final day nailed her piano lid down. You can laugh if you want but you wouldn't if you heard her play. And what's more, she's a proper alecan as well. If she breathes on you after dinner your Mam accuses you of being out on the booze when you get home. They won't let her on any of the pub pianos in town, you know, 'cos she's bad for business. One solo from her and everyone goes home.

'Course, she thinks she's God's gift to teachin', like that kind always do. You never leave her class without there's chalk dust covering the whole room and four pages of notes no one can understand in your exercise book. If in doubt, copy out. That's her motto, and she's all made up with herself when we just sit there instead of throwing wobblers or desk lids like we do in some other lessons, but what she doesn't know is that we're not really interested, not at all, not for one minute. We're just bored to fuckin' death.

I spend most of my time in her lesson looking at Josie McKenna's tits. She really has got the biggest knockers in the school, and that includes the teachers. Though Mr Heywood, the art teacher, runs her a close second. Not much of a face like, but those bumpers of hers, they're like the tip ends of torpedoes. I know one thing, she never had them that size at the start of the fifth year. It must be something to do with spring. Come next October, they'll probably drop off into her full cup one morning as she's bending down to put her shoes on. Either that, or her dad's old socks have all gone missing.

So there I was, a thousand miles away, thinking about bouncing up and down with Josie and her amazing knockers on some beach somewhere in the hot sun with no one around except my man-servant and a couple of slaves, when I heard Mrs Faconfield asking me a question.

''Ey, wha'?' I said.

'That is no way to speak to a lady member of staff, Scully,' she said. 'Try again before I send you to learn some proper manners the hard way.'

'I do beg y'pardon, miss,' I said. 'I was not listening there for a moment. I was thinking about the Triple Alliance. I don't understand that, miss.'

'Well, tell me all you know about the Triple Alliance. Anything at all. You should have read it for homework, if you remember.'

'I know,' I said, 'but there was somethin' interestin' on the Open University an' I watched that instead.' I saw her eyebrows rise and her brow make those lines like in a farmer's field and then I added, 'Me dad's goin' f'his degree,' which got a couple of giggles from those who knew my dad.

'Well, come on then, we haven't got all day. You

must remember *something* about the Triple Alliance. We did spend at least a fortnight on the subject.'

'I've got it!' I said after I'd thought and thought and really thought. 'I know what it is now. It's a new kind of long jump.'

I didn't think it was worth going down to get the stick for. It was only a joke, the miserable old cow. No sense of humour, that's her trouble. The last time she smiled her mouth had to have stitches.

When I got to the headmaster's office I stood outside for a bit and had a good look at his time machine. It's a circular wooden board nailed to the door and divided up like a clock into twelve parts. In each of the parts is a small red light bulb, and all typed out neat and tidy on a piece of paper is some place in the school, like 'Assembly Hall' or 'The Gymnasium' or 'The Science Block', except for three sections where there's written 'Come In', 'Wait' and 'Out'. The arse bandit woodwork teacher, Gaffer, did it for him when he first came, and before the week was out we'd all written in things like 'gone for a wank' or 'fucking the secretary' in the spaces and the Gaffer had to do them all again and cover them with this plastic stuff. At the side of this board there's a notice that says, 'Press This Button' and so I pressed it. A red light started flashing on an off in the 'Art Department' section. I didn't go looking for him though. It was no emergency.

He hasn't been our headmaster long; since Christmas when the woman we had before, Fatty Arbuckle, kicked it at the start of the autumn term. We all thought our deputy head would get the job but he never. They imported this new feller from Kirkby and he thinks he's dead hard and smart and got us all worked out. I still don't know his name and he's one of them fellers that doesn't even ask you yours. He just bursts you and tells you to go, like as if he's a marshal in a frontier town on the telly. When you get to the door holding your hands or your bum, you always think he's going to say, 'Now get outta town.'

I must have been waiting there about twenty minutes when Steve came limping down the corridor with Snotty Dog's class. It was the first time I'd seen Steve in weeks and he was even more crippled than ever with his bad knee that he got smashed up when he was a star winger with Blackburn Rovers just after the Boer war. He's my hero, Steve, even though it was him that told me that I wouldn't make the grade as a footballer myself and wanted me to try and be an actor instead 'cos I was the star of the school panto-mimes. An actor! Frigging hell, what next – ballet lessons instead of metalwork? I told him I couldn't as I didn't have a decent enough handbag, and he's never said any more about it since, and he doesn't hold it against me, just like I don't hold it against him 'cos he told me the truth, and no one else would. They'd just laugh at me behind my back.

'Hello, Scully,' he said. 'In trouble again?'

'Who me, Steve?' I said. 'Don't y'know me better than that after all these years? I'm just here t'get me new prefect's badge.'

'Who sent you down?'

'Well, er, Mrs Faconfield.'

'Come with me,' he said. 'I'll fix it for you. You'll be alright.'

'With that one? Are y'sure?'

'She's alright, Scully.'

'Yeah, she might be a whole bundle of fun in the staffroom but you try sittin' in a desk an' chattin' to her.'

'Suit y'self then,' he said, 'you stay here if you

want a sore behind for tonight's match—'

'Are y'comin', Steve?'

'Coming?' he said. 'I'm taking you.'

'Y'not are yer? Ace. We're a different side now, y'know. Y'won't recognize us.'

'So I've heard. What's all this about havin' a black Bruce Grobbelaar in goal?'

'Oh, Dole, yeah—'

'Who?'

'Tommy Kew. An' it's true, Steve. Just you wait till y'see him, y'don't have t'take the word of an expert, but I'll tell y'this; he's safer than the Midland Bank.'

We was outside school in the rain by this time, walking through the back playground towards the junior school and the church.

''Ey, hang about,' I said. 'Where y'takin' me?'

'Confession,' he said. 'This class always goes on the first Tuesday of the month.'

'Oh Jesus no.'

'Well, take y'pick, lad. Confession or the cane.'

'There's not much in it, Steve,' I said but I carried on walking with him and the rest of the class. I could stand my soul suffering but I wanted my arsehole safe from destruction before the match.

I went and stood outside the confession box. It was my turn next and Snotty Dog had just gone in. You have to stand by the door, 'cos if you don't, you'll get killed in the rush when the door opens, and you may as well get it over with. It's like going to the dentist's: You don't want to hang around in the waiting room all day, listening to the screams. I was leaning on the wall, catching everything that Snotty Dog was saying. You should have heard him. He was going on as though he was the Virgin Mary.

'Pray Father, give me your blessings, for I have

57

sinned. It is three weeks since my last confession.'

Now that was a dirty lie for a start. He always skives off school when it's confession day, same as we all do. The only reason he'd come in today was because of the big match tonight. Mind you, there's no point in telling the priest the truth 'cos that's asking for trouble right off, that is. I was in there once with Holy Joe O'Malley, our parish priest, and when he asked me how long it was since my last confession, just for a laugh I told him May the third, 1935, which is the day my Mam was born. And you know what? The lousy frigging penguin lifted the curtain up and had a good look at me. It's breaking the rules, that is. I was so surprised, I just stared back at him for ages and then ducked down with my coat around my head. But it was too late, he'd recognized me and went straight over and told our old headmistress. I had to kneel down on the stage in assembly the next morning and say the Hail Mary and start the singing.

'I have told lies to my parents and to my teachers, Father,' Snotty Dog was sayin' in this funny little voice like he has when he's readin' out loud in class with his finger on the line, an' he's sayin' the words all slow. 'And I have sworn and blasphemed a lot, and hit me little brother when he gets on me nerves a lot . . . and . . . and . . .'

'Is that all, my son?' It was Father O'Connell who was on duty. He's alright as priests go, Father O'Connell, but he's always doing a bunk to Africa. He's been twice since we've been in the Seniors, and when we were in the infants he was there when they had that big war in Biafra or somewhere, and when he came back he only had one arm. The Protestants must have shot him, like they do in Ireland. It doesn't half get in his way, only having one arm, especially when he's saying

58

Mass. Not only does it look sort of daft, a one-armed man praying, but he has to have an altar boy walking around with him, like you have a runner in cricket.

'Yes, Father, that's all, I think,' Snotty Dog said.

'That's good,' Father O'Connel said. 'Very good indeed.'

'Arr, it was nothin',' Snotty Dog said.

'Now are you sure there's not somethin' y'haven't forgotten?'

'No, Father, honest t'God.'

'And you attend Mass every Sunday?'

'I never miss, Father.'

'And communion.'

'Every time, Father.'

'That's very pleasing, I wish there were only more like you,' Father O'Connell said in a voice that sounded very much as if he was taking the piss himself, but I don't suppose he could have been. 'And there's no thievin', my son? No apples from the greengrocer's, a packet of sweets from the newsagent's. Little things like that, here and there?'

'Oh no, Father. I never do nothin' like that.'

What a liar! He's worse than me. I felt like bending down and shouting through the keyhole about all the shirts off the lines and the gallon of white emulsion from the wallpaper shop we screwed when his dad was doing the decorating. And what about Freddy Johnston's football boots that he reckons he lost on the bus going home from Sefton Park, that he's got underneath their bed till Freddy goes to Australia next month.

I didn't say a word though. I mean, I was going in there next to say the same old crap as everyone else.

'Well now, that is a good confession, and for you

penance I want you to say five Hail Marys and will you finish your confession with a good Act of Contrition.'

'Oh my God, because thou art so good . . .'

As I stood there in front of the door a big pile of tiny tot infants came rushing through the big open doorway at the far end of the church, all wide-eyed and wondering, looking up at the cross and the flowers on the altar and the big dripping candles, whispering and bowing and crossing themselves the wrong way around. I knew what they'd come for; some practice for when they did their First Holy Communion in May. Once, a long time ago, me and the others had stood there, barely able to peep over the edges of the seat in front of us.

Watching them there, all scared and happy and soaking it all in, I sort of had this kind of memory, like, of when I was a little kid in the Infants and the start of the Juniors, when I believed in God and Heaven and the Sugar Candy Mountains. School was alright then, too. I never used to skive off in the Infants.

There was this teacher who took 1B in the Infants who thought the world of me, and that's no lie. Her name was Mrs Ainsworth and she was a widow though she couldn't have been very old, I don't think. She told me her husband fell off a ladder fixing the roof and then he was paralysed for a while and then he died. She was always in church. Straight from school she'd shoot in here and get down on her knees at the altar rails. I suppose she had nothing better to do. We used to follow her in and she taught me some prayers. She taught me the 'I Believe' and it was dead long and I was the only one who knew it right the way through. I can still remember bits of it now, I think. 'I believe in God the Father Almighty, Creator of Heaven and Earth, and in Jesus Christ, his only forgotten son . . .' or something like that. She always said she'd take me home with her one day, this Mrs Ainsworth, to play with her kids and I worked my little balls off for her. I came top in her class at Christmas and she got me moved up into 1A, the top class. She thought she was doing me a favour but I didn't want to go. Did I buggery. I screamed all the way down the corridor and tried to run home. In the end, the caretaker had to carry me and I bit him on the arm.

I only lasted a week. It wasn't because I was thick or anything like that. It was because of what I did with my plasticine. She was a bigger boot than anything out of Timpsons, the woman that took 1A. Her name was Miss Horey and she had a carrot head and a neck like a milk bottle, and most important of all, she hated me. I'd only been in there a morning, and she was hitting me over the knuckles with a ruler, just because I didn't know my four times tables. I was only five. And what's more, we'd never done any multiplying in 1B, only adding up and taking away. Then one afternoon, I'll never forget she gave us all a dollop of plasticine and told us to make a man.

Well, I didn't know. Nobody told me. I made this feller perfect. I even give him a nose and eyes and a mouth with this safety-pin my Mam made me wear in my shirt in case my pants fell down. And I give him a chopper as well. You know, a dick. I suppose it was a big one, but I had a lot of plasticine left over. All the other kids were dead jealous as well, you know. They were. Another five minutes and they'd all have given their little men one as well.

My big mistake was going out to Miss Horey's desk to show it to her. I bet if I'd made him like Father O'Connell and left his arm off or given him two heads and three noses, she wouldn't have been bothered, but just because I made him exactly like

61

he was, she yelled blue murder. As I stood there thinking to myself I've done good here and this is bound to impress her, she tore the dick off my feller and dragged me screaming down the corridor again, past my old class, and into the headmistress's office and she threw my dick on the desk. Then the two of them went screwy together. There they were, raving away about me being filthy and dirty and bad, and all the time the dick was lying on the desk, all bent and mangled, and every so often one of them would sneak a look at it. If you ask me, I think they never knew before that blokes kept it there. They must have thought you carried it under your arm and it came out of a tap.

There wasn't anything they weren't going to do to me that day. Expelled in first-year Infants. Now, that's something isn't it? But when the shit stopped flying, Mrs Ainsworth took me back in, and I was never in any more trouble then till I got in the Juniors. But every chance she got after that, Miss Horey'd get me into lumber or give me a clout. And she used to do it to our Arthur too, when he was in the Infants, just 'cos he was my brother. Poor Arthur, until lately he'd have been as shocked as her if he'd seen my little plasticine man.

I never felt the same about school after that though, not really, and it was no different with church. I liked it for a bit, and I took everything in as well at first, but that's a phoney too, just like school. The thing that really put me off about going to church was that I knew for a fact that two of the fellers that came around with the collection plates were robbers. My dad used to go on jobs with them, that's how I know. He still does on the quiet, which is another reason for the holiday in Rhyl if you ask me, but if my Mam finds out she'll throw him all over the house and then out of it if previous form is anything to go by.

It's a bit much though isn't it? I mean, when you're a little kid, and you don't know any better, and you think these fellers that walk around with the plates are dead holy, almost priests themselves, and you think to yourself, 'Now, that'll go towards a new candle for the Virgin's statue' or something, and then you're at home the next night and your dad walks in with these same fellers and two hundred dozen nighties they've robbed from Marks and Spencer's. I tell you what, it makes you wonder where your money goes after it leaves the plate. From what I can see, if you go to our church and you put silver on the plate it's got a better than evens chance of going out of church the same time as you, and down the pub in someone's coat pocket.

So, I stopped going. One Sunday, just before we went in the Seniors, I was walking past the park on the way to ten o'clock Mass when this lad from the Protestant school, Eddie Valentine, he give me a shout to make up his team for a game of five-a-side, and I climbed over the railings without even thinking about it. The only time I ever go now is Midnight Mass at Christmas, and I only go then to see all the drunks heave up and faint. It's better than anything on the telly, but I don't think I'll even go to that anymore, not after last Christmas Eve when a woman sitting behind me was sick all over my head.

That is of course unless I'm stuck here, standing outside of confession first lesson of a Tuesday afternoon, listening to Cardinal Snotty Dog saying the longest Act of Contrition ever heard. The trouble was that when he got halfway through the short one, he realized he couldn't remember all of it, and so he had to go back and read out the long one written up on the wall, but he kept getting stuck on all the big words.

He finally finished and opened the door, coming

out with a huge grin, digging me in the ribs like as if he'd just pulled off a big robbery and then going over to the altar for a big sniff and five Hail Marys. Farter Alcock had gone on before him and he was still at the rails saying his penance. He must have had about a thousand Our Fathers to say. I wonder what he must have told the priest to get all them? One thing you should never do is tell them about playing with yourself. They really spin in their vestments if you let that slip.

The red light went on and I opened the door and there was a big pile of pushing and shoving going on behind me to see who went in next. I knelt down and took hold of the Cross that was hanging at the side of the wire grille in the wall that separates you from where the priest hides. Behind the grille is the curtain and that's the trouble. You never know for certain if they're there or not, 'cos you can't lift up the curtain and have a look. I always hold my breath and listen for them. All the old ones have bad chests. It's the ciggies you know. My Mam reckons they've got to have something to do with their hands when they're not praying. As soon as I can hear them wheezing I start. It's bad enough having to be there, but I couldn't stand it if I was left on my own, talking to a curtain and a cross and a bit of wire, while the priest was having a slash in the priest's house.

He coughed, so I started but I kept me voice well down. 'Pray Father, give me your blessin's, for I have sinned. It is four weeks since my last confession. I have told lies to my parents an' to my teachers, Father, an' I have sworn a lot . . .'

When I came out with me usual dose of five Hail Marys, Farter Alcock was still at the altar rails. Only when I went and knelt by him did I hear him snoring. Steve left him there when we went back over, and Father O'Connell woke him up halfway

64

through half six Mass when he started farting in his sleep.

We lost the game that night one frigging nil, and threw away any chances that we had of the championships. It was a good job it wasn't a cup game or else the whole season would have been finished. We didn't really stand much chance of being champions of the league but we were in the semi-finals of the under-sixteens cup, so maybe if we had to have an off day we picked the right one at least. It could easily have been five-nil the way we played, and it would have been ten if it hadn't been for Dole, though in the end it was him that gave the goal away.

I think the reason we were so bad was that we were all out to impress Steve and show him how good we were, so that all the passing and helping and working for each other that we'd always done before went completely to cock in the first half. Even after half time when Steve told us what was wrong we still didn't play like we can do. Another reason was that it'd pissed down for about an hour before the match and the ground was already heavy to start with. No disrespect like, but niggers don't play so well in the mud you know. I think it might be something to do with them not being used to it where they come from, or else all their skills got stuck in the slutch, but we just couldn't get going. To add to all that, they were a good team that we were playing. Top of the league and already in the final of the under-sixteens cup. And cocky with it. They all come from a big comprehensive in Halewood about three times the size of our school. The trouble with Halewood, if you ask me, is that it's an estate on its own like, with countryside nearly all the way around it, and 'cos of that anyone that comes from there thinks they're something special. If they have one of them coat of arms things, it should be an open gob in a cabbage patch.

We held out until ten minutes to go and it began to look as though we might get a draw or even snatch a quick goal, especially as they were getting tired of seeing Dole make it all look unbelievably easy and hard at the same time. The only bit of luck he had was when a long shot hit the crossbar, came back, hit Dole on the top of the head as he turned around and then bounced back off him over the bar for a corner kick. He was still laughing when he fisted the corner out towards the right wing and safety. 'Out, boys, out,' he said as he went and leant against the goal-post.

Our attack, if that's the right word for it, soon broke down and their left back heaved the ball out of the mud, high in the air and towards our goal. Brian Bignall and their centre forward both jumped up and missed it and the ball went skidding down the pitch for their little front runner to run onto. He was in the clear, just him and Dole – who was hurtling out of his goal towards the ball stuck in the mud five yards outside the penalty area. Dole made ground on the little toad, but not enough, and just before he got there Poison Dwarf managed to scoop the ball away from Dole's dive and carried on towards the empty net.

We'd all stood there like wanky actors waiting to go on stage, as if it wasn't anything to do with us that the curtain had fallen down, and even when the kid beat Dole we all stayed still, stuck where we were. All except Dole. He picked himself up and raced back and whatever you say about fair play and being a good sport and all that shite, Poison Dwarf asked for everything that Dole did to him.

You see, it's a common trick around our way when you're just knocking around in the park or on the playground, with coats as goalposts, to dribble around the goalie and then with everyone beaten, stop the ball on the line, whip down on your hands and knees and head it past the coats. It's just a bit of a pose, a joke in a kick around. And you never ever do it in a real match. Not if you want your three score and ten you don't.

But this little snot rag did. He saw Dole was still yards away from him, and he got down on all fours at the side of the ball and wiggled his bum. I wouldn't mind, but he was only about the same size as the ball when he knelt down, but when Dole saw his arse jigging about, he let out a big long scream like Tarzan with his balls caught in some brambles, took a fit, took a run and took off, bounced just behind the kid and then skidded into the net with his arms around him. Dole was still filling his face with fist when Brian Bignall came and hooked the ball off the line and then the net collapsed over Dole and Poison Dwarf as if they were the two gladiators in that smart old film, *Ben Hur*.

The kid's face was in bits when they got pulled apart. Like an Identikit. He got carried off to all corners of the pitch. Dole took one look at the referee, stammering and going purple and tugging at his notebook jammed in his little black pocket, and he said, 'Alright, ref, I know, I'm goin',' took off his jersey and went and stood by Steve, poor Steve, who'd turned around and turned his collar up and his trilby down and was pretending to watch the match on the next pitch.

'He oughtn't t'have gone an' done that, Steve,' Dole said. 'It wasn't polite.'

'It's . . . well . . .. never mind,' Steve mumbled and he lifted his hands as if to comfort Dole but kept them in his pockets so all that happened was that his mack shot up in the air, and Dole trudged off towards the dressing rooms right across another pitch full of players.

It was like getting dressed in a coffin that night. Our first defeat, a penalty and all, the first time Steve watches us, Dole sent off, a report sure to go in, Mad Dog standing outside telling everyone it wouldn't have happened if he'd been in goal, and all the Halewood halfarses singing and shouting in the changing room next to ours, 'We are the Champions, We are the Champions' and nobody saying anything in ours, just shuffling about in the damp, but every one of us hoping we'd meet them in the final and have the last laugh. Well, that was what I was thinking anyway, and if the others weren't thinking that, they may as well go and hang themselves.

Not even walking part of the way home with Dole's sister and thinking about Thursday night with Marie Morgan seemed to make any difference. We'd been beaten. Again. I should have been used to it by now, after the previous four and a half years, but I wasn't. I fucking well hate being beaten.

4

Well, I washed under my arms, had a shave, threw some of our Vera's left-over talc down my undies, splashed about a pint of my dad's knocked-off after-shave on my cheeks, combed my hair, took a pair of trousers from between the mattress and the bed, and sneaked out the front door without even our Arthur seeing me go. Then I sneaked back in again, 'cos I'd forgotten the most important thing of all – my protection.

I hadn't had the nerve to get them myself so I'd dragged Mooey down to the barbers, gave him some money, convinced him he needed a haircut, wrote him a note saying, 'I want a packet of Durex, please, urgent' and sent him in. I'd have done a lot to get some Johnnies, but I wasn't going to let Hatchet Harry, the mad barber, have a go at my scalp. Not the same day as the night I got my hole anyway. The last time he cut my hair I could have got a part in a cowboy film, playing a Mohican. Half an hour later Mooey came out with what I wanted and a smart basin cut for himself.

Back out of the house just as someone opened the kitchen door, around the corner, at the bus stop, told this mate of Brian Bignall's and his girlfriend that they'd just missed the bus and it'd be at least half an hour before the next one. Saw them flag down a taxi; nobody else waiting with me at the stop, too good to be true. Marie turns up looking as near to normal as she'll ever get; not a soul in the whole road, a miracle for a sunny Thursday night at half past seven. Get a hard-on lighting a ciggie for her, watching her sucking the smoke in, breathing it out again, burn my fingers on the match but it doesn't matter, light the filter tip on mine but sod it that doesn't matter neither. The bus rolls up, first stop after the terminus. Nobody I know downstairs, we go upstairs and then - disaster, absolute frigging unmerciful disaster.

How was I to know the whole flaming youth club'd be going down town to see some stupid basketball finals at the YMCA? Hey, how was I to know that?

'Alright there, Scull, la', copped off at last have yer?'

'Aye aye, no dogs upstairs, please.'

'Or bitches.'

'Nor scrubbers.'

'Where'd'y'pick her up, Scully? The abattoir?'

'Nah, the cemetery, wasn't it?'

'He was diggin' a hole at the time.'

'An' he'll get his hole t'night an' all.'

'God help him.'

'I hope y'wearin' somethin'?'

'Yeah, an' it'd better be rust protected.'

'An' germ resistant.'

'Got the vaseline ready have yer?'

'Wha'? On a rebore?'

'Course, I had to sit there and grin and bear it and say nothing. There were about fifteen of them, and as you know yourself, if I'd even looked as though I might be getting upset, they'd have only given me more, and the next thing you know, I'd be fighting the whole frigging top deck over Marie Morgan of all people, and the next day the whole sodding estate'd have me married off to her.

Mind you, give Marie her due, she had an answer for all of them. After all, she probably knew all the questions, before they started. Anyway, between suggesting that one of them got his mouth retreaded, and telling Mike Powell to grow up and be a man or don't you do impressions, informing Alan Jones that the last time she saw a gob like his a gamekeeper was feeding it bananas sideways, she gave as good as she got till our stop came at Old Swan.

'You were quiet up there,' she said as we waited for the 61 bus to Otterspool.

'Ah, I take no notice, me,' I said. 'Y'know, sticks an' stones...' I tried to grab her hand as she leaned against the bus shelter but I didn't want to look at it and take aim like a game of darts. I just wanted to try and casually find it, and then act as if it was a big surprise to me when I had hold of it, like it was natural and relaxed and I'm a big boy now, even though I was caking it inside. The only trouble was I could never find it. I put my hand in her coat pocket twice and then I gave up until the bus came.

I know it was a bad move asking the bus conductor for scholars, but after Mooey's expedition to the barbers and one thing and another I hardly had any money left. 'Be prepared' our Tony always used to say. Fat lot of notice he took of himself, but I wasn't going to make the same mistake as him. Not with Marie Morgan anyway.

'But I'm only fourteen,' I said.

'What about y'mother, here, then?' he asked as I fumbled about in my pockets to see exactly how much I had.

'That's not my mother, don't you insult my younger sister.'

'An' I suppose y'goin' t'y'aunty's?' he said. 'What a nice little boy.'

'That's right, how did y'guess?' If I paid full fare now, I couldn't buy her no chips afterwards and we'd have to walk halfway home.

'Well, I tell yer what, son,' the conductor said, 'if y'are goin' t'y'aunty's an' she's anythin' like mine, y'd better not let her see these.'

And he bent down and picked up my packet of
Durex off the floor. I almost died in my seat as the
bastard and all the bus pissed themselves silly.
But what could I do? If I said they weren't mine, I
may as well get off the bus now.

'They're me dad's,' I said. 'I've just got them for
him. He er can't get them himself y'see. He's er
paralysed.'

'From the waist down?'

'That's right,' I said, grabbing at straws. 'He fell
off our roof last year, we're expectin' him t'die
shortly.'

'Is that a fact?' the conductor said as everyone
laughed at me and I wondered why. 'The next
thing y'll be tellin' me, there's a balloon shortage
an' y'goin' t'a party.' He tossed them in my lap and
sauntered off down the bus all made up with
himself.

What a smart start to my sex life. Marie muttered
something about not knowing what I'd brought
them for and had a little laugh to herself, and from
them on till we got to the terminus the people
around us were either moving away or coming
closer for a better look.

It's a bit of a dump this Otterspool Promenade,
really. Just a big pile of grass and stack of trees
and car parks. It looks out over the Mersey and
that's so dirty and muddy anyone can walk over it,
never mind Jesus. At low tide all you can see is
muck and rubbish, bed frames and old bikes. In my
Mam's day they used to call it the Cast Iron Shore
and nothing's changed much from then, I can tell
you. Except they've dug some gardens and planted
a few flowers.

She didn't know very much about football,
Marie, and those Duran Duran give me a pain in
the arse, so we didn't have much to talk about,

though the weather and the telly got a good going over from us, but after that, there didn't seem as though there was anything left to say. It was then that I pulled my master stroke from out of me pocket, where they'd been goin' soft anyway.

'Here y'are,' I said, 'don't say I never give y'nothin'.'

'I don't like chocolates,' she said. 'They kill me teeth.'

Fucking hell.

I took aim and fired. I was desperate. So desperate that I grabbed the Milk Tray as well and squashed the box, but at least I had hold of her hand. Her fingernails were bitten near down to the knuckles.

'It's a nice night,' I said. Again.

'It's alright.'

Another fifty yards, two bike frames, a gas oven, an old three-piece suite and a burnt-out car. One of the bike frames looked as though it could have been saved.

She took her hand away to light a cigarette.

'It's me last one,' she said, and then stuck her hand straight back into her pocket before I had a chance.

Fucking fucking hell.

I stopped and leant over the promenade rails and wondered what I could say about the oil jetties at Dingle that would excite her, and then I looked down at the shore. There was a mattress off a bed lying half covered by the mud, with what tide there was just dribbling over it.

'Well, that's a coincidence, Marie,' I said. 'It really is.'

I looked around. The bitch was thirty yards away, just walking along on her own. I had to shout her back, didn't I? And then she didn't exactly run romantically towards me. Not like she

73

was supposed to. Not even in slow motion.

'Wha' is it?' she said.

'Here, come here, look.' I made her stand right by me. 'See that mattress over there,' I said. 'See, the green one with the brown patches, well, that's the same mattress as the one on my bed. That's a coincidence that, isn't it, Marie?'

'Is that all?' she said. 'Jeez, I thought y'd found the Crown Jewels,' and she flicked her ciggie in the water.

If you want to know the truth, I'd never seen a mattress like it in my life before, but I had her now, leaning against me, and I put me arm around her shoulder and wished I could stop trembling.

'What does a mattress make y'think of, Marie?'

'Sleep,' she said.

But I carried on and turned her towards me and she moved her head up to face me and I closed my eyes and I kissed her.

On the nose.

Right on the tip.

Thank god it wasn't Snotty Dog.

'Here,' she said, and reached into her pocket. 'Y'd better have a chocolate.'

So, she was the first girl I'd ever kissed. So there, now you know. So. *So*? You make your mistakes don't yer? Nobody's perfect first go. You live and learn, that's right isn't it? Like I told the others. It was a case of old wood and pigs' livers.

I just hoped she wouldn't tell anyone, that was all. She could tell Mooey all she wanted, he'd probably think I thought I was an Eskimo, but if she told anyone else and the word got around, I'd leave our estate, I would. Do a Mickey Brown and join the Foreign Legion in Llandudno; join the Dogs on the road to the North Sea. Anything, 'cos life wouldn't be worth living around our way.

We got to the end of the Promenade where it was

74

all boarded up, and we turned back. I'm not saying I'd given up the ghost, but I wasn't sure what to do next. What to mess up next, that is. It was going dark as well, which was smart in one sense, but I was frightened to death of not being able to see what I was doing. It was bad enough not *knowing* what I was doing.

But I didn't have to do anything as it turned out. She did it all for me. We'd just got back to the famous green and brown mattress when she linked my arm and came closer to me.

'It's gettin' a bit colder, isn't it,' she said.

I hadn't noticed, I must say, 'cos I was sweating so much I wouldn't have been cold in a snowstorm, but the way I agreed and hugged myself and shivered and went, 'Brrr, it is, isn't it?' you'd think I was Mooey's Eskimo caught out in the knacker.

'Have y'got a job yet, Franny?' she said.

'Nah, I haven't looked.'

'Don't y'want one?'

''Course I bloody well do; just there doesn't seem much point in tryin'. I read in the *Echo* the other night that there's somethin' like one job f'every hundred school-leavers in Liverpool this summer. Fat chance I've got of landin' one of them. They want O-Levels an' good conduct badges t'tarmac the roads these days.'

'I'm leavin' at summer an' all,' she said.

'How come you an' Mooey can leave school t'gether when y'not twins?'

'I'm ten months older than him,' she said. 'Our Karen's gettin' me in her place.'

'Me dad can't get me on the Corpy; they've already told him.'

'It's a smart job our Karen's got. They have the radio on all day long an' they knock off at three of a Friday.'

'What she do, your Karen?'

There was a bench and some bushes about thirty yards away. My plans were to get her down there before she changed her mind about being nice to me. I started to limp.

'She's in the meat paste factory on the industrial estate. She takes the guts out of chickens.'

An old couple walking past us must have reckoned I had a wooden leg, the way I was walking. I thought Marie'd never notice. It's her kind that try and shake hands with fellers with no arms.

'But they're goin' t'make her supervisor soon.'

'Is that so? Oooh, ouch.'

'Yes, she's the fastest degutter in the factory.'

'Fancy that. Ouch, oooh,' I said as we got nearer to the bench.

'What's the matter?' she said at last. 'Gorra stone in y'shoe?'

'Ah, it's nothin' much,' I said, but I made certain I stopped right by the bench. 'It's just a broken bone I got stoppin' a certain goal the other night. Playin' me up a bit, that's all, but it was worth the agony. I'll be alright in a minute.'

'Sit down f'a while,' she said and I almost forgot my limp in the panic to get there.

'Aren't you sittin' down?' I asked after a bit.

'Suppose so,' she said and I got two ciggies out of my packet and put them both in my mouth like lovers always do, and I lit them and passed one over to Marie.

'No thanks,' she said. 'I've just put one out.'

She bit her nails and I smoked my two ciggies as if it was the normal thing to do, and it got a bit darker and no-one came past except a couple of kids on bikes and I stuck one of the ciggies behind my back. When I'd finished, I rubbed my hands together like I meant business and then put my arm around her shoulder, mentioned the cold weather again and ploughed in for another go.

No messing this time – straight on the gob first go, and me hand around her waist. I waggled my lips about for a bit and then pulled away. I'd wondered about sticking my tongue in her mouth like you're supposed to, but I thought better of it. Just as well, I can tell you.

'I hope it was nice,' she said.

'Wha'd'y'mean?' I said. 'It was great.'

'Well, y'know, it's like . . . y'never tasted nothin'?'

''Ey? Tasted? Y'a girl, not a packet of fish fingers.'

'Well, y'know, it's me mouth.'

'There's nothin' wrong with y'mouth,' I said. 'It's in the right place, underneath y'nose, on top of y'chin, y've got two lips, they open an' close. What more d'y'want?'

'It's not exactly me mouth,' she said, 'it's me gums.'

'Y'gums?'

'That's right.'

'What's wrong with y'gums?'

'I've gorra disease.'

I went sick inside. VD of the gob. I knew of only one way she could possibly have got that.

'Er, like what kind of disease, Marie?'

'It's pyorrhoea.'

"Oh.' I was almost pleased. It wasn't nearly as bad. It only felt as if someone had shit on my lips.

'An' me gums bleed somethin' awful sometimes.'

I lit another ciggie and stood up.

'By God, that rest's done me leg the world of good,' I said, an' I began t'jog up an' down on the spot t'prove me point. 'Can't be broken after all, hardly feel a thing now. Fit t'walk another five miles, I reckon. Come on.'

We were back on the road towards the bus terminus before I could even bear to look sideways at her again, though she didn't seem to notice very much. She still had tight hold of my left arm and if I lifted my elbow I could feel her left tit. I had visions of seeing the gang tomorrow and Mad Dog asking me what I got, and me saying I got a feel of her left tit with my right elbow. That was what pulled me into the field at the side of Jericho Lane, if you ask me, not Marie giving me a tug and saying it was a short cut to the chippy. I'd been down around Otterspool often enough to know that it was no quick way to anywhere, except your hole in one.

'Look at the moon,' she said, 'it ₁ almost full.'

'They've got a terrible housin' problem,' I said, but she just ignored me.

'I could lie down an' look at the moon f'hours,' she said, and then she did lie down and look at the moon.

'It must be wet, that grass,' I said.

'Oh, only a bit, an' I've got me polythingy coat on; it dries dead quick.'

'Well, I haven't. I'm not goin' home lookin' as though I've been f'a swim.'

'Y'don't have t'lie on the grass,' she said, all husky an' deep. 'Y'can lie on top of me.'

Oh fucking hell!

'There's a bull in this field somewhere, isn't there?' I said, looking around me and playing it cool while my cock stood secretly to attention.

'Posin' again?' she said, and me old man nearly tore a hole in my undies and I lay all over her and wondered if you could get pyorrhoea in half an hour flat.

It's funny you know, but I hadn't noticed nothing before when I kissed her, but now, not only did she seem to taste horrible, but there was a real bad smell around and all. I wanted to ask her if what she had smelt as well, but I didn't like asking, not now.

I began to suspect something was wrong when I got her bra off. I'd rehearsed that bit the night before with one of my Mam's fastened around the wardrobe door when everybody was asleep, and I thought at least she'd be impressed by the way I did that, but all she did was giggle. I hadn't had anyone's tits to practice on, but I'd heard enough stories to have some idea and she stopped laughing after a while and I knew I was getting her worked up, so I put my hand on her knee and her legs opened. She put her arm across the inside of my thigh then and her hand went be'ween my legs and it was so good I had to concentrate on not coming. I thought of the inside of her mouth and my flag fell straight to half mast so I stopped thinking altogether and got on with the job.

My hand went up the ladders in her tights till I got to the top and I pulled at them as she lifted herself up and I took them down past her knees and my balls were aching past themselves, especially when she moved her fingers across my zip and then up and down it as if she was going to pull my trousers down any minute.

Fat chance.

I'd just got going on trying to take her panties off when she started sniggering away again. I'm not kidding, it was like trying to fuck the Laughing Cavalier.

'What's the matter, Marie, f'Christ's sake?'

'Nothin'. I just think it's funny, that's all.'

'Wha' is?'

'It's y'first time, isn't it?'

'Gerrout, what makes yer think that?'

'It is though, isn't it?'

'So wha' if it is? There's no need t'be acting like

79

it's Cannon and Ball.'

'It's not that I'm laughin' at,' she said. 'It's somethin' else completely.' She had another little chuckle to herself and with no warning at all grabbed my nudger through my trousers and squeezed my copper's helmet, and I almost landed on the frigging moon with the excitement and the agony of it all. I felt in my jacket pocket and got the packet of Durex out and I started struggling with the flip top opening. One fell out and I tore at the plastic wrapping trying to get at it as she pulled and tugged at my nudger. There was still a foul smell about and my knees were soaked and she was still laughing, but the state I was in, she could have been singing 'The Teddy Bears' Picnic' at the top of her voice and rubbing gin on her gums and I wouldn't have cared.

Her other hand reached out towards mine and helped me get the wrapping off and right at that second she'd asked me if I loved her I could have said 'yes' and not giggled as much as she was. That is, until she got the rubber thing free and took it out of my hands, wrapping an' all, and bloody well threw it away in the dark. I went chasing after it on my knees and then come back to get another one out.

'I'm not doin' it without one, Marie,' I said. 'Not bareback. We might get caught out.'

'Y'won't be doin' it at all, Scully,' she said. 'Not t'night anyway.' She said something else as well, but I couldn't catch what it was 'cos she was almost crying. With laughter.

'Wha'd'y'mean?' I said. 'Y'can't stop now. Not now.'

'I can,' she said when she'd got her breath back, 'an' I am.'

'But why, Marie? What for?'

'I've got to. Y'see, I'm on.'

'Y'wha'?'

'I'm on; I'm havin' a period.'

'Y'll be havin' a broken nose if we stop now.'

'There's nothin' y'can do about it.'

'Y'lousy bitch. Y'lousy stinkin' rotten slag.'

'I knew y'd say that.'

'Take it out, go on, take it out!'

'I can't, I'll bleed.'

'From the fuckin' nose, if y'don't.'

'Touch me, Franny Scully, an' I'll make you the laughin' stock of Liverpool before the week's through.'

I put my hands behind my back and cracked my knuckles instead of cracking her one.

'Y'knew all along, didn't yer 'ey? Y'did, didn't y'? Go on, own up. When y'saw me at the beginnin' of the week, y'worked it all out.'

'What if I did?'

'That's mean that is. An' sly.'

'Serves y'right.'

'I beg y'pardon? Serves *who* right? Wha've I done to you? Wha've I ever done t'deserve this?'

'It's not just you,' she said, 'it's you an' all of them. I know what y'all call me. I've heard. I know.' She wasn't laughing now. 'Think I'm easy, don't yer 'ey? "Willin' f'a a shillin'." I've got ears, I'm not deaf.'

'Here,' I said. 'Here's two bob, give me hell.'

'See what I mean? See?'

'It's y'own mistake, girl, you started it. Nobody asked y' t'do it in the first place.'

Well, it wasn't my fault. How was I to know? Who could have guessed saying that would start the flood taps on full? Talk about from sex to suicide in thirty seconds. Buckets she was weeping, and I was lying at the side of her, getting wet and trying to work out what was happening.

'I never started it,' she said. 'It got started for me.

One day . . . one day—'

'Oh fuck, Marie, look, it doesn't matter, let's—'

'I was ten . . . last year of the Juniors, Miss Golding's class . . . he met me after school—'

'Yes, love, I'm sure he did, now—'

'My Uncle Harry, said he'd come t'take me home . . . to his house . . . for tea—'

'Good old Uncle Harry, I bet it was a nice tea,' I said all of a gallop and trying to lift her up, but she was a dead weight. 'Steak an' chips, somethin' like that, 'ey we could get some ch—'

'Through the new estate . . . across the waste land . . . it was winter an' it was dark—'

'Look, it's dark now an' it's gettin' late as well—'

'He put his arm around me 'cos it was dark, that's what he said—'

'Yes, fine, alright, Marie. it's alright, you don't have t'tell me anythin', just please stop fuckin' cryin' will y'?'

'He put his coat on the banisters . . . the front room door wasn't quite shut . . . but there was no one else in the house . . . he'd seen t'that alright.'

'Marie, *Marie*, I know what y'goin' t'tell me, I've already guessed it, *y'don't have t'tell me—*'

'He put me on the couch, lifted me up like a baby an' put me—'

'*Marie!*'

'Took all my clothes off . . . an' I cried an' cried but he took no notice, none at all . . . my knickers ended up over the fireguard, an' as he was doin' it t'me I screamed an' screamed an' *screamed*!'

And then she couldn't say anymore and I bent down and hugged her and as I knelt there close to her I could hear the tiniest screams you've ever heard coming from what seemed like right inside. By the time she stopped and I got her to her feet she'd already woken up three cows and one was on its way over to see what the action was.

'Look, Marie,' I said as we trailed back towards the road like two rejects from the Good Samaritans, 'look, let's forget about the whole thing 'ey? That's the best thing t'do, isn't it? No hard feelin's an' a secret shared is a secret somethin' or other, I can't remember right now, but y'll feel better in the mornin'. I didn't know about y'uncle, y'should tell the police y'know, well, someone anyway, 'cos he might try it again, the lousy sod, why doesn't he pick on someone his own size? I've got a good mind t'get a gang up an' beat the livin' shit out of him right now. Where does he live 'ey? Come on, Marie, I won't laugh at yer any more, promise, an' I won't tell anyone about it, y'can trust in me, y'know that, don't yer? Look, here's that chippy, d'y'want some? Do yer? Y'did say "no" then, didn't yer? That's good, we won't have t'get scholars on the way back, an' see, there's a bus in the terminus, we'll be home in no time, have a bath when y'get home, that always does y'good, y'know. I always have one after a hard game of football. Just lie there lettin' all the dirt fall off me, makes y'feel all refreshed like, an' ready t'start all over again. Good for yer, a ba—'

'Why don't you just shut up?' she said.

Marie didn't say another word all the way back to Old Swan and she managed to stop crying, but I reckoned that you could tell people knew there was something wrong between us by the way they kept looking at me and Marie all puzzled and then moving away as if they realized we wanted to be on our own. Either that or it was the smell moving them. As I sat there folding my ticket over and over again, I wondered if it was just simply something to do with her gums, or maybe it was her period or another reason that she hadn't told me about but whatever it was, the stink was really strong. The same conductor as before was on the bus but even he didn't stay for a chat, and he never went up the stairs again.

Mind you, it wouldn't be a show without Punch. When we got on the bus at Old Swan to go home I said my first prayer in years that the youth club wouldn't be on it, and my prayers were answered. They weren't, but He'd sent our Tony and Mrs Barrett instead. And made sure that the only two seats left on the top deck were in front of them. Tony near slid off the seat with joy when he saw me and who I was with. Mrs Barrett would have done the same, but there was no room for her to slide anywhere, the shape of her.

'Alright, Tony,' I said, putting a brave face on, 'hello, Mrs Barrett.'

'Mrs Scully, if you don't mind,' she said and flashed the wedding ring on her pudgy old finger.

'Oh aye, yeah, won't be long now, will it?' I said, sort of hoping that if I got her talking about babies, our Tony'd leave me alone.

'No, it won't,' she said. 'I went the ante-natal clinic this mornin' an' they said the head was engaged.'

'When's it gettin' married?' I said before I had a chance to swallow my tongue.

'I was just about t'ask you that, kidder,' our Tony said. The couple in front of us turned around as our Tony was talking, had a good look at me and Marie and moved three rows further up as the bus emptied.

'Don't know what y'mean, Tony,' I said.

'Doin' a bit though aren't yer 'ey?'

'Who me?' I said. 'Y'kiddin'. I've just been t'see the youth club playin' basketball. Ace game it was an' all. The finals, y'know. Marie was there an' she came home with me. Right that, isn't it? Isn't it, Marie?'

'If you say so,' she said and a feller with an

umbrella across the passageway from me started going 'tut tut tut' and looking at me and waving his brolly like a fan. As soon as someone else got off the bus, he moved away. I had a good mind to go up there to him and tell him it was her who had the bad mouth, not me.

'Where've y'been anyway, Tony,' I said. 'Shouldn't be goin' about draggin' expectin' mothers out on the ale, y'know.'

'If y'must know,' Mrs Barrett said, 'I haven't touched a drop in months.'

'No wonder that woman in the off licence's had a long face lately, Mrs Barrett.'

'*Scully.*'

'Sorry, Mrs Barrett, Mrs Scully.'

'We've been down t'the Cathedral t'see a film on havin' a baby, actually,' she said. 'It was all about the birth an' everythin'. It's beautiful, that's what it is. An' fulfillin'. It makes y'see the divine light.'

I knew what divine light she'd be seeing in about a month's time; their bedroom light at three o'clock in the morning, as she tried to rock the little devil asleep while our Tony snored his socks off. But I didn't argue. She was too old; she knew everything. It's a fact that, stay alive forty-odd years and you know all there is to know, nobody can teach you anything. That's what most people that age seem to think anyway.

'An' Tony's goin' t'be at me side right through it all,' she said and got hold of his hand. 'Aren't you, sweet?' He gave me a sickly grin and I had to laugh. Can't look at a pound of liver without fainting, our Tony.

'I don't like t'say this,' our Tony whispered when he'd got his hand free, 'but there's an awful smell of shit hangin' around you two.'

The top deck was almost empty. I could hear the conductor saying, 'Standin' room only downstairs, fill up the top deck now please.'

'It's her,' I whispered back, 'it's her gums.'

'Her gums?' our Tony said in this voice like the Kop choir of a Saturday afternoon, and leant halfway around me to try and see into her mouth, while Marie leant across to give him a mouthful.

It was then that the three of us saw it. Two spread out mounds of cow shit, one on each knee of my trousers. I must have carried the load halfway across Liverpool.

A nightmare, that's what it was. It had to be. I'd wake up in a minute with a hard-on for Joanna Kew, our Henry'd be steaming around the cockloft and Hovis'd be crying for 'The Three Bears'. And everything'd be alright.

But it wasn't a nightmare and it wasn't alright. Marie'd started laughing again, our Tony was singing 'Down on the Farm' and Mrs Barrett was opening all the windows and trying to get out of her seat in case the smell upset her baby. And I was attempting to wipe it off with two rolled-up tenpenny bus tickets.

The only consolation I had was that it was our stop next. I shot off the bus and started rubbing my knees against the privets and then I found an old newspaper and got rid of most of it. Onto my hands mainly. But at least that gave me an excuse not to walk Marie home, not that either of us really wanted one. And anyway, it was all her fault. If she hadn't thrown that Johnny off into the dark, none of this would have happened.

'Thanks, Marie,' I said, for something to say to get away as I held me hands out in front of me.

'Yes, well, I'll be seein' yer,' she said. 'It's been . . .' And then she couldn't say any more. I almost ran after her to tell her I'd keep her secret if she kept mine but she was laughing so much there didn't seem much point. I could still hear the bitch when I was halfway up our road with Tony and Mrs Barrett. He stood at the gate with me while she found the key and opened the front door.

'Glad I came t'night,' he said. 'Wouldn't have missed that for the world.'

'You're welcome,' I said. 'As long as I can come an' see you throw up an' pass out when she goes into labour.'

'Jeez, d'y'have t'mention that?' he said. 'I had me eyes closed f'an hour an' a quarter there. Every time I opened them there was blood. Still, it was worth it, just f'the bus home. Y'know what they say, don't yer, Franny? If y'go out with cows, y've got t'expect shit on y'knees, an' Marie Morgan's the biggest cow I've ever seen.'

'Think y'funny, don't yer?' I said as Mrs Barrett chased him into the house. 'Well, y'd be surprised, Tony, I'm tellin' yer. It was nothin' like y'imagine it t'be, nothin' at all.'

He blew a raspberry through the letterbox, but what he didn't know, thank God, was that I'd never said a truer word.

5

A week later to the day, the following Thursday, my dad fell into the house at ten past eleven with what was left of his pay packet, holding his letter making him redundant from the Corporation, crying like a baby and spilling crisps and peanuts all over the floor.

'"Thank you for your services,"' my Mam spat, reading the letter. '"We will contact you if opportunities for re-employment arise in the future." Like shite they will, I've seen this comin' f'ages, them friggin' councillors, couldn't organize a funeral in a cemetery they couldn't. It's a waste of time votin', God knows it is. They're only interested in one thing, that lot – themselves; featherin' their own nest.' She stood there, looking at my dad, and then she threw the piece of paper in the fire and tried to pick him up. 'Give us a hand with your father, Francis, will yer.'

We carried him up to bed and then my Mam lay on the eiderdown with him. I could hear her trying to comfort him as I came back down the stairs, and I heard my dad suddenly shout, 'Don't throw me out, Bernadette, please don't throw me out,' and then they were all quiet, and I got back to watching this old gangster film with some feller flicking coins all the time.

My Mam went up to the council the next morning and had my dad's foreman up against the depot wall, but there was nothing she could do. My dad was just one of about a hundred painters, decorators, binmen and cleaners that got laid off, and it was nothing to do with the foreman anyway. They wouldn't let her in the offices to see the real bosses, the ones that sit there at their desks on their fat arses all day long, playing little games with people, making all the decisions and cocking them up and running out of money and then lobbing the men out of work, while none of them ever got the sack. Promoted, no doubt, some of them. My Mam saw one of the councillors in the Labour Club that night and poured her Guinness down his neck, but it made no odds. My dad was back where he'd been too often before.

And then to make matters even worse, Mrs Barrett went into hospital to have a rest till the baby came 'cos she was run down. I always knew our Tony'd try and push her into the traffic one day. But my Mam had a right few days of it, what with my dad moping around the house threatening to blow the council buildings up and our Tony hanging about complaining 'cos he had nobody to cook for him and no one to play with.

I don't know how we got through the next week without our Tony cutting his wrists and me dad boring everyone to death, but by the Friday tea-time, my Mam'd had just about enough. 'Look,' she said t'me. 'I'm takin' y'dad out f'a drink t'night, christ knows he needs one f'a change. There's some stew in the oven, be a good lad an' take it next door t'that useless brother of yours an' try an' cheer him up, will yer? I had t'give him two quid t'go down the pub this afternoon I was so desperate t'get him from under me feet.'

'I'll cheer him up, Mam,' I said, 'but who's goin' t'do the same with me when I come back? Ten minutes in his company's enough t'get anyone depressed.'

I tried to get our Arthur to take it next door, but he's not as soft as he was now that he's stopped playing with the girls and wanting to wear his hair in pigtails, and when I wouldn't pay him he told me to get lost and ran away before I could catch him. There was no chance of getting our Henry to do it either. He'd just heard about the Common Market and was digging a channel tunnel in the cockloft and learning the French for 'puff-puff'. Me Gran'd left the house two minutes after my Mam and dad looking like a cross between Ziggy Stardust and Bette Davis, and so there was only me left, sucker me. I waited till there was only some Wightman Cup tennis on the telly and then I went over with the pan.

I expected to find him on their settee writing love poems to Mrs Barrett and covered in soggy paper hankies, but there he was, large as life, bouncing about in front of the telly, dressed all in white and holding this tennis bat that must have been second-hand when McEnroe was in nappies. I could hardly believe my eyes. Our Tony playing tennis? Watching it on the Box even, dressed like Virginia Wade and waving his bat about like an epileptic butterfly? Even worse, whatever the players were doing, Tony was there copying them, jumping all over the living room. Everytime there was a high lob, he took cobs out of the ceiling.

'What the hell're y'doin'?' I said. 'Have y'taken leave of y'senses?'

''Course I haven't, Jesus did y'see the spin on that second serve?'

'Well, y've gone mad then, instead.'

'I've not gone mad, our kid, but I am mad; madly in love. I've struck it rich at last,' he said as he volleyed his wedding photo off the mantelpiece and dived for the base line behind the couch.

'What's happened? Mrs Barrett laid a golden egg?'

'Nah, sod Florrie,' he said, 'her savin's are nearly gone an' anyway I've just copped off, lah,

90

this afternoon down the Hope an' Anchor.'

'They don't let yer in there without a tie.'

'I wore me belt around me neck, said it was a leather one. Smart 'ey? Quick thinkin' that, wasn't it? I had t'hold onto me pants all the friggin' time like, but it was worth it.'

'Y've got another woman?'

'Not another woman,' he said in a rush 'cos he had a difficult back-hand return to make, 'not just another woman, Franny, *the* woman, I'm tellin' yer.'

'But what about Mrs Barrett?'

'Warrabout her?'

'Y'lousy get. Y'can't do that, she's in hospital now because of you. Mothercare's oldest customer.'

'It's not my fault I'm so irresistible,' he said, bending forward ready to receive serve. 'These older women have always been me downfall an' anyway I was much too young t'get married. I know that now I've met Gloria. I was trapped by Florrie, y'know. Trapped, that's what I was. Just a fool t'meself an' all the women what've been missin' out the last six months.'

'But what y'doin' dressed up like a pillock for?'

'She's ace at tennis, an' I'm gettin' some practice in 'cos I'm playin' her t'morrer. It's the tennis season now. She told me.'

'Y'can't play with that bat,' I said. 'Look at it. The frame's so bent y'could stand behind a corner an' still have a game.'

'Gloria's lendin' me her new one,' he said. 'It cost thirty quid an' it's not a bat, it's a raquet.'

'You can say that again.'

'She can afford it,' he said as he stood at the net curtains, wiping his bat down with the dishcloth and gargling his cup of tea. 'She's stinkin' rich y'know. Doesn't even draw her dole, they've got so much money in the house. Stop laughin', it's true,

an' 'ey, I'll be the one with the big grin when I get
me divorce through an' go an' live with Gloria in a
big mansion in the country or somewhere like
that.'

'Y'a real head-the-ball, you are, Tony. Only
yesterday y'was showin' me Florrie's sleepin' pills
an' sayin' that if anythin' happened to her, y'd be
off like a shot over them pearly gates after her.
That y'couldn't bear t'live a single day without
her. An' now here y'are plannin' a divorce.'

'Y'know what it was like,' he said as he served to
save the match, 'meetin' her f'the first time. It was
like that time in *West Side Story* when that white
feller an' the wop tart meet across a crowded room,
an' suddenly there was only them, they only had
eyes for each other. Well, me an' Gloria were
exactly the same, except she's no soddin' nigbo or
nothin'. I was standin' over by the women's bogs
in the Hope an' Anchor an' she'd just come off the
pinball machine in the arcade over the road, an'
our eyes met as the heel of her shoe got stuck in the
grid, an' they never left each other until she
tripped over the step comin' into the lounge, an' I
rushed over to her side an' picked her up an' she
bought me a short an' twenty Embassy. An' then
she drove me to our corner on her motorbike, just
like Peter Fonda in *Easy Rider*.'

'But two Corporation bin men shot her t'death as
she was goin' home.'

'Don't talk flamin' daft. I'm seein' her t'night.
She's goin' t'wait for me outside Mill Road
Maternity after visitin', an' we're goin' t'drive off
into the sunset t'gether.'

'Have y'told her about you an' Florrie then?'

'Well, not exactly. I said she was me Mam when
she asked.'

'I tell y' this much,' I said as he knocked two
ducks off the wall and fell over the ironing board,

'y'might be serious about this Gloria tart, but y'll never make a tennis player in a month of Sundays.'

'Why not? I haven't missed a return yet.'

'But y'don't concentrate enough. While y've been talkin' the tennis's finished an' y've been playin' shots against a dalek in *Doctor Who* an' that's a microphone in his hand, not a bat.'

'It'll be different t'morrer,' he said. 'I'm one of those players with the big match temperament. I rise t'the occasion. I, like, respond t'the atmosphere.'

'Where y'playin' t'morrer?'

'Them tennis courts over at Sefton Park.'

'Oh, y'll really have the Centre Court crowd behind yer there.'

'I hope you're not bein' sarcastic,' he said as he put his jumper on and stuck the tea cosy over his bat. 'Why don't y' bring Marie Morgan along an' we can have a game of doubles. Play in them trousers y'had on the other night. We're bound t'get a court t'ourselves then.'

'Listen,' I said, 'it was just an accident that we were there like that, I've told yer. I can get better than her. I'm not short of someone t'tap up.'

'Well, go on then. Play tennis with us t'morrer. See what y'bring.'

'I don't like tennis, it's borin'.'

'Y're all talk, you are, Franny. The only woman you could bring with yer is me Mam.'

'At least I didn't marry someone the same age as her, near enough.'

'That's all over with now, haven't I explained? Forgotten. Me an' Gloria is today. Florrie was yesterday.'

'Twenty-five years yesterday, more like.'

'Well, come on, mouth, let's have a look at what you can do. Christ, when I was sixteen it was on me mind so much I had nose bleeds regular every

93

month. If the best y'can come up with is Mooey Morgan's sister . . .'

'Right,' I said, 'I'll show yer. Just you wait till t'morrer, y'll get the shock of y'life.'

When I got outside the house I walked up the road and thought about who I could tap up in time. If it'd been someone who didn't know me well, I could have got one of my cousins to come and no one'd know the difference. Our Eileen in Dingle's a cracking bit of stuff and all, and she lives by Sefton Park, but Tony wouldn't count that. There was Josie McKenna, Tits Anonymous, in school, but I didn't even know where she lived, and anyway it was Friday evening. There was always the youth club dance, if I could get in, but everyone there would have heard about me going with Marie Morgan, so that was out. So I had to come back to me first choice, the girl I really wanted to take with me; no-one else. Dole's sister, Joanna. Black Beauty. And I want to be a jockey. *The African Queen*. I could be Humphrey Bogart.

The only trouble was that I was shit-scared not only of asking her, but of meeting up with her dad in one of his Jack the Ripper moods. I wasn't bothered about her being a darkie. Christ knows, if I could get on a bus with Marie Morgan, I could have a game of tennis with a bit of shade. Especially one as smart as her. I stood there on the corner by the Leighs', being brave for ten yards and then getting frightened again and coming back. Fuck it, I thought finally, you don't get anything unless you ask for it, and I decided to go and get it over with and ask her. And then I decided to try and hide the sodding pan of stew I'd carried all the way from our Tony's.

'Good ev—'

'Who the bloody hell're you? We've paid the milk.'

'Er, hello, Mr Kew, er I was just wonderin' if your Tommy was there, that's all. F'a minute like. I won't keep him.'

'I wish y'flamin' well would.'

I was alright. He was in a good mood.

He went in and shouted up the stairs and Dole came down covered in colours again. Talk about dip, don't dazzle; red T-shirt, orange pullover and green cord trousers. He looked like a walking set of traffic lights.

'I haven't got it,' he said after we'd stared at each other for about ten seconds before I had to shield my eyes.

'Wha'?'

'Y'tongue,' he said. 'Y'have lost it, haven't yer?'

'No, yer, well, it's like this, Tommy. I want y' t'do a favour f'me.'

'Take a bath in a bucket of whitewash so your honky friends won't talk about you?'

'Y'can do that after if y'would, but right now, it's somethin' even more urgent than that. It's about t'morrer, I've er like, got this game of tennis, y'see . . .'

'Tennis?'

'I know, that's what I think an' all, daft isn't it, but the problem is I've got no one t'partner me, an' I was wonderin' if maybe—'

'I'd love a game, I'm really good y'—'

'No, no, it's not you I want. I mean, I can't play with you, 'cos it's *mixed* doubles, an' it's not allow—'

'But I'm black an' you're white, that's mixed enough, isn't it?'

'Stop takin' the piss, Tommy, look, y'know, d'y'think y'could ask your Joanna if she fancied a game. T'morrer it is, Sefton Park. Y'can tell her she doesn't have t'be any good. In fact, the worse she is, the better, 'cos we'll all be bloody useless, y'can

guarantee, an' I'll pay her fare down there, an' a
can of Coke after an' that ... y'know ... it should
be a good laugh ... I'm sure she'd enjoy herself—'

'Have y'finished?' he said.

'Er, well, yes.'

'You ask her y'self,' he said, and opened their
front-room door. 'Jo, there's someone here want
t'talk to yer.'

And the only thing I wanted to do was find my
pan of stew and run.

Dressed in white. Black and white. Newcastle
United's colours. No make-up. No need. Big eyes.
Bloodshot. Standing at the door, taller than me,
cheating 'cos she's stood on the step; Dole going
back up the stairs two at a time. Me and her. No
one else. Even her dad keeping quiet. I could hear
the scrape of knives and forks in the next room. My
tongue in Lost Property again, but she looked so
incredibly beautiful, like a painting on the wall.

'Hiya, Franny.'

Oh no. No. *Please* no. Oh. Oh. Oh. Oh Jesus.
Christ I have, I've come in my pants. Like a little
kid. Frigging hell what's wrong with me? Sky-blue
jeans and all. It's going to show through any
minute. She'll think I've wet meself.

'What's the matter?' she asks as she leans
forward.

I'm bent double, see, staring at her doorstep and
her slippers.

'It's the pains in me back,' I said. 'I get them
every so often, cripplin' they are, I'll have t'go
home right now an' lie down, I'll be alright in a
bit.'

I turn around and hobble down the path, one
hand on my back, another covering my cock. I see
a whole lifetime of fuck-ups ahead of me; never
getting my end away. Growing old on my own, a
virgin pensioner, with my prick forever in my

96

pocket, never seeing nothing but bog seats and long johns.

'But didn't y' want to'see me about somethin'?'

I can't turn around, the patch is spreading, so I bend down a bit more and look through me legs. 'Oh it was nothin'. I was just wonderin' er, Joanna, I've gorra game of tennis t'morrer an' I need a partner, a girl like, an' if y'not doin' nothin' . . .'

'I've never played tennis.'

'All the better.'

'What time?'

Here it is – the old brush-off. Whatever time it is, she's doing something else.

'About two o'clock.'

'I'll borrow our Tommy's racquet.'

I nearly turn around and reveal all. I can't believe it.

'Y'mean y'll come?'

''Course I will, but what about your back? Will it be better by then?'

Christ, I've gorra dick like a water diviner, it's at it again.

'A good night's rest an' I'll be fine,' I said. 'I'll see yer then, thanks, Joanna, I've got t'go now, it's hurtin' again.'

I'm out the gate and behind the privets and I look up above the hedges, and she's laughing, two rows of shiny teeth, white from ear to ear, looking like a cross between a row of gravestones and a toothpaste advertisement. I can't blame her for laughing. She probably thought I'd been gettin' some tips off Mooey Morgan on how to chat birds up. Mind you, the way my luck was running, she was certain to be down for a sex change operation the next morning.

I had a hell of job the next morning explaining to my Mam what I'd done with the stew-pan. I'd left it in Mooey's garden but it was gone when I went back. Mooey's old girl must have reckoned Christmas had come early this year, but I was buggered if I was going to knock on their door and try to explain to her that I wasn't Santa Claus, or even one of the reindeers. And anyway, the last time I called for Mooey, Marie answered the door and did nothing but look down at my knees and choke on her piece of toast.

Tony didn't come back the previous night after visiting Mrs Barrett so me and Joanna had to make our own way down to Sefton Park. I was wearing my white football shorts under my jeans, plus three pairs of undies and a jock-strap full of toilet paper just in case I got a look at her knickers and couldn't control myself. There was only our Tony's old beaten-up and bent racquet, but I wasn't too bothered, as I didn't expect to be hitting the ball very much.

It was funny going down there with her, people looking at us and everything, but when she linked my arm when we got off the bus and walked throught the park, I couldn't give a toss what they were thinking or saying to themselves; to hell with them. I thought I might get a lot of·cracks about her colour, but apart from a gang of spades on a corner who looked at her full of hate 'cos she was going with a white bloke, there was nothing actually said out loud. No doubt even a few of them on the bus or walking past us thought I was a lucky sod, and you know what that is, don't you? 'Cos I was a feller and she was a tart. It's alright for a white lad to knock off a coon; everyone thinks he's having a whale of a time and look at you all greedy like as if they wish they were having a slice themselves. You're not doing anything wrong in their eyes if it's that way about, but the shit hits the fan if you're a white girl and you're getting a taste of some nigger's sweat. 'What's the matter?'

they all say, 'can't she get a white bloke?' Or else they go on about the size of a nigger's cock. I know that for a fact, 'cos I've thought it myself when I've been down the town and seen some white tart with a nig-nog. It's stupid really, but I know that if I was a tart, I wouldn't go out with no shines or chinks or nothing, however smart they were, 'cos I couldn't stand everyone looking at me all dirty like they do.

Mind you, there was no chance of Tony's new woman getting looked at with anything except maybe horror. I can't say I was surprised when I saw her 'cos he's got a natural born talent for picking up tarts that need plastic surgery in a hurry, and this Gloria In Excelsis Deo was no exception. I'll tell you something else; after seeing her, I know for a fact that money isn't everything. If I'd been on my own I'd have got the next bus home, but I wanted to have a pose with Joanna. Not that our Tony was impressed, like, but that's him all over. 'Never mind the quality, just look at the colour.' If he had a choice between Diana Ross and Hilda Ogden, he'd spend all his time in the Rover's Return.

'What's the big idea?' he said as we stood behind these bushes and took our kecks off while the girls went across to the ladies' bogs.

'Wha' big idea?'

'Bringin' a spade with yer.'

'So that's what it is. I knew it didn't look like a tennis racquet.'

'No, her – the Queen of the Jungle.'

'Piss off, Tony, at least she's all there where it counts. Look at the figure on her. Turn her upside down an' y've boiled an egg in three minutes.'

'A blackbird's egg,' he said as he put both feet in one leg of his shorts.

'Get knotted. I wouldn't mind if you'd turned up

with Miss World. Is she any good at tennis, Tony?'

''Course she is, she's entered championships.'

'Has she? I can just see the headlines now,' I said. '"Quasimodo Wins Wimbledon".'

When she came out of the bogs, this Gloria one, I'm not kidding, she looked like a tractor wearing a dress, and when she started playing, she trundled about the courts with all the speed of our Tony searching for work.

As for Joanna, well, thank God I was well protected from public view, 'cos her walk alone was enough to get me going; all easy and loose and relaxed and yet just as if she was going to spring into life any minute, like their Tommy, and go flying towards the top right-hand corner.

Mind you, when it came to playing tennis, she was as criminal as the rest of us. Whoever served lost the game. It was as simple as that. The first time it was Tony's turn, he threw the ball up, took a flying swing, missed, let go of the bat, the ball hit him on the head, and the bat knocked Gloria to the ground.

She was one of those, Gloria, who knew everything there is to know about the game: how to score and where to stand and when to change ends and all the rules, but didn't have a fucking clue how to play. It was great. She'd spend ten minutes moving us all into the right positions to receive her serve and then she'd welly eight serves on the run into the boating lake at the other side of the park. Tony spent more time paddling about looking for lost balls than playing tennis.

By a quarter to three, with the first set at something like 102 all, Tony suddenly realized the pubs were shutting, and inspired by a vision of brown over bitter and cloth over the taps, he flung across four aces in a row. As soon as Joanna flopped her services into the net or over the trees, our Tony was there, galloping towards the net, arms out, eyes shining, victory his and Massey Ferguson's.

Not only was he useless at tennis, he couldn't even jump over the net proper. He got his foot caught in one of the holes and fell onto our side of the court like a doped-up donkey jumping Bechers Brook, broke his nose, gave himself shale-marks from his kneecaps to his forehead, and buried the handle of the bat halfway into his stomach.

He missed his pint and all. Gloria had him on her motorbike in a flash, but it was half-past seven before he got released from the Royal Infirmary Out-Patients, and even then he had to fight his way out 'cos they wanted to keep him in overnight for observation. A waste of time that would have been. I've observed him all my life and I still can't make any sense out of him, so they wouldn't have much chance.

Me and Joanna took their clothes home. Gloria's tent dress weighed a ton, but I'm not surprised. You could sleep a family of five in it. I didn't want to take our Tony's shoes with me on the bus, not after the shame of the other night, but Joanna poured about a pint of perfume on them, so that was alright. Especially as I'd already thrown his socks into the lake.

I wanted to walk her to their door but she wouldn't let me at first, so I asked her at the corner of her road. You know, about seeing her again.

'It's me dad,' she said.

'Y'don't have t'tell him.'

'That makes it even worse,' she said, 'if he finds out an' I haven't told him.'

'Well, then tell him. Jesus, y'sixteen aren't yer? Y'out of nappies, y'been t'school, y'can tie y'own shoelaces, y'know y'alphabet; what's he think y'are? A baby?'

'He just goes mad f'nothin' sometimes,' she said. 'Absolute mad. Can't even get the words out; sprayin' spit everywhere.'

'I don't know how y'take it,' I said. 'Every time I call for your Tommy, I'm frightened from y'doorstep, never mind in the house.'

'When we were little kids he didn't . . . he wasn't like this, I know he wasn't. We used t'go the park, fly kites, play things. Him and our kid . . . always had a ball at his feet. Teachin' Tommy like. Now the only thing he teaches him is how t'duck an' run. But our Tommy's gettin' older. He won't take it much longer. He wouldn't take it now except f'me Mam. He always gives in on account of her.'

'Well, if he was alright once, what's t'stop him bein' alright now? At least he's got a job, more than my old feller . . .'

'It's not that, although in a way it's part of it, 'cos he thinks he should have a better job, an' that he's never got any promotion due t'the colour of his skin. An' y'see, what he wants t'do, what he never stops talkin' about, is t'go home, y'know t'Lagos, take what he's learnt over here an' get a big job back there.'

'Is that where you come from an' all, that place?'

'Lagos? It's not home t'any of us. Me Mam comes from Wolverhampton an' we were all born in Liverpool. But me dad reckons he was a big man over there; someone t'be reckoned with. He could walk down the street an' people'd know him. Not like here, where he's just another . . . you know. So, that's it really. But the frightenin' part is that he's gettin' worse as he gets older, an' he sort of sees that he's never goin' t'go nowhere.'

I felt like a Father Confessor. First Marie and now Joanna. Tears making shiny rivers down her black face. I could always be a priest if times got really hard. Five Hail Marys for a good weep. Ten

Our Fathers for raving hysterics.

'Come on,' I said, 'it'll be alright, y'won't be livin' here for ever, y'll be leaving one day, come on, take no notice. It will, it'll be all right, I know it will.'

I took the tent off her and we walked towards her house although she said she didn't want me to. Mooey was in their front garden, digging. Looking for buried pans of stew.

'Look,' I said, 'I'm going t'this party t'night, over in the village. I was goin' t'go with some mates but I can easy ditch them. It should be ace. Why don't you come with us, we'll have a laugh. Tell y'dad y'going t'y'aunty's or somethin'. He won't find out.'

'I can't,' she said, 'not t'night. I always stay in with me Mam of a Saturday night.'

'Next Friday then – after the semi-finals of the cup? Come over an' watch the game an' we'll go straight out. 'Ey? There's this ace film on in town. *Scarface* it's called. Al Pacino out of *The Godfather*. I've been wanting to see it f'ages but the only trouble is y'have to have y'face slashed before they let yer in.'

She tried a bit of a smile and then she looked over my shoulder and her mouth opened so wide I had an ace view of her tonsils. In good nick and no sign of pyorrhoea, I made sure of that. Then I turned around and a massive big black hand got hold of my tennis shirt and lifted me onto me tiptoes, like a wet arse ballerina winched onto a crane.

'Er hello, Mr Kew, er nice day for it, isn't it?'

'What're you doin' sniffin' around my daughter?' he said.

'I beg y'pardon?'

'You heard me the first time, y'little pink gobshite.'

'Dad . . .'

103

'Shut it you an' get in the house.'

'It's very simple, Mr Kew, let me explain. I was on the bus from town, y'see, just been t'the youth club basketball finals, downstairs I was as a matter of fact, havin' just given up smokin', an' Joanna here, well, she fell down the stairs at the roundabout didn't she? Caught herself a terrible clout on her head. These bus drivers y'know, not a thought in their heads f'the safety of their passengers, they go around those roundabouts like madmen as y'probably know y'self. Well, I was sittin' in the seat nearest the stairs, an' so I picked her up an' dusted her down an' brought her back here. Proper shocked she was. Be bruised somethin' awful in the mornin', I shouldn't wonder. Y' very lucky y'know, er dark-skinned people, like, that's what I always say, 'cos y'bruises never show. It's good that, isn't it?'

He let go of my shirt and looked at the two white buttons in his hand and then gave them back to me. 'Won't take a minute t'sew back on, Mr Kew,' I said, 'don't worry.' And then he give me the biggest backhander I've ever had in my life. Right across my face, teeth rattling like marbles in a tin, blood in my mouth and nose, and I'm spun around and looking at Mooey's amazed face over the privets.

'I wasn't bein' funny,' I mumbled with my back to him. 'It's a fact that about the bruises.'

'An' I suppose it's also another fact that y've both been playin' tennis in two different bloody parks,' he said and grabbed hold of Joanna and tore into their pathway. He shoved her at the door as he got his key out, and when he opened the door he pushed her up the stairs. 'Get up there,' he said, 'an' don't come down until I tell you to.'

'Doesn't he like tennis?' Mooey said.

'It's not that,' I said as I wiped at the blood and

104

felt around my teeth with my tongue. 'He just doesn't like me. Or anyone.'

'I do,' Mooey said.

'Wha'?'

'I like yer.'

'Thanks Mooey, but it's not much of a consolation.'

'I really really like yer,' he said, leaning on his spade. 'You're my best friend.'

'Lost a tart an' found a friend,' I said. 'That's about par for me these days.'

'Y'goin' t'take me t'that party aren't yer?' he said. 'Y'are, aren't yer? Y'promised y'would, an' Mad Dog told me about gettin' me Mam's nerve pills an' I've got them. It was her description. I said I lost it.'

'Five foot three, needs a bath, always got holes in her tights.'

'Er, wha'?'

'I'm describin' y'Mam.'

'Y'don't have t'do that, Scull. I know her already.'

'Oh fuckin' hell, don't make me laugh, Mooey, it hurts too much.'

'It's smart, this description she gets, you know. She's got a season ticket. I just sign the back an' she can have anythin' she wants. I got a Donald Duck bubble bath for her last week.'

'That's what I call a good swop.'

He was still shouting after me about the party and waving his spade in the air as I turned their corner and walked up our road.

When I got home my dad was in the front room with the two fellers who pass the plates around in church, and I could see by the daggers I was getting that I wasn't welcome. Maybe they were getting him a job on the plates till things picked up. Me a priest and my dad on the plates; what a smart church that'd be. We'd make a bomb.

All the excitement though was in the back kitchen. My Gran and her feller with the Steradent smile with her and I'd never seen her so happy since the day my grandad died. Hers was the only happy face though 'cos my Mam was wearing a frown that went down to her shoulder blades and the only reason my Gran's feller was smiling was because his teeth were made that way.

'Look, Francis,' my Gran said, 'look!' She flashed a diamond ring under my nose and pretended to be all bashful.

'Aye aye, been robbin' Woolies again, Gran,' I said just before my Mam kicked me under the table.

'I'm engaged,' she said.

'Just like Mrs Barrett's baby's head,' I said and they all looked at me soft. I could tell her pensioner fiancé was going to give me a speech about the younger generation so I went into the hallway as our Henry opened the front door carrying a big box wrapped in brown paper. He muttered something about a new transformer and he was so desperate to link it up to everything else, he went straight into the back kitchen, right past my Gran holding her hand up and my Mam laying the law down about trial marriages, took his meat and potato pie out of the oven and went upstairs to the cockloft.

Hovis came out of the garden then with his bow and arrows, but after he shot my Granma and hit her feller in the bollocks with his tomahawk, he got chased out of the back kitchen. He went straight into the front room and me dad and the Sacred Mafia legged him out of there as well. So he sat with me at the top of the stairs for a while, having a little moan 'cos he always has to be the Indian and never gets to play the White Man. It wasn't long before my Mam shouted up to me to get him in the bath and I ended up joining him in it, wiping the caked-up blood out of my nose, and wondering if it looked as broken as our Tony's looked a couple of hours earlier in the park. After I dried us down we had a game of blow football but he always cheats and used his hands. Anyway, every time I blew down the tube my nose hurt. By twenty to eight he was buggered, and I'd only got as far as the porridge being too hot for Goldilocks and he was out to the world.

I went into me and Arthur's room. He was already in bed reading a book on rockets and all that crap. He's going to be clever, our Arthur. My Mam must had it away with the school's attendance or the insurance feller, 'cos his kind of brains don't run in our family. He knows more about some things now than any of us ever will, and he's still in the Juniors. I used to hate him, really hate him, when he was a little pansy but he's alright now and I've got used to him anyway. We leave each other alone most of the time and so we get along.

I got dressed in my faded jeans and best shirt after I'd had a shave. I didn't expect to cop off at this hippy party, but there was no harm in trying. The knocker went as I was coming down the stairs and when I got to the door it was Dole.

'I know,' I said, 'don't tell me, y've come with a written apology from y'dad, plus a five-pound note t'cover the cost of a reconditioned face.'

'Me Mam sent me around t'apologize.'

'It was me own fault. I should have known better. Your kid warned me not t'come down the road with her.'

'Are y'alright?' he asked me. 'Y'nose hardly looks puffed up at all.'

'Don't sound so friggin' disappointed,' I said. 'Anyway, wha're y'doin' now?'

'Nothin' much.'

'D'y'wanna go to a hippy party with us?'

'Don't mind.'

'Is that all y'can say? Y'should be jumpin' at a chance t'go to a white man's party without bein' the butler. I don't know, Dole, y'don't know y'born, you niggers don't. Y'come over here, we let yer in *our* country, feed yer, give y'clothes, put yer on the Social Security, let y'have the pick of any slum y'wanna live in, an' then when y've got a golden opportunity t'be one of us f'a night, all y'can say is, "Don't mind."'

'I think me dad should have hit yer in the mouth.'

'He did,' I said. 'Well, are y'comin' or what'?'

''Course I am.'

'Y'wouldn't like t'go an' persuade—'

'No I wouldn't, there's no chance.'

'Does she, y'know, does she, like—'

'It's laughable, y'know, Scull, it really is. Y'both actin' like love-sick pigeons.'

'Don't be daf – did you say "both" then?'

'I'm afraid so. I haven't heard her talking about marryin' Michael Jackson f'over a week now.'

'That's how I feel about Kenny Dalglish an' all.'

I shut the front door behind us and walked down our path. One thing I didn't do before I went out was rob my Mam's nerve tablets. It was a waste of time even looking. My Mam's got no nerves.

6

'Why've y'got a paper hat on y'head, Mooey?' I
asked when we all met up at the corner by the
Leighs' house.

'It's a party, isn't it?' he said.

'We took the mistletoe off him,' Snotty Dog said,
'but he ran away when we tried t'get his hat.'

'Mistletoe at this time of the year, Mooey?'

'I found it behind the couch,' he said. 'I think it's
plastic.'

'I don't believe it,' I said as I looked the three of
them up and down.

'An' you lot want t'cop off?' Dole said.

'Fuck off, big lips,' Mad Dog said. 'I'm alright.'

'Oh aye yeah,' I said coming between them, 'but
whose idea was it t'put a dickey bow on?'

'It's a touch of class that is,' he said. 'A master
stroke.'

'It goes really well with y' open-neck shirt.'

'Y'haven't got a pair of shoes in the house I could
lend, have yer, Scull?' Snotty Dog said. 'The sole
came off mine as I was comin' out.' I looked down
at his feet. There he was in his shirt and tie, clean
trousers, hair combed, nose disguised, the lot; and
on his feet he had a pair of wellies. It was like the
Duke of Edinburgh turning up at the Royal
Command Performance with a punk rockers T-
shirt on. Even Mickey Brown'd stand a chance
against these three. Mind you, so would I, the more
I thought about it. At least we'd get a crowd
around us. I was just going to tell them that wellies
were the latest fashion with the in-crowd when
Crackers and her Tea Lad came out of their house
and declared war on us before they set off for the
snug at the Boundary. She had her cat-fur coat on

and a hat even softer than Mooey's with a bowl of fruit salad on top of it.

'Wha'd'you think y'doin' standin' there?' Crackers screamed at us. 'Go an' stand by y' own lamp-post.'

'You heard, push off,' the Tea Lad said. 'Hangin' about decent people's houses, blockin' the way, looking f'trouble, haven't you got better things t'do? Where're y'parents, that's what I want t'know. What are they doin'? How would they like it if y'stood outside their house all night long?'

Usually, that's about it. We'd stand there and let them get it off their chest and sometimes we'd form a chorus with them 'cos we know the speeches off by heart, and after they'd put the world to rights they'd go off and get pissed on two pints of shandy, an' we'd stay where we were. But not tonight. The Tea Lad must have had a bit of promotion or a pat on the head with his briefcase 'cos he marched right up to us and stood there waving his hands about like one of them monkeys on the PG Tips adverts. 'I've watched you lot day in an' day out f'nigh on twenty years—'

'I'm only sixteen,' Mooey said.

'—an' y'haven't changed an inch. In fact y've got worse as time's gone by. Y'neither use nor bloody ornament, the lot of yer.'

'We haven't got any balls, mister,' Mooey said. 'That's why.'

'I don't want t'know about your sex life, sonny,' he said and then him and Crackers hung onto each other sniggering away like two little kids who's shouted 'fuck' for the first time and found out your tongue doesn't drop off and you don't get struck blind by Jesus and all the Apostles. Sneaky old gets like that make me sick. All smug and proper and so-called decent, but give them a chance for a sly titter and they're near to wanking in their woolly undies. But if Mooey'd said 'bollocks'

110

instead of 'balls', we'd have had the Law holding us by them inside of ten minutes, 'cos they'd have both taken a sanctimonious fit.

'I tell y' what,' I said seeing as they were in such a happy mood, 'give us back what's rightfully ours an' we won't bother yer no more.'

Frig me, that really got them suspicious, that did. You'd think I'd offered to paint the outside of their house with Snotty Dog's stolen paint, cut the privets and polish their dwarfs, the way they looked at me.

'How d'we know y'll keep y'promise?' the Tea Lad said.

'Well, it's easy isn't it? If we don't, y'll still have all the balls back within a week, won't yer? An' look at it another way, it's nearly summer an' we won't have need of y'soddin' lamp-post any more.'

'It's a fact that,' the Tea Lad said. I almost had him on our side, the soft get.

'Oh no,' Crackers said, pulling her coat across her attempt at tits, 'we couldn't have that.'

''Course we couldn't,' her feller said. 'Er, why not, Mary? Sounds alright t'me.'

'Because,' she said, 'because I'm not havin' you lot goin' around causin' disturbances, even if it is in the next street. An' that's my final word on the subject. Never let it be said that I've let my fellow neighbours down. It's only by all of us gatherin' together that we can keep trash like you down.'

'An' who're you t'say who's trash an' who isn't, 'ey?' Dole said.

'I've only got two words t'say t'you, young man,' Crackers said. 'Enoch Powell!'

'He's right though,' I said. 'Who do you think you are? What gives you the special right t'tell us what's right an' wrong, who's good an' bad?'

'Yeah, yeah, too true,' Mad Dog said, supporting Dole for the first time ever, with his forehead all creased up in a frown and his knuckles white and bony, which were always the danger signs with him, 'yeah, you're nobody special, you aren't. If y'so fuckin' smart, why don't y'move out? 'Ey? Answer that one, go on.'

'How dare you use such—'

'Go on, bugger off up t'the village with y'sack full of balls. Buy y'own house—'

'An' y'own lamp-post,' I said.

'—if it means that much to yer. D'y'think the rest of us like y'living here?' Mad Dog finished off in a scamper, throwing the words like bricks onto the prefabs. 'What makes y'think we want yer in this street?' The telltale slobber of a rabies victim was on his bottom lip, and the Tea Lad backed away.

'You don't even live in this street,' Crackers said, all prim and proper.

'An' I wouldn't neither, not with you two miserable toffee-nosed twats at the top of it.'

'Lawrence! Lawrence!' Crackers screeched at the Tea Lad but he was having nothing of it 'cos Mad Dog'd just sprayed him with what could have been a fatal dose and he was scraping away at his face with his hankie. 'Lawrence, don't just stand there, call the police, do something about it, f'God's sake.'

'Why don't y'piss off back t'Arabia, Lawrence,' Mad Dog said.

'That's right,' Dole said, 'buy a motorbike an' put us all out of our misery.'

Lawrence was doing a smart impression of the contents of a spin drier and backing desperately into their pathway, so Crackers took up the good fight on behalf of all the decent citizens of our estate and naturally enough threw herself at the biggest gangster of us all: Mooey Morgan, standing there perfectly still at the edge of the storm, like a lighthouse. A forty-watt bulb in the top of his head and we'd have had our own portable lamp-post and all our problem's would have been solved.

Crackers must have been a good fighter in the

Infants 'cos she'd scratched all down Mooey's face, knocked his hat off and grabbed hold of him by the tufts of his hair that were hanging down from his basin cut before he realized that the storm had hit him.

''Ey no, get off, that hurts, I just put lacquer on,' he said as she tried to knee him in the futures and he bent down to get hold of his paper hat and got her knee in his face instead. He knew then it was serious and not some kind of new game that no-one'd told him about, 'cos when she tried to send the head in, he grabbed hold of her hat and pulled her right off the ground. It wasn't his fault she had about fifteen hat pins stuck in it. Her head looked like a patchwork quilt by the time Mooey started biting the fruit salad on top o. the hat.

'Lawrence,' she screamed, 'Lawrence, in the name of Christ, I'm bein' attacked, quick before he gets me Russian mink!'

'Ow! Ow!' Mooey joined in, 'I've broken a tooth on y'grapes,' and he threw the hat on the floor and jumped all over her mixed fruit. Crackers called for Lawrence again but he wasn't even in the road. You could just see his head poking out of their alleyway, and I knew then why he worked in an office. Forms and documents and desks don't boot you in the balls when the going gets tough. I felt almost sorry for him as me and Dole dragged Mooey away and stopped Mad Dog taking her hat. We got to the other side of the road while Mooey chased his own hat, and I turned and give her some verbal just before she give it to Lawrence.

'It doesn't matter about the balls,' I said. 'Y'wouldn't give us them back whatever we did, an' y'know why, 'cos it's y'only bit of fun out of life, isn't it? Standin' there waitin' f'a ball t'come over, runnin' off an' addin' it to y'collection. Y'wouldn't want t'live anywhere else would yer? It wouldn't be the same elsewhere. You like it here, y'think y'the

113

King of the Castle, Lord an' Lady Muck, looking down on the rest of us. D'y'know what youse are, do yer? Yer worse than any of us, worse than anyone around here. You're a—'

But it was a big word an' I couldn't think of it.

'Hypocrite,' Dole said.

'That's the word,' I said. 'That's what y'are, what he just said. Y'not worth wastin' breath on, come ahead, let's go, lads.'

'Y'd better go an' all,' Crackers said, finding her voice as we walked away, and being joined by her hangdog husband who knew he'd done wrong and was due for a whipping, 'I'll have the police here the next time you set foot outside this gate; hooligans, downright hooligans, I'll see your parents, don't you worry. I'll make them pay for this hat, hand-made, it was—'

'We really showed her then, didn't we 'ey, boys?' Snotty Dog said, doing a bit of shadow boxing as he walked. I had to laugh. He hadn't opened his mouth once.

'That's not all we'll show them neither,' I said. 'Give it a couple of weeks t'die down an' we'll have them good and proper.'

'Wha' we goin' t'do, Scull?' Mad Dog asked.

'We're goin' t'get back what's rightfully ours.'

'Like what we planned with Mickey Brown?'

'Dead right, but unlike Mickey an' all his big plans, we're goin' t'do it.'

'Can I have me mistletoe back?' Mooey said. 'Me hat's all ripped.'

'Sod y'mistletoe, Mooey,' I said. 'The important thing is have y'got what I told yer t'bring?'

'These alright, Scull?' Mooey said, and got a big bottle of pills out of his pocket.

'Great, Mooey, just great. Them hippies'll pay fifty pence a go f'those. Well, come on, you two, wha've y'got?'

The two Dogs just stood there looking sheepish and looking away and then Snotty Dog put his hand in his jacket pocket and pulled out a bottle of Junior Aspirin.

'Friggin' Jesus, who're these for?' I said. 'We're not goin' to a play-school outin', y'know.'

'I told yer,' Mad Dog said, turning on Snotty Dog. 'I said they were no good. Our Dog End ate a whole bottle of them last year an' nothin' happened. An' he's only three an' a half now.'

'Well,' Snotty Dog said, 'I asked me Mam an' she said all her nerves were gone.'

'I'm not surprised,' I said.

'Wha've you got anyway?' Mad Dog said. 'Where's your drugs?'

'Look, pal,' I said, 'I'm just the brains in this organization. I set things up. Supplyin' the ideas is the hardest part.'

'Yeah,' Mad Dog said, 'for you it would be.'

'It doesn't matter anyway,' I said. 'The state some of them'll be in t'night, y'could feed them Carter's Little Liver Pills an' they'd be no wiser till the mornin'.'

'I don't know whether I wanna go anymore,' Snotty Dog said. 'Not in me wellies.'

'Y'll be the centre of attraction in them, Snotty Dog, no kiddin'.'

'I know. That's what's worryin' me.'

'Don't y'believe me?'

'Well, y'know me,' he said. 'I don't like t'be different. An' whatever y'say, drainpipe jeans an' wellies don't go.'

'An' I'm havin' second thoughts about me dickey bow an' all,' Mad Dog said. 'It's hurtin' me neck.'

'F'fuck's sake,' I said, 'y'tie it to yer shirt, not y'Adam's apple.'

'I can't fasten me shirt at the top, it's too tight.'

'Don't go then,' I said. 'Alright, miss the chance

of a lifetime, but don't forget, while you two are at home playin' with y'hot-water bottles, we'll be thinkin' about yer while we have our third orgy of the night.'

'Er, well, er . . .' Snotty Dog said.

'Just think, la',' I said, 'all of them long-haired hippy tarts, self-startin' knickers an' not a bra between them. Just dyin' for it, all of them; achin' t'get real fellers like us into them sleepin' bags they're always carryin' around. They don't really want them divvys they knock about with, y'know. All them fruits with beards an' dirty armpits an' haversacks, 'course they don't. They want us if the real story was told.'

'If y'are goin' home,' Mooey said, 'can I have y'wellies an' y'bow tie?'

'Did I just hear you right then?' Mad Dog said, putting his arm around Mooey while Snotty Dog got his mistletoe out of his pocket and smiled at him.

So, they swopped Mooey his school tie and his baseball boots for Snotty Dog's wellies and Mad Dog's dickey bow and we headed for the village. What's more, we even got in one of the pubs up there as well, 'cos when we walked in, the manager took one look at the state of Mooey and thought he was the comic that he'd booked for the back room. For half an hour till the real comedian turned up, Mooey was on free drinks and crisps, and people were standing at the bar laughing with him instead of at him.

When they threw us out we sat on the wall of the pub's car park and Mad Dog and Snotty Dog kept their courage up by telling each other about what they were going to do at this party and about all the women they'd had and both of them knew they'd never had anyone in their whole lives, and

116

Mooey hung onto every word in the hope of picking up some tips.

'An' there was this tart once in a Rolls-Royce,' Mad Dog said, 'when I was comin' home from Formby in the rain an' me bike'd broken down, an' she stopped for me an' put me bike in the boot, an' she had a cocktail bar in the back of the car, an' a colour telly an' a telephone, an' she had a big house where she lived all on her own, a stately house t'be exact, up in St Helens, an' she took me back there t'dry me clothes off, an' she had black leather drawers an'—'

'But that's nothin' t'the time I was pickin' spuds over in Ormskirk,' Snotty Dog said. 'The farmer's daughter there, I'm not kiddin ' yer, she had—'

'Two best King Edwards up her jumper,' Dole said.

'An' a chip on her shoulder?' I asked him.

'Sod off, you two, she was all real, an' she knew the best spots on the farm t'do it too. Jesus, there was times when I'd come home with about ten-pence in me pocket an' less than a bag full of spuds picked all day, but absolutely knackered. Knackered! The things she could do on top of a hay wagon, well, at times, y'know, she even defeated me, an' that's sayin' somethin'. There was once when—'

''Ey up,' I said, 'here's trouble,' as a blue and white police mini came teararsing into the car park, lights flashing, siren going, brakes squealing, the lot. They make you laugh, the Law; thick, that's what they are. They are though. I mean, look at the big signs all over their cars – 'POLICE'. I ask you, it's a dead giveaway, isn't it? You don't see robbers going around with a big notice on top of their cars saying 'THIEF' do you?

No sooner had the car stopped when Isaiah and another older copper I'd never seen before came galloping out of the doors like greyhounds out of a trap and straight towards us sitting there on the wall.

Well, of course, your first reaction is to run, isn't it? After all, it's natural. What would you do? Wait for a truncheon up your nose? Even Mooey knew enough not to hang about for a blue-bottle special. We left Snotty Dog still on the wall getting to the part where she was balancing on the back of a tractor in the knacker in the tea break while he was stood on two hundredweight of spuds doing something called the Irish position, and we were off across the car park, down the alleyway at the side of the pub and over a brick wall. That was as far as we got 'cos there was a dirty big alsatian in there guarding all the empty ale bottles and when it took a cob out of Mooey's wellies we threw ourselves back over the wall and surrendered.

I don't think Snotty Dog ever knew we'd been gone. Isaiah had to push him off the wall to make him stop.

'Now then,' Isaiah said, 'runnin' away's as good as a confession in my book, so y'may as well get it over with now.'

'Y'frightened us,' I said. 'All we saw was you two runnin' from y'car an' so we ran away an' all. We thought someone'd planted a bomb in there.'

'I'll plant somethin' on you in a minute, young Scully,' Isaiah said, 'an' it'll be just as painful as a bomb.'

'We haven't done nothin',' I said. 'It wasn't us.'

'It wasn't you who what?'

'Did whatever it is we're supposed t'have done.'

'No one else around here'd be soft enough. It had t'be you lot.'

'Any of you kids know anythin' about fish?' the other copper said.

'I'm no kid,' Mad Dog said.

'I'm down the chippy every night,' Mooey said.

118

'Tropical fish, bollocks.'

'They don't have no West Indian chippies around our way,' Mad Dog said, 'an' I'm no kids neither.' Sometimes he doesn't have to froth at the mouth for you to know he's mad. Isaiah went over and lifted him up by his sideboards and then jumped on his baseball boots.

'Y'what, lad?'

'Er, nott'n, I was talkin' t'meself. Er, d'y'know that hurts?'

'No, whistle me a few bars,' Isaiah said, proving he read the jokes out of Christmas crackers, but we all laughed with him, holding our ribs, chuckling fit to bust.

'It's a serious bloody offence, this,' the other copper said and Isaiah stopped laughing and so did we. 'What we want t'know,' he said, getting out his notebook, 'is who put the ten frogs, two sea snakes an' half a dozen piranha fish in the paddlin' pool at the new sports centre, don't you laugh, don't you dare laugh, it's no laughin' matter. My youngest was in there at the time, almost swallowed one of them, he did. Good job he had the great presence of mind to alert the proper authorities. Strip a body in a matter of minutes they can.'

'Can they?' Mooey said. 'Can they really? Isn't it amazin'? It must have been toads I kept then. They never stripped me once.'

'Don't play funny buggers with me, brick head,' the copper said and started pulling him towards the police car. 'You're goin' down the station you are.'

'Oooh, smart, ace, can I have another "DANGER" sign?'

'Y'can have a night in the cells, that's what you can have. I'm not havin' the likes of you givin' me lip.'

119

'I didn't throw no pyjamas in the water,' Mooey said. 'It wasn't me, I haven't got any pyjamas.'

'It couldn't have been us,' I said as the copper dragged Mooey out of his shirt and what was left of his mind. 'We're banned from the sports centre, anyone'll tell yer that. Y'll never pin that one on us, we couldn't even get in the front door, never mind the water.'

'He's right, Jim,' Isaiah said. 'I remember now. I was called out t'them. Playin' table tennis with the billiard balls an' then straight into the baths for more lumber. Threw a lifeguard in the water. Nearly drowned the poor sod.'

'How was we t'know he couldn't swim,' I said. 'It was his own fault. We had t'rescue him an' all.'

'I wasn't there,' Mooey said.

'Are y'ever—' Isaiah said.

'Have y'been in trouble with the Law before?' the other copper said, spotting him for a dangerous villain just like Crackers did.

'Only once,' Mooey said.

'Yeah,' Isaiah said, 'but tell him what it was.'

'Do I have to?' Mooey said, going all coy.

'We can still take y' down the station,' Isaiah told him. 'Find somethin' t'get yer for.'

'Well, I was ridin' our Joey's go-kart in the road.'

'Is that all?'

'But which road, bottlebrain?' Isaiah said. 'Go on, tell my mate which road it was.'

'It was a big one.'

'Too bloody true it was,' Isaiah said. 'The M57 motorway t'Southport. Rush hour an' all.'

'I was on the outside,' Mooey said. 'There was no traffic there.'

'The hard shoulder?'

'No, the fast lane,' Isaiah said.

'I was in a hurry t'get t'the beach,' Mooey said. 'An' er anyway, it was me first offence.'

'No it wasn't, Morgan, me lad,' Isaiah said. 'Your first offence was bein' born.'

The radio in the police car started crackling and a voice came over their loudspeaker, doing all the 'Z Victor One' stuff. Isaiah's mate rushed over to answer it but Isaiah stayed where he was, just looking at me and the others, his eyes going up and down each of us in turn till he came to Dole.

'Been havin' too many washes in coal-tar soap, have yer, son?'

'No,' Dole said.

'Oh, I see. Y'were about t'join the Black an' White Minstrels, but y've lost y'way.'

'No,' Dole said.

'Now, what could it be? Y'dad was a pair of Polaroid sunglasses? Y'mam was a licorice stick? Somethin' like that.'

Dole never said anything this time, but if looks could kill, they'd need a new police recruit on our estate. Isaiah knew he'd hurt him and that's what he likes doing more than anything.

'An' as f'you, Scully,' he said, leavin' Dole, satisfied with a job well done, I'm just waitin' for yer, y'know. Waitin'. Y'll turn up one of these days, right on time, an' I'll take yer down a one-way street straight t'the depot.'

'Are you a bus driver as well?' Mooey asked him.

Instant death that would have been from one of us, but Isaiah just laughed at him. 'You can come along f'the ride, if y'want,' he said, pleasing Mooey no end. He started back towards his car and then came back for one last parting shot at Dole.

'I'd like t'say I'd remember your face,' he said, 'but t'tell y'the truth, y'all look the same t'me.'

'I'll remember yours,' Dole said, looking him straight in one eye and just over the other one. 'What's left of it, that is.'

I turned away, not wanting to see the sight of

Dole's blood and features all over the pavement.

'Come on will yer, f'God's sake,' the other copper shouted. 'There's murder down at the Boundary.'

Isaiah was torn in two as he struggled to try and catch Dole to strangle him and also to get in the police car at the same time. He changed his mind at least three times before he heaved himself into the front seat and they went off, skid marks everywhere, down towards the Boundary. Isaiah was so keen to get another look at Dole that he ended up in the back seat as they took a corner by the church on two wheels.

'Anyway,' Snotty Dog said, 'we were there on this tractor, y'see, me an' this farmer's daughter . . .'

'What number is it anyway?' Mad Dog said.

'Posh houses don't have numbers,' Snotty Dog said. 'They just have names, some of them.'

'There's one down there called "No Hawkers",' Mad Dog said. 'Daft buggers, there's no hawks f'miles around here.'

'Shall we just go in, like?' Snotty Dog said.

'Wha'd'y'mean?'

'Well, y'know, Scull, just knock at the door an' join in with the others.'

'Wha'd'y'expect us t'do?' I said. 'Sing Christmas carols outside?'

'Can we?' Mooey said.

We found the house in the end but there didn't seem to be anything going on, not like at a party up our way where you can hear the noise in the next parish. It was all dead quiet, though there were lots of cars in the driveway and outside the gate, so we knew there must be something doing in there.

Not even Mooey'd go up and knock on the door and say 'Hello,' though he would have gone and sang 'Good King Wenceslas' without any prompting. We stood there for ages, just inside the front gate, kicking their gravel about and wondering what to do next when we heard footsteps coming down the avenue. I poked my head around the iron gates and saw it was Mickey Brown. I knew it was Mickey Brown 'cos he was dressed like a prick. We waited in the bushes till he was just level with us and then jumped out at him.

'Surprise, surprise!' I said.

It was and all. He crumpled in a dead faint in my arms and it took us ages to bring him around. What finally did it was Mooey giving him the kiss of life. He was up and wide-eyed in a flash. Mooey must have found out about French kisses.

'What're you lot doing' here?' he said as he checked all his pockets and wiped his mouth. 'Y'give me the fright of me life there. I thought it was the Law. I've been followed by a plain clothes cop all night, but I managed t'shake him off in the Cemetery.'

'What's the Law doin' followin' you?' I asked.

'Never you mind,' he said, all mysterious, 'an' I'm not speakin' t'you after that trick y'tried t'play on me about Marie Morgan. Good job I didn't take it serious, y'must think I'm soft, an' if y'think y'bunkin' in here, y've got no chance, none at all. I know this lot personally, I do; friends of mine, they are, an' I'll tell yer this much, I was here last night an' they've been at it ever since. They won't want any gatecrashers now, an' anyway, it was by invitation only, t'start with.'

'Wha're you doin' there, then?' Mad Dog said.

'Ah well then, that's the question, isn't it?' he said. 'I'm supplyin' their needs, y'might say.'

'They want someone t'laugh at.'

'Listen, Scully,' Mickey said out of the corner of his mouth, 'without me there'd be no party. That's how much I'm worth t'them. I'm an important man, I am.'

'He's got the concessions f'cockles,' Snotty Dog said.

'Anyway,' he said, 'I've got t'go. I'm late as it is.'

'Yeah, well alright, Mickey,' I said, 'you run along in there, don't bother about us, we don't count, we're only y'mates, after all.'

'You're no mate of mine,' he said. 'Not anymore.'

'Fair enough,' I said. 'I can't say I'm happy

about what y'doin' to us after we've been through so much t'gether, but you go y'own way, you look after number one.'

'I'm sorry lads, but this is the big-time league y'mixin' in now. Y'd only be out of y'depth, y'know how it is.'

'Wha'?' Mad Dog said. '*You*, big time, y'little—'

'No, no, we understand, Mickey,' I said, giving him a brotherly pat on the shoulder to show there was no hard feelings and then looking down at his feet to make sure I wasn't seeing things. 'It doesn't matter about me an' the boys. I know y've outgrown us lately, it's fair enough ... but there is just one thing before y'go. D'y'know y'stood in a puddle of pills?'

'Oh shite,' he said, on his hands and knees, protecting his pills like a kid with a sandcastle. 'I must have a hole in me pocket.'

'More like a hole in the head,' I said. 'I bet y'didn't lose that copper at all. He'll just be stalkin' yer on all fours, followin' y'trail of pills.'

'There's no need t'worry about that,' he said. 'I was just makin' him up.'

'Wha're y'doin' with all those pills anyway?' Snotty Dog said.

'I'm openin' a friggin' chemist's, that's what I'm doin',' he said as he transferred all the pills out of the pocket with the hole in.

'We'll be y'assistants,' I said. 'Just f't'night, like.'

'Y'won't.'

'We fuckin' well will, Mickey,' I said, ''cos if we don't get in there I'm goin' t'make sure that copper you invented turns out t'be real.'

'Y'wouldn't,' he said, 'not t'one of y'mates.' And then he had a good look at me and then at Mad Dog with his forehead touching his chin. 'Y'would.'

'Too true we would, now get down that path.'

'Y'pushin' pills, that's what y'doin',' Dole said.

'An' y'nothin' but a stupid get. If you get caught y'won't see the light of day f'five years, but all of them in there'll be alright though, won't they? Twenty-five-pound fine paid for by daddy, that's all they'll collect. It's you who'll be the sucker.'

'It's worth it,' he said, 't'get in there, an' anyway, I'm only the delivery boy.'

'We already know that,' Mad Dog said. 'At that butcher's in Bootle.'

'No, soft. That's what they call me in the business. I deliver the goods. I don't push them or nothin'. I wouldn't do anythin' like that. Someone else does things like that, I just turn up with the order. Ah come on, get lost will yer, I'm dead late. I almost missed me connection.'

'Y'don't need a bus t'come up here,' Snotty Dog said. 'Y'can walk it in a quarter of an hour.'

'Oh God spare me,' Mickey said, holding his head and looking up at the sky. 'Don't you lot know nothin'? Me connection's the feller what pushes the pills. "Uncle" we call him. I don't know his real name an' he doesn't know mine. That's how it works.'

'Well, come on then,' I said, 'cut the crap, let's get in there, an' if they say anythin', y've got some really hot stuff with yer an' we're y'bodyguards.'

'You five?'

'That's right,' Mad Dog said. 'Wanna argue, wise guy?'

'It's a waste of time y'comin', honest it is,' he said. 'They're all much older than you f'a kick-off. Y'll never score, not unless there's a cradle-snatcher in there.'

'D'you want t'knock on the door,' I said, my fist ready, 'or shall I do the honours?'

''Ey? Oh no, no, don't touch it, I've got me own special knock,' he said and then gave the door about fifteen 'rattattattats' just like out of a British spy film. As soon as he'd finished there was a voice from the other side of the door.

'Yes, who is it?'

'The Man from Uncle,' Mickey whispered.

'An' James Bond an' the Spy Who Came In from the Cold,' I said.

'An er, an' me, er Mooey Morgan, I'm here too.'

'Where are you from?' the voice said.

'Over the seas an' far away,' Mickey said, going deep red and putting his head down.

'I didn't know y'lived in Birkenhead, Mickey,' I said as the door swung open and standing there, blocking the entrance, was this really wild freak with hair stood on end as if he had two million volts up his arse. He was just dangling there like a puppet on a string, his eyes trying to focus on us.

'What the . . . who's . . . where . . . these? Look, man, I . . . who the fuck are they?'

'Y'alright,' Mickey said as he shoved past him and we tried to do the same but got the door shoved at us. The guy wasn't that freaked out he couldn't recognize trouble anyway.

'No, I'm not alright,' he said, 'not with them.'

'They're safe, I'm tellin' yer,' Mickey said. 'They wouldn't know grass if they walked on it.' From one of the rooms off the hallway there was the sound of someone quietly murdering a guitar but that was all. Some party. But I wasn't going home now, not without a fight.

'See,' I said, 'we're safe, y'can put y'trust in us, we won't let yer down.'

'No, er . . . no, you can't.' Freaky said, holding onto the door as Mad Dog backed off into the pathway and got ready to charge his way in. As it happened, he didn't have to bother 'cos freaky turned away from us and made a grab at Mickey, leaving the door free and Mad Dog bouncing into the back of Mooey as we piled into the hallway.

First base. There was only Freaky in there and some tart on the stairs coming out of her dress.

'Look, man, get these kids out of here, will you? We don't want any risks, you know that. When you came last night you had no one with you then. I mean . . .' He seemed to lose all interest in us all of a sudden as he pulled Mickey against the door to the room where the guitar was. 'You have got the stuff, haven't you? You did bring the goods? Come on, brother, where is it?'

'Er excuse us,' I said as I tried to squeeze past him, 'if you don't mind . . .' But Freaky obviously did. It was worse than trying to bunk into the match of a Saturday.

'What is this – a rip-off?' he said to Mickey. 'Where do you think you are now, eh? We're not into little street-corner deals, you know. There's enough with you for a month for all of us, or there better had be, so cut the shit an' get this fucking rabble out of the way.'

The voice on him when he said 'shit' and 'fucking' was real posh. I didn't know rich people swore like that.

'What rabble?' Mad Dog snarled. 'Who're you talkin' about? An' the mouth on you as well.'

'There's no harm in them, pal,' Mickey said. 'They're mates of mine, I can vouch for them. I've known them years.'

'That in itself is no recommendation,' Freaky said, 'now listen here, Sonny Jim—'

'Who're you callin' Sonny Jim?' Mad Dog said. 'I'll wipe the floor with you, mophead, if y'call me that again. I didn't come here t'be insulted, I came f'a fuck an' I can't see any.'

'Okay, okay, point taken, apologies all round, now look, do us a favour will you? We've got a bit of business to do, no offence meant to anyone present, but clear off out of it will you? Fast?'

'We're not leavin' Mickey . . .' I said.

'The Man from Uncle,' Mickey whispered.

'Whoever he thinks he is, we're not leavin' him. Who knows what'll happen t'him after he's handed over the goodies? Delivery boys around our way are always gettin' beaten up. We're here t'look after him an' that's what we intend doin'.'

'We're not movin' from this spot,' Mad Dog said, 'an' that's final. Not unless it's t'go in there an' see an orgy.'

'Fucking hell, I don't know,' Freaky said, 'I really don't. If it makes you happy, go on in, and what's more, if you see an orgy come straight out and let me know.'

'Ta, la',' I said, pushing at the door leading to the other room. 'An' hey, Mickey, if he tries any rough stuff, just give us a shout will yer. That's what we're here for.'

Inside the room there was a thick cloud of funny-smelling smoke and a sea of sleeping bags, like as if it was five o'clock in the morning. It probably was to them the state they were in. The stereo was on dead low and the feller committing cruelty on the guitar was still at it in a corner. In another corner by the window there was about a dozen hippies passing a ciggie around while one of them rolled another.

'Where's the orgy then?' Mad Dog said.

'It'll be upstairs,' I said. 'This'll just be the waitin' room.'

There was heavy breathing at me shoulder, then a hand gripping it and then a groan and then another one. I turned around and it was Snotty Dog, his eyes hanging out on his cheekbones far enough down for him to see what a mess his nose was in. But it wasn't his nose that he was staring at.

'My God!' he gasped, 'it's true, it's really really

129

true, look at that will yer. Just look at that!'

We all looked over to where his shaking hand was pointing and there, about to climb out of a double sleeping bag, was a skinny little tart totally in her knacker, wearing nothing but a smile and a bead necklace. She started to step across some bodies towards us, her tiny tits bouncing about, and Snotty Dog and all of us just stood there, wide-mouthed, eyes bouncing up and down with her tits. Every secret thought come alive; even Mooey, and he never had any secret thoughts. She stood in front of us without flickering an inch, as though she was dressed for a winter walk along Blackpool promenade. And all our Towers were lit up.

'Excuse me,' she said.

'Alright there, girl, I'll excuse you any day,' Snotty Dog said in his own special ham-fisted style of chatting birds up that doesn't even work on the scrubbers down our way.

'You are obstructing the doorway,' she said.

'That's an indirect free kick, that is,' Snotty Dog said, and she give him a sarcastic smile as we stepped aside for her. But sarcastic or not, any kind of smile was good enough for Snotty Dog.

'I'm on, I'm on, boys! She laughed at me joke. She give the come-on, I've hit the jackpot! Out of me road, let me get in there.' He trampled on at least three heads as he raced over to her sleeping bag, and when he got there, he threw the cover back and jumped in, shoes and all.

I took a look at the group over in the corner passing the rollie around amongst themselves and giggling away at nothing. That was all they was doing. It was like Ring a Ring a Roses. The weird thing though was that they were all laughing at the wrong speed, like a single played at thirty-three revs a minute.

'Would y'look at them, Mad Dog,' I said. 'Disgustin' isn't it 'ey? Deserve t'be robbed soft, they do. Must be students, y'know. Me dad says they're all like this in them colleges. Mind you, where there's dope, there's dope. Give us them Junior Aspirin, will yer.'

I walked into the centre of the room and tried to imagine I was in Kirkby market of a Saturday afternoon, like I used to be, selling spuds with our Terry, my cousin that has the potato business.

'Alright then, alright then, who's after the trip of a lifetime! You want drugs, 'course you want drugs, well, y've come t'the right man. "Tune out, turn in, drop on," that's what I always say. Now this little lot I have right here in my hand, straight from the casbahs of Monaco no less, a bottle full of Turkish delight, an' I'm givin' them away t'night, ladies an' gentlemen, givin' them away. I should be a registered charity at this rate. Not eighty pence a pill, not seventy-five, not even sixty, an' believe it or believe it not, I don't even want fifty-five for them. Don't all rush at once now, step right this way in an orderly manner f'a rocket trip t'the moon at *fifty* pence a go, that's right, you heard, fifty pence; come on now, roll up, roll up . . . alright, don't form a queue, I'll come t'you. 'Ey, that rhymes! Any poets in here t'night?'

I shuffled back to the others. 'Soddin hell,' I said. 'What's wrong? They're not interested.' The only movement in the whole room was about half a dozen of them burying their heads in their sleeping bags.

'Not interested?' Mad Dog said. 'I don't think half of them're alive, never mind interested. Are y'sure this isn't a funeral parlour?'

'I'm beginnin' t'wonder,' I said as the tart out of the sleeping bag banged the door into us as she came back in the room. 'Hey up, though, we'll see some life in a minute, y'can bet on that.'

'Here I am, love,' Snotty Dog shouted, waving from the sleeping bag, trying to look like every film star he'd ever seen but only succeeding in looking like Snotty Dog with an enormous hard-on. The sleeping bag'd become a tent. 'I knew y'd come back. Baby. I kept it warm for yer; guess what I'm talkin' about. Come on then, darlin', get stuck into here, great invention these double sleepin' bags aren't they 'ey?' He moved over for her. 'This is y'big chance, an' boy, do I mean big! Y've had nott'n till y've had a man ... *like me!*'

She stood above him with a real smile on her face and Snotty Dog opened his arms, closed his eyes and pursed his lips. For a second or two we almost believed he really had copped off, until she bent down and whispered into his ear.

'Fuck off, little boy.'

Snotty Dog threw himself out of her sleeping bag as if someone was about to practise the *Nutcracker Suite* on him, and he stood there sniffing and spluttering, trying to get the wind back in his sails sufficient enough to tell her what he really thought of her, while all the time she lay on her back smoking a roll-up of her own and totally ignoring him.

'Well ... well ... didn't fancy yer anyway ... just doin' yer a favour, that's all ... an' another thing, where's y'pride, goin' around in the knacker like that. They'll sag when y'get older y'know, them tits will, walkin' around with no support, not that y've got much there t'sag in any case. Friggin' disgustin', that's what it is, nothin' but a scrubber with ingrowin' tits, that's all you are ...'

I went over and pulled him away just as he started quoting the Bible and the Act of Contrition at her. 'Come on,' I said, 'We're goin' now, sod this place, it's a phoney.'

It was only when we got back into the hallway

that I noticed that Dole wasn't with us, and hadn't been since we were in the doorway, and the reason I noticed was because he was sitting on the stairs with that good-looking tart we'd seen earlier wearing a dress that must have been a handkerchief once, but what was inside that handkie, you'd never find in anyone's trouser pocket. Snotty Dog summed the situation up in a second with his usual flair for fucking things up and strode over to the banisters.

'Alright there, girl,' he said, 'er, y'can go now, Dole. There's a tart in a sleepin bag back there wants a few words with yer. Nice night isn't it, love, d'y'wanna know my vital statistics, do yer? Gerraload of this, 38–28–38 an' 12.'

'Twelve's his shoe size, love,' I said. 'Take no notice.'

She wasn't taking any notice neither – not only of Snotty Dog, but of any of us except Dole. She couldn't take her eyes off him; so much so that we all started looking at him as well. And it was then I realized niggers have got another big advantage apart from not showing their bruises, and that's that they never show their age neither. Seeing him for the first time, he could have been anything between fifteen and twenty-five, and this tart was willing, it was obvious, to believe he'd long ago forgotten his twenty-first birthday party.

'Getting back to you,' she said, turning a knock-out arse towards Snotty Dog, 'you must have problems with your colour. I mean, it must present difficulties.'

'Yeah, I have murder getting' a suntan,' Dole said, and she laughed and took hold of both his hands and put them around her waist.

'Why haven't I seen you before?' she said to him as Snotty Dog got his head jammed in the banisters and his knickers in a twist.

'I haven't been here long,' Dole said.

'Own up will yer,' Snotty Dog shouted. 'It's 'cos it's dark. Put the light on an' make y'decision, girl. Y'won't regret it.'

'This is my brother's idea, all this,' she said.

'Wha' about me?' Snotty Dog said. 'I'm talkin' to yer an' all.'

'It's very boring, don't you think?'

'It was till ten minutes ago when I met you,' Dole said.

'I was goin' t'say that as well, love. He took the very words out of me mouth.'

'My parents will be absolutely livid when they find out.'

'Where are they?' Dole said. 'At the alehouse?'

'On a cruise.'

'Yeah, I bet,' Snotty Dog said, giving up and coming over to us. 'Belfast an' back.'

Freaky and Mickey were still stood there, further down the hallway, haggling over money, and Mickey was counting the pills and the little packets and looking in his turn-ups and down his kecks.

'Y'sister's wearin' falsies, isn't she?' Snotty Dog said to Freaky. 'I'm right aren't I? 'Course I am. Look at y'face. Thought as much.'

'They're not the only things false in here, if they are,' I said. 'They're off another planet that shower in there. It's last this place.'

'There's the door,' Freaky said. 'If you turn the handle the door opens and you can all crawl back to where you belong.'

'Don't worry, pal, we're goin' right now. We don't wanna stay. I'd rather be back where I belong if this is a sample of your idea of a good time.'

Dole was too busy to say goodbye so we left him to it. The last we saw, Mickey was taking his shoes off and Freaky was telling him he was finished as a delivery boy. Snotty Dog nearly took the hinges off the door when he closed it and Mad Dog swung on the gate till it came off but no-one'd come out and give them a fight or even a chase so we walked off down the avenue just as the village church bells were chiming midnight.

'Well, that was very nice,' Mooey said, 'but can we go t'the party now, 'ey? Can we?' He hadn't said much all night, Mooey, but he'd just about summed it all up for us. We hardly said two words to each other all the way home, though I could hear the Dogs muttering about Dole being a lucky sod because he was black and it was personality that counted in the long run.

I left them at their gate and walked back to our house part of the way with Mooey. I was tired and I was fed up too. Another night wasted frigging about. What did we do tonight? We did nothing. Even going up the village and seeing inside one of them houses wasn't what it would have been once. The Dogs were right in a way when they said they wanted something else, but my something else wasn't the same as theirs – whatever theirs was. Whatever mine was. A few months ago I wanted to be a footballer. Not only wanted, but was certain I was going to be one. I'd closed my eyes and told myself that was what I was going to be, whatever the odds. It sort of kept me going through all the shitty boring days at school and around here. But there was nothing down for me, I knew that now. I must have been out of me head to believe I was our estate's answer to Bobby Robson's prayers, but at least I had something to dream about. Now, I seemed to have nothing. Nothing big enough to take me away, that was certain.

When I got in, our Henry was standing at platform eight and the telly was blaring in the front room. There was a noise from the top of the stairs as if Hovis was starting to cry but I didn't want to know about that so I went in the front room where my Mam was sitting on the couch eating marshmallows while my dad was asleep at her side with the *Football Echo* over his head and one shoe on and one shoe off.

'I thought it was y'Gran,' she said. 'Been anywhere nice?'

'No.'

'Someone called here f'you just after y'went.'

'Oh, who was it?'

'Some darkie.'

'Oh.'

'A girl, Francis.'

'Oh aye? Probably had a message f'her brother. I've been out with him an' the gang t'night. Er, say anythin'?'

'She said she wanted t'catch you before y'went out.'

'As I say, it'll be about Tommy.'

'Where did y'say y'went again?'

'I didn't, but we went to a party. It was last. There was nothin' happenin'.'

'Y'should have taken y'girl friend,' me Mam said, just dropping it in like she always does.

'What girl friend?'

'The one at the door before.'

'Arr, come on, Mam. She's the sister of one of me mates, that's all.'

'Him with the father? Is that Hovis cryin' up there?'

'Yes.'

'Go an' fetch him a glass of milk will y'? I can't miss Gary Cooper.'

It was *High Noon* on the telly and the lead had started to fly. Cowboy films are my Mam's weakness, about her only one. Every year when *High Noon* comes back on the box she stands there by

136

the couch, joining Gary Cooper as he defies the town and waits for the twelve o'clock train. Still, it got her away from Joanna and me out of the room. Hovis'd fallen out of bed and when I put him back he didn't want anything except to go to sleep again, so I went to the cockloft with the milk and stood outside on the ladder. It must have been peak hour on the tracks 'cos I knocked and knocked but Henry wouldn't answer, not even when I shouted through the crack in the door, 'The train now arrivin' on platforms four, five, six, seven an' eight is comin' in sideways.'

There was uneasy peace on the streets of wherever it was when I got back on the couch with my Mam and she knew there'd be nothing happening a bit so she started on me again. She never watched the bits that Gary Cooper wasn't in anyway.

'I've seen her mother at the shops. Nice woman, always got a kind word f'everybody she meets, makes y'realize how lucky y'are sometimes. Her daughter's very good-lookin' as well. For a nigger.'

'An' what does that mean?'

'What I said, that's what it means, son.'

'But y'wouldn't like it if she *was* me girl friend would yer?'

'It's not what I mind it's what other people'll say.'

'Christ, Mam, since when have you cared what people say about us?'

'I don't, Francis. I don't give a frig about other people. But can you stand it?. That's the question.'

'But she's not me girl friend, Mam. How many times do I have t'tell yer?'

'Y'sound just like St Peter after the Last Supper, the way y'denying' it.'

'Arrey, come on, Mam, lay off will yer. It's late.'

'I've got nothin' against the darkies,' she said,

'nothin' at all. We're all the same underneath, God knows, but y'll come in f'some slangin' if y'take her out on this estate, y'know.'

'Nobody said anythin' this afternoon,' I said and she just looked at me all wise and somehow like an old statue and she didn't need to tell me she'd caught me out.

'Well, be warned,' she said, 'an' if it goes onto its natural end—'

'I've only known her proper f'three days, Mam, give us a chance.'

'Y've got t'think of the kids an' all,' she said. 'Look at little Hovis, God bless his cotton socks, y'couldn't wish t'meet a happier kid now, but when he starts school he'll soon be made t'feel out of it. Bloody Vera, I wouldn't mind if she'd found a Sambo she could trust, the stupid bitch.' She shovelled the last marshmallow into her mouth and Gary Cooper stepped out of the bar into the street, heading for the railway station.

'Yeah, well I'm off t'bed, I'm knackered.'

'Make us a pot of tea before y'go, will yer, son? It's got a great end to it, this film.'

I'd just got the pot in my hand from the coffee table when there was a big thud like someone was breaking through the wall upstairs.

'What the hell's that?' me Mam said. 'Go out an' have a look will yer?'

I opened the front-room door and stood at the edge of the stairs. At first I couldn't hear anything and I was just off out into the back kitchen when a little groan came from the landing at the top of the stairs

'Hovis has fell out of bed again, Mam.'

'Take another cup of milk up for him then, there's a bottle in the pantry, only be quiet, it's nearly High Noon in here.'

I couldn't be bothered getting him another drink,

138

so I went straight up the stairs and onto the landing. When I got there I stepped over our Henry and went into Hovis's room. And then I realized what I'd just done and came rushing out just in time to grab hold of Henry's legs as he began to slither head first down the stairs.

'Mam,' I shouted, 'Mam, come quick, it's our Henry.'

'I can't,' she said, 'the train's just come in.'

'Mine's just blown up,' Henry said and tried to commit suicide by falling down the stairs.

'Mam, it's serious.'

'But Gary Cooper's trapped.'

'Christ, Mam, he's really hurt himself.'

He had and all. His eyebrows were all singed off, what was left of his hair was still stood on end and his face was covered in miniature train oil and little burns. Stuck right into his forehead was half a dinky train wheel and tangled up in the hair at the back of his head were two plastic passengers and a porter's cap.

'What the soddin' hell's goin' on here?' my Mam said from the bottom of the stairs. 'Wha've y'done t'y'self, Henry?'

'Me buffers, Mam,' he gasped. 'I've burnt me buffers.'

'I'll jump on them in a minute,' she said, going back in the front room where the real action was.

'I think he's bad y'know, Mam, have a look.'

'Is he buggery,' she said. 'Y'can't hurt y'self with a child's toy. I'll send y'father up, he's not doin' nothin'.'

Me and my dad cleaned Henry up as best we could. There was bits of trains stuck all over him like pins in a new shirt but nothing turned out to be very serious, and when *High Noon*'d gone my Mam made him a cup of tea. He sat in the back kitchen with an even emptier look than normal on his face and none of us could get any sense out of him at all. He only took two swigs of tea and he was back up the stairs. Just in case any of his passengers were trapped in the wreckage, I expect.

When I went up to bed, he was stood at the door to the cockloft just shaking his head and mumbling, 'Gone, gone, all gone.' I climbed up there to have a look and I saw what he meant. Everything was in bits and pieces like a metal jigsaw puzzle. The Inter Cities had all collided at Crewe junction, the Sheffield train was at the bottom of the Pennines, bridges had collapsed on tunnels, the British Isles was spread all over the cockloft, while the new cross-Channel train had driven straight off Dover harbour into the old toilet bowl that stood for the English Channel, leaving hundreds of little imitation passengers lying splattered everywhere in sight.

I think he really would have taken an overdose there and then, but when he got to the medicine cupboard all we had in was a packet of stain remover for dentures and three Beecham's Powders, and I kept him away from the bottle of bleach in the larder. Otherwise, you could have guaranteed, our Henry'd have been there, booking his one-way ticket to the Great Terminus in the Sky.

8

I didn't even bother going down the labour exchange but Mad Dog and Snotty Dog went and the bloke behind the counter told them that if they didn't want to be unemployed the best chance they had was to stay on at school and go in the sixth form. Mad Dog had to be carried out fighting when he heard that, but it was a waste of energy. There were no jobs for us. Even the suckholes were finding it hard and having to take what turned up. I had to laugh. Five years stuck to the tit of every teacher in the school and still no job.

'I'm goin' the Shetlands on me own if you lot don't come, so there,' Snotty Dog said as we walked over to school. It was the afternoon of the semi-final and I had my boots and my towel under my arm.

'There won't be anythin' there except sheep an' Texans,' I said, 'an' anyway, with your sense of direction y'll probably end up a waiter in a Spanish night club.'

'That's alright then,' he said. 'Anythin'll be better than here. There's bound t'be somethin' goin' when we get there.'

'Yeah, a bus goin' back t'Liverpool,' I said. 'That's all. An' we'll all be on it.'

'Honest, Scully,' Mad Dog said, 'you haven't half changed.'

'He's in love,' Snotty Dog said.

'I'll pretend I didn't hear that,' I said, 'f'the sake of what passes for your nose.'

'Y'have though, Scull,' Mad Dog said. 'I knew yer

141

once when it was always you wanted t'go places an' it was the rest of us had t'be persuaded. Now, it's the other way around.'

'That's right,' Snotty Dog said, 'like the South-ampton trip last year t'watch the Reds. We would never have gone on that if it hadn't been f'you.'

'An' what happened?' I said. 'It pissed down all the time, we got as far as friggin' Aldershot an' the game got called off. Real smart that was.'

'But we had a lot of laughs along the way,' Snotty Dog said.

'It was alright at the time, I suppose.'

'Well, come on then,' Mad Dog said, 'let's go. There's nothin' stoppin' us, we've got nothin' t'lose. They're bound t'want tea lads on the sites up there. I heard there's houses an' roads goin' up left, right an' centre. We needn't work on an oil rig or divin' or nothin'.'

'A tea lad?' I said. 'Is that what y'wanna be?'

'It's better than what we've got here – which is nothin' at all.'

'He doesn't wanna leave his tart behind,' Snotty Dog said. 'Can't trust her, that's what it is.'

'One more word about her, bollocks,' I said, 'an' y'll have a face like a bag of spanners.'

'I better not say what's on the bog door at school then,' he said, just before I got hold of the lapels of his jacket. 'I didn't do it, honest.'

'Wha' is it?' I said, 'come on, tell me.'

'Y'just said y'didn't wanna hear another word about her.'

'Tell me, or else.'

'Look y'self.'

'*Tell me.*'

'"Snigger snigger snigger, Scully's screwin' a nigger,"' he said and put his hands over his face but I threw him away instead.

'Well, it's a fuckin' lie.'

'Still an' all, it's better than Marie Morgan,' Mad Dog said.

'Jesus, y'know more about me than I do meself.'

'That's on a bog door an' all,' Snotty Dog said from ten yards away. 'There's even a drawin' f'that.'

'I was only practisin' what I preached anyway. I told yer before.'

'We know,' Snotty Dog said. 'Bulls' eyes an' scrap wood.'

'At least I got more than you did at that party the other night, Snotty,' I said.

'I wasn't tryin',' he said, and what's more, he believed himself and all.

'Come on, will yer,' Mad Dog said. 'Y'can't say nothin' t'you lately without y'lookin' f'a fight.'

'Me? Lookin' f'a fight? I don't have t'go lookin', Mad Dog. I just wait around long enough an' some idiot opens his mouth an' asks f'one. An' another thing while I'm about it, whoever it is writin' that crap on the toilet walls, if y'know who it is—'

'No, we don't—' Snotty Dog said.

'Whoever it is, tell them from me that if I ever catch them—'

'I hope y'don't think it's one of us,' Mad Dog said.

'Look, I never said that at all, all I'm sayin' is—'

'Y'must have known when y'started goin' out with her it'd be like that,' Snotty Dog said. 'I'm not bein' funny, like, but y'askin' for it, knockin' off a nigger.'

'I'm *not* knockin' off a nigger.'

'Alright, alright, don't scream, y'don't have t'spell it out; y'just good friends,' Mad Dog said and then the both of them got out of the way quick and I legged them into the playground just as the first whistle went for the start of school so that

143

everybody was supposed to stop runnin', cos that's
the daft rule in our jailyard. One whistle you stop
whatever you're doing, and you stand still where
you are, two whistles you get into class lines and
three whistles you march into registration like a
bunch of infant kids.

'Course, it all depends who's on duty, 'cos some
teachers just blow one whistle and run off back to
the staffroom for the last ciggie before the battle
starts, and others don't turn up at all and you can
drift in through the doors when you feel like it, but
naturally enough, this particular afternoon when
us three are hot footing it around, we had to have
the Gaffer, and there's nothing he likes better than
a good set of rules and regulations.

'You three,' he shouted, giving us 'Rhapsody in
Blue' on the whistle and then giving us a chase,
'what d'you think you're playin' at, come back here
this minutes, don't you know the rules yet, just you
dare go in that door before I blow the third whistle,
I know who you are, don't think you can get away
with this . . .' And when he got back to the playground only the first-years were still in line while
the rest of the school were fighting and shoving
their way through the other doorway.

But, of course, he got us. Before registration was
over he was at our classroom door with his cane,
fetching us down to his woodwork room, prodding
at our backs like a slave driver on a rowing boat.
When we got down there he just pointed to one of
the benches and the other two leant on it with their
coats up their backs. Not me though, no chance.

'Come on, Scully,' he said, 'you know the score,
bend over and be quick about it or I'll give you
two.'

'I've got piles,' I said. 'They'll bleed.'

'First I've heard.'

'Y'don't go around advertisin' the fact, do yer?

"Hello, my name's Franny Scully, I've got piles."'

'Oh, a comedian, right, you can have two on the hands.'

'That's not justice,' I said. 'It hurts just as much on the hands. Why should I get two?'

'Three then?' he said. 'Any advance on three?' So I give up and got two right across the fingertips. The look on his face was comical. Teeth clenched, eyes closed, breathing through his nose like a pig at a feast. I almost laughed out loud except I didn't want two more.

'Don't go away, boys,' he said as we raced for the door. 'I've got a job for you, just up your street – lifting something, but it's not a shop I'm afraid.' He walked down the workshop to this thing wrapped in a big tarpaulin at the back and he stood at the side of it like a painter with his latest picture. 'See this here,' he said, 'you three are going to help me carry it down to the headmaster's office, one to each corner, don't stand there whining, it's only two flights of stairs and five corridors, come on, liven up, anyone'd think you'd just been caned.'

'I can't lift anythin',' I said. 'Me fingers're paralysed with pain.'

'There's no such word as "can't", boy,' he said, 'and if you drop this your piles'll be coming out of the top of your head. Now take a corner each and hurry up about it.'

After the third time I said I was definitely going to drop it, he believed me and he took the whole back end to himself and finished up doing a smart impersonation of a ruptured duck while I guided us down the stairs and along the corridors till we got to the headmaster's office. The head greeted us like long-lost friends and we gathered around, big pals together for the grand unveiling of what was hidden under the tarpaulin. Only the Gaffer had other ideas about that. He didn't want three

yobboes like us lowering the tone of his performance when he was doing his arse-lickin'.

'Right, you three, off you go to your classes now,
and next time, Scully, remind me to hit you
afterwards instead of before.' He chuckled away to
himself and then had a sidelong glance at the
headmaster who wasn't laughing at all and so he
stopped in mid 'hoh-hoh-hoh'.

'Scully,' the headmaster said, 'Scully, I know
that name, now let me think. Yes, it must be nearly
a fortnight now, Mrs Faconfield sent you down to
me for giving cheek.'

'I can ex—'

'And when I came back at the end of the lesson
Mrs Faconfield had arrived but *you* had dis-
appeared. Since then I also seem to recall another
teacher has spoken to me about you, one of the
male members of staff—'

'That'd be—'

'Be quiet, boy. Got some explaining to do,
haven't you? Thought I'd forgotten, didn't you?'

'Yes, but—'

'Stand in that corner, I'll deal with you in a
moment, but first, a pleasant surprise for a change.
Shall I perform the honours, Mr Leslie?'

'Certainly, sir,' the Gaffer said, like as if he was
talking to the Queen. 'The pleasure's all mine, sir.'
If he'd have been wearing his leather apron I
reckon he would have curtsied he was in such a
state.

'Right then,' the head said, 'here goes!' and he
pulled the tarpaulin away and then stood there,
going 'oh' and 'yes' and 'super' and 'my my my'
and getting proper excited, and all it was for Christ
sake, was a fucking desk!

The only difference I could see between it and
any other desk I'd seen was that this one had
press-button drawers instead of handles. The head

146

didn't think so though. He spent the next ten minutes sitting at it and touching it and playing with the buttons, watching the drawers slide open one by one. When the Gaffer revealed his master stroke and pressed a button at the side and all the drawers came out together as if the desk was having a breakdown, the head got so excited he reminded me of our Hovis stood under the tree at Christmas ripping the paper off his plastic ducks and books of fairy stories. Give him a week, this feller, and he'd have his teddies and all his toys in the drawers.

'I can't thank you enough, Mr Leslie, I really can't. A truly impressive piece of craftmanship.'

'Thank *you*, Headmaster.'

'Excellent, first class.'

'Just something I knocked up in my spare time, sir.'

'A quite remarkable feat. I'm sure nobody else in the whole authority will have one as big as this.'

I don't know, the state of them. They were supposed to be in charge of us and the way they were acting, they were hardly in charge of themselves.

'Now, the next thing I would like to see would be a portable stairway for the stage in the hall. As it is at the moment, one has to enter into assembly through the back stage. I was thinking it would be rather more impressive if I could march right down the hallway through the gathering and ascend the stage directly from the front. What do you think eh?'

'I think that's a splendid idea, sir,' the Gaffer said. 'I'm sure it could be arranged.'

And I was sure it could and all. By the end of next week no doubt. The same feller was six months mending one of our goalposts last year.

'Right, and now for the unpleasantries,' the

headmaster said, and I knew it was my turn and that he wasn't going to play with me. 'Come here, Scully. Now there is one thing I cannot stand and will not tolerate in a child . . . here, boy, I'm not going to bite you . . . and that one thing I will not stand for is downright cheek and insolence. I don't care if the child is a first year or about to leave as you, thankfully, are. Do you understand that, young man?'

He stopped and I knew he expected an answer so I said 'Yes sir' and he drew breath and started again.

'Well, if you do understand, why on earth do you end up outside my door, and not for the first time, I'm sure of that.'

'Y'see, it's all a mis—'

'Yes, Headmaster, I've sent him down to you on at least two occasions this term,' the Gaffer chipped in.

'There you are, you see. You don't even have any respect for a teacher who could be of great benefit to you in the learning of a trade. A considerable help in these difficult times.'

Another joke. All we'd ever made in his class are plywood table-tennis bats with no pimples and coffee tables with a slant. The rest of the time he has us copying out of these big books about chisels and fret-saws. I know all about them but it's a long time since I've as much as seen one in his lessons.

'And do you listen, do you co-operate in your woodwork classes? Do you accept guidance and advice? Obviously you don't. I can tell by the look on your face now that you think you know it all already. Well, you might know everying there is to know after four o'clock, Master Scully, but while you're in my domain, you're going to stay exactly as you are: one of the many and with nothing much to recommend you by. Go to that cupboard, boy, and take out the cane, then lift up your blazer at the back . . .'

'But I went to Conf—'

'Not a word, not a single word, I won't listen to anything you have to say to me. You had your chance earlier.'

'But . . .'

'Are you deaf?' he shouted down my earhole. 'Now bend down and touch the desk. On second thoughts, that chair over there.'

'I've got piles,' I said. 'I'll bleed all over the place.'

'Right, it'll have to be the hands then, face this way, come on hurry up with you.'

'I've just had two on the hands off him, an' what's more this is all—'

'Don't talk to me in that tone of voice, no wonder you are always in trouble, get that hand straight, stop trying to cup your fingers, do you think I was born yesterday, keep them still. No piles on your hands, have you? Good, and remember,' *Crack!* '"do unto others", other hand up now, up, up, "as you would," ' *Crack!* ' "they should do unto you." Stand up straight for goodness' sake, where's your backbone, don't slouch there like a puppet and stop whimpering, boy, what good will that do? Now walk down that corridor with your head held high—'

'But—' I said at the open door.

'Don't interrupt me, walk down that corridor with your head held high, as if you belong to the human race, and—'

'But, sir—' Every other time he'd ever hit me he hadn't opened his mouth, and now when I wanted to say something I couldn't get a frigging word in edgeways.

'Come back in this room, hold out your hand

again! Right out, you impudent young devil.'
Crack! 'Now perhaps that will teach you to interrupt me, and I am warning you, look at your
bootlaces once or even open your mouth and I'll
have you back in here for another lesson, now go!'

I walked down the corridor admiring the ceiling
and knowing that if ever everyone was soft enough
to start one of them revolutions that they have in
history, the first place I'd come with a sub-machine
gun would be right here, in this school, and I'd
shoot that bastard's knob-pressing fingers off, and
the Gaffer's chiselling hand. Old Faconfield'd
never ruin another hymn again neither.

I wouldn't mind, but the third time he'd hit me,
all I'd tried to do was tell him my classroom wasn't
down this corridor, it was at the other end of the
school. You can't talk to people like that, you know.
It's impossible. I'd have to traipse all around the
bleeding school now to go to my lesson. But I'd get
my own back, nothing was more certain. The day'd
come alright, and I wasn't going to wait for no
fucking revolution neither.

My fingers were still sore as we got changed for the
big match that night, but I soon forgot about it as
we put on our all-red kit and Steve came around
giving us a bit of, like, encouragement and advice.
The team we were playing were St Patrick's from
Kirkby, and their part of Kirkby is even tougher
than our estate and that's saying something. They
reckon that if you see a cat with a tail down there,
it's a tourist.

We'd almost finished getting ready before they
arrived and to be honest when we saw them the
temptation was there to get back into our clothes
and get away while we could. It was like the
arrival of that train in *High Noon*. Everyone

150

through the dressing room door was bigger than the one before, until the last one scraped the top and sides of the doorway.

'Jumpin' Jesus,' Dole said when he saw what was standing behind him. 'I didn't know they had a zoo in Kirkby.'

It wasn't so much that he swung his arms about as he walked, or that he could scratch both knees without bending down; it was his face that was the deciding factor. I'm not saying he had a low forehead but even if he'd had a crew cut his hair still would have got in his eyes. His lips covered his teeth alright, but his chin must have collapsed with the effort when he was in the cradle. His crowning glory though was his pimples. They made his cheeks look like two plates of beans on toast.

'I've seen better skin on a sausage,' Brian Bignall said as the Planet of the Apes walked past him. Ten yards later, at the other side of the room, he turned around like an elephant stuck between two trees.

'What did you thay, thunthine?' he said as we all hung onto our hooks laughing. Poor sod, looked like the Missing Link and talked like a poof.

'Give uth a kith, thweetie,' Brian said and while the Apeman was pushing the insult up to his brain and down again to his fists, their teacher walked in.

You don't half get them in teaching you know. You do. You should know that by now. All the wankers in the world're stuck away in schools. That's a fact that is. And they're all different to each other. You could handle them if they were all the same; mass produced at some factory some-where – 'Dopes Unlimited'. But every single looney and creeping Jesus or pocket Hitler is nothing like the next one. I don't know why we have to suffer

151

them, I don't, but they still keep turning up at the school gates.

One thing they do all have in common is that they all want you to believe they're something special, that they've done a bit before they became as useless as they are now, and they never tire of telling you what it was they were supposed to be good at. Probably not allowed to speak at home, and so they save it up for us like so much garbage for the binmen.

Now, this teacher had a navy blue blazer covered in little wings, a walk like he was practising the military two-step and a drop-handlebar moustache. That could only mean two things. He'd never been in the RAF and he couldn't ride a bike. But he wanted everyone else to think he had. And talk? He never stopped from the first minute he saluted the shower curtains.

'Come on, boys, quickly now, quickly, we're late enough as it is, good afternoon, you must be the teacher in charge of St Malachy's, how do you do, my name's Hulme, deputy head at St Patrick's, don't usually come to the away games these days, though I was a PE man in my prime as you can probably tell, it doesn't leave you does it, however the PE chappie's fell down a mountain and I volunteered to lend a helping hand, especially as the last time his team played away from home they almost caused a third world war between Bootle and Kirkby, but they'll be no trouble tonight, I can assure you of that, little gentlemen you'll see out there, I've told them already, that's what they like underneath it all you know, a good bit of discipline. I take it we have a neutral referee, this being the semi-final of the cup, and that you'll want me to run a line, for which I've brought my flag, my own personal flag this, you know, yes, I was a Grade One referee for many years, controlled all the important games in the Armed Services, linesman in the Football League as a matter of fact before I called it a day; perhaps if you follow the professional game you might have seen me. Yes, well, my team will be ready soon, let's hope it's a first-class match, I'm sure it will be, good luck, boys, all of you, may the best and most sporting team win. I'll just go and inspect the pitch if you don't mind, advise the captain which way to play if he wins the toss. The pitch with the slope isn't it? Fine, fine, good, good,'

And then he was off through the doorway with his stiff upper back and his battalion walk and all their team give a big sigh of relief while Steve just shook his head. A linesman in the Football League and he told the world, and there's Steve, could have played for England if his leg hadn't fallen off, and he'd never dream of telling anyone. But that's it, isn't it? Teachers like Steve, who've done something really smart and hardly crack on about it at all, they're so few and far between I've never met any others.

Still it turned out to be a great game, despite the Mad Airman flying up and down the touchline with his flag, pretending to be David Coleman as well as the Blue Max. He must have taught football at a blind school before he went to St Patrick's.

You know what? Within five minutes of kicking off I scored with my first touch of the ball, and if you don't believe me, we'll just pick up Brian Moore's commentary on the game with four and a half minutes gone of this exciting cup tie: 'Yes, good ball, John, well played son, good thinking. Mike, Mike, Mike, *Mike!* That was your ball, don't stand there waiting, come to it. Look, Mike, that was yours too, wake up. No, son, it's no use saying you were looking at me, you've got to watch the ball as well, and you're completely out of position now. Look, look, there's their inside left, your inside left, and he's making ground, your ground ... he's through, he's ... scored. He only had one player to beat, he should have had at least two, now don't argue, just listen to me, it was your error just as much as Tony's, letting the ball go through his legs, and I don't care what sort of a goal it was, applaud, St Patrick's, applaud. I told you to applaud if they scored. Now I want to hear it!'

They did too. Big hard cases from the scrag ends of Kirkby, standing there clapping a goal that wasn't one of my best to say the least. And what's more, every time one of us fell over he made the nearest player pick us up. The best joke of all though was at half time. They were so full of this feller's bullshit, they all came over and shook hands with us. At half time! We were bound to get our tits felt at full time at this rate.

All through the shouting and ranting and giving of orders in the first half, Steve had just stood there in his overcoat and trilby, putting his hankie up when the ball was out of play or if they were offside, but the last thing we wanted was some raving ex-referee and linesman giving us dictation notes on how to play. When we sat around him at half time, he just told us to carry on playing our normal game and to take no notice of anyone, and then he did his little pilgrimage around each one of us, pointing out things that we'd done which were smart and those that weren't so smart, while over on the side of the pitch some of St Patrick's were being sentenced to death and perpetual detention.

I reckon if the Mad Airman left them alone they might have done a lot better, 'cos they were a hard side with the added ingredient of Archie the Apeman playing centre forward and giving Brian Bignall as rough a time as he'd ever had. Three times in the first half he grunted and hit shots into the pit of Dole's stomach from the edge of the penalty area that had Dole grunting too.

Midway through the second half he scored twice in five minutes, two cruel volleys that gave Dole no chance of getting near, and probably some relief that he had no chance. 'Thee, thee,' he said the second time he ran past Brian, 'that thowed yith.' All around Steve, what few spectators we had all went quiet, remembering, like I was all the times we'd been beaten before, and some of them started drifting off home. In the lead for the gates were Mad Dog and Snotty Dog. Just before they went out of sight I saw Mad Dog diving about, showing everyone how he would have stopped those two goals.

Over on the far touchline the Mad Airman was hopping about waving his flag and going weak at the knees. 'I told you so, Archie,' he shouted as he held onto their substitute, 'I told you he could be beaten, what did I say, he's over-rated, he's too small, let's have some high crosses now and finish it off, come on St Patrick's, another one past him and it's all over.'

The game was far from finished yet, but Steve was. He didn't mind him picking on his own players but he wasn't going to let him pick on any of ours as well. Underneath it all, he isn't soft in the least, Steve isn't. I've seen him screw people into the ground when the crunch had come, and the crunch had just come again. He put his hankie in his pocket and marched onto the pitch and stood by the referee as he tried to write Neanderthal Man in the scorers' column of his little book.

'Excuse me,' Steve said.

'I know what you've come about,' the referee said. 'It's Gob Almighty over there, isn't it?'

'That's right,' Steve said. 'He's coaching from

the line and it's not allowed, particularly abusing our goalkeeper.'

'He's giving me a headache as well,' the referee said.

So the two of them went over towards the head of the Luftwaffe, who, seeing the game was up, started yelling last-minute instructions to everyone in sight. It was like that fight years ago between Muhammad Ali and Joe Frazier with the referee standing between them in those smart shorts they wear that start underneath the armpits. But he was really laying the law down and pointing his finger at their teacher as if he'd just butted Steve in the bollocks in the final round.

When the fight started again, they played a lot better without him, but so did we. You don't realize how bad something is till it's gone, and we hit the crossbar three times almost as soon as the foghorn had stopped, and the third time it happened we scored to make it two all.

It was from a corner taken by our right winger, Stanner. I reckon his great-granma must have had a visit from the foreman of the local plantation one night, 'cos although he's definitely a darkie, he looks like a white lad covered in two hundred-weight of liquid Dairy Milk. He's got Swan Vesta legs, straight hair, glasses an' a long pointed nose. No big lips, arse and frizz for him. But what was for him were all the corners on the left wing, taken with his right foot so that the ball would swing in towards the goal-line.

This corner did just that, and after everyone jumped and missed it, the ball slapped against the crossbar and dropped about three yards from goal, right in the middle of everyone who'd just jumped. For about fifteen seconds it bounced around the goalmouth like a giant pinball before Brian Bignall, lying on the floor with the Apeman on top of him

156

not sure if he was Lester Piggott or Larry Grayson, managed to hook it over the line for his first goal of the season.

A quarter of an hour left, two all, and anything could happen. It did too. Like the best save I've ever seen outside of a life-guard manual, and of course it was Dole that did it. I told you before how good he was, and I'm telling you now. I've been following Liverpool ever since I learnt how to jump over the turnstiles, and I've seen all the goalies – Gordon Banks, Shilton, Phil Parks, Brucie Grobbelaar, Pat Jennings, and even Ray Clemence, but I've never seen them do what Dole did five minutes after we scored.

The move started when their right winger got the ball on the touchline and Joey Duncan, our full back, was trying to force him over towards the corner flag 'cos they can't score goals so easy stuck on the touchline as they can facing goal. As they got nearer the goal line the winger stopped and rolled the ball forward, showing it to Joey, inviting him to try and kick it away. When that happens, you know that one of them's going to get skinned and the other's going to be away down the pitch with Cheddar cheese all over his face. Joey took a chance and took a swing and their right winger took off for goal for the first time in the match.

Now that meant that Brian Bignall had to either come over and leave the Apeman on his own, or stay with him while the winger took a clear run at goal. He was on a hiding to nothing, but he had to go for the winger. As he legged it over there, the lad looked up and saw him and headed for the goal line. Dole all this time is standing at the near upright like he's supposed to, cutting out the angle. Brian just gets to the winger as he's near the line, at the edge of the six-yard box, but it's too late. As

Brian slides into him, he gets a really vicious centre in.

Any centre forward worth the Vaseline on his forehead'll tell you that the best centres to head are those that come over hard. You don't have to put no effort into them. Get the direction right and just a nod at the ball in passing and it's making that funny whirring noise as it spins in the back of the net.

This cross is beating Dole from the instant it leaves the winger's boot. He's cut the ball back across the goalmouth away from Dole, two yards outside the six-yard box, and the Apeman is totally unmarked, facing the far upright and the open goal.

And he heads the ball neat and proper, sends it just where it should go, low and fast, inside the far upright.

As all this goes on, Dole is running the eight yards across his goal from post to post, racing the winger's boot, the flying ball, the approaching centre forward, working out angles, speeds and distances without even knowing he's doing it, yet knowing with certain knowledge where the ball's going to go.

I suppose it only took a second, maybe two, I don't know. And it'd be daft to say that time stood still, 'cos it didn't. But I just have to close my eyes to see Dole do it all again, and every time I go past two uprights and a crossbar, I see him there, sideways, horizontal, a yard off the floor, knees bent, legs together, his black body like the wood of a crossbow, arms stretched, the ball still, held, silenced by his hands.

The fall of the body, shouts and applause, everyone suddenly hearing sounds again, the Apeman banging his head on the ground in disbelief, lisping at the grass, and a long lazy kick upfield, a big grin on Dole's face and it's all over. I tell you, things like that don't happen every day, and when they do, you hang on to your memories and you don't forget them the day after.

Geoff Long got the third goal for us. He's our outside left and built like one of them old-fashioned trains that Butch Cassidy used to hold up, with big pistons banging up and down, making the wheels go around, while the rest of the train just rattles on above. And Geoff was just like that. He only ever seemed to run from the knees down. The rest of him, even his arms, appeared to be still, and although he had all the skills, he didn't have many tricks or shuffles, but when the mood took him he could beat man after man as if they weren't there, heading down the track; destination goal. Our Henry would have been proud to have him on his tracks. If he'd still got a train set that is.

It was a simple enough goal, like the great ones often are. Geoff took a short pass from me as he moved across their penalty area from left to right, running straight towards the opposite touchline, avoiding not beating tackles, finding space in the inside right position, and then when everyone was expecting a simple pass out to Stanner on the wing, he swivelled on his left foot and hit the ball with his right, towards the opposite corner of the net. Their goalie just looked at it, helpless as a cripple with fleas, while the ball cut an angle across him and into the net.

We'd scored over a hundred goals since Christmas alone, more than anyone else in the league, and we thought we didn't jump on each other's backs and hug and cuddle anymore, but everyone was over to Geoff for that goal. Just as less than two minutes later we were all over and around

Dole, unconscious, out cold at the edge of the penalty area.

It was almost exactly the same as the Halewood game. A high ball down the middle, Brian missing it, and one of their forwards with only Dole to beat. But this time it wasn't Poison Dwarf that he had to worry about, it was Archie the Ape with the ball at his feet, trampling down the middle. Dole came out towards him and they met head-on just inside the area. It was like a crash I'd seen on the news the night before between a petrol tanker and a Jag on the motorway.

As the Apeman pushed the ball that bit more forward so that he could hit it properly, Dole slid through the muck and grass, timing his dive perfect for that little loss of control as Archie lifted his size seventeen and brought it down full tilt on Dole's head and shoulder as he held onto the ball. Dole had no chance. Archie would have needed a ten-minute warning in writing to have stopped himself.

The ref lifted Dole up and then he put him down again and called for a stretcher. Steve limped off towards school followed by our substitute and we all gathered around Dole.

'Drop the ball, son,' the ref said. 'Come on, it's okay now, it's all over.'

'Fuck off,' Dole mumbled, 'you'll let them score.'

'Now now, less of that language, I could have you off f'that.'

'It's the bang on his head, ref,' I said. 'He doesn't swear normally, he's an altar boy.'

'Very well, how many fingers am I showing you, goalie?' he said, holding three fingers to Dole's face as he held on to the ball. Good job he didn't show him two fingers, he might have got another mouthful.

'Three,' Dole said straight off. Nobody could believe it. Close up, you could see his eyes weren't so much glazed as bricked in. The ref didn't believe it either and tried again.

'How many this time, son?' he said, holding one finger up.

'Three,' Tommy said, and then promptly passed out.

Have you ever seen anyone trying to climb off a stretcher as he was getting carried off? It took Steve about ten minutes to find the key to the medical room and by that time Dole was sitting up with his head between his knees and still refusing to let go of the ball till Steve arrived back. When they finally lifted him up, Lole kept pushing backwards and knocking over our substitute who was at the back end of the stretcher until in the end Steve carried him off like he was walking a wheelbarrow behind his back and Dole was punching thin air.

He crawled back onto the pitch twice but the referee wouldn't let him back on and me and Brian Bignall had to lift him over the line for his own good. Brian took his jersey off him after a brief punch-up, gave him his to wear and then went in goal. Me and Geoff Long dropped back to centre half and the substitute kept well away from Dole's place on the line 'cos Dole was convinced it was all his idea. When we got back onto the pitch Archie was there, laughing to himself and weighing Brian up as he stood in goal. Archie was about six inches taller than him and he walked over and stood towering over Brian, giggling away and making imaginary headers into the net.

'I don't know what you're laughin' at,' Brian said. 'Y' just the right height f'me. When I send the head in, I'll knock all your bottom fuckin' teeth out.'

'Oooh, ref,' the Apeman howled, 'he'th threatenin' me.'

Although we only had ten men and a scared substitute, there was less than five minutes left to play, and we hung on. They had a stack of corners right near the end, one after another, but each time Brian or one of us managed to scramble them away. Archie was limping after his collision with Dole, and anyway it wasn't as hard as we thought. Every time he opened his mouth it got easier.

If someone says to me in thirty years' time, 'football' just like that, I know I'll think straight away of that game and the final whistle at the end of it all. It's the best moment I've ever had on a football pitch and something tells me I'll never have another quite like it. Everything we'd ever done as a team since all the darkies came to play for us seemed to have led up to that point, that day, on a sloping pitch, with a handful of spectators, two team managers, and a fat referee. Dole holding his head and trying not to laugh, Archie sulking off saying, 'Jammy black thambo bathtardth,' the Mad Airman, his voice broken at last, his words all gone, gathering his team around him, Steve shaking hands with everyone and hugging us as if we were his own kids, and all of us heroes to ourselves.

There was only us in the world that afternoon. The changing rooms didn't need lights, the showers didn't have to be hot, Joanna didn't have to be waiting outside for me and Dole, the rest of the world could go and fuck itself. We were in the final. So, go on, say 'football' and I know what I'll be thinking of from now till I'm making friends with the daises and the worms.

9

'I can't come out t'night,' she said as we stood one on either side of Tommy, holdin' him up.

'Arrey, Joanna,' I said. 'Why not? It would have made the day complete. Apart from bein' caned five times, t'day's been perfect.'

'That's what I came around t'tell yer last Saturday night,' she said. 'An' every time I've seen yer since, y've been with the others.'

'Y'must have just missed us on Saturday as well.'

'That was the night t'end all nights,' Dole murmured. 'I just sit on the stairs all night long now, tryin' t'relive it all, but it's not the same.'

'I bet it isn't, Tommy,' I said.

'What're you talkin' about?' Joanna asked.

'Oh nothin',' I said.

'More than me head hurt after that, I'll tell yer.'

'He fell down the stairs, Joanna, take no notice.'

'Did y'Mam mind me comin' around like that?' she said.

'Oh no, not at all,' I said. 'She was just down t'church the next mornin' t'see if the banns'd been read out.'

'I've had a talk t'my Mam,' she said, 'an' it'll be alright at the week-ends, y'know, Friday an' Saturday. She won't mind.'

'Y'mean t'get married or go out?'

'It's me dad,' she said, giving me no surprises at all. 'He goes out drinkin' then.'

'Instead of drinkin' in the house,' Dole said.

'T'morrer then,' I said. 'Friday'll be alright, won't it?'

163

'It'll be great. I'm sorry about t'night, honest I am.'

'I'll come with yer instead if y'want, Franny,' Dole said.

'As long as I can hold y'hand.'

'I'd rather y'held me head.'

'Come on, Tommy,' I said, 'we'll take you home.'

'It's the hospital we should take y',' Joanna said. 'That's where y'teacher wanted t'take you.'

'I'm alright,' he said. 'Leastways, I would be if I could breathe. You two're so desperate t'link each other I'm gettin' squashed t'death here.'

We got him to their corner, and without a word of a lie I was going to leave them then 'cos I didn't want another knuckle butty off their dad, but he must have been doing a Crackers and spying on us from their front window. No sooner had I stopped and we were trying to fold Dole's arms around Joanna than he was out of the gate and down towards us. I suppose I should have done a gallop there and then, but I thought I'd be brave in front of Joanna and show her I could stand up for meself. I didn't stand up very long though. The first thing he did was throw me in the gutter. Whirled me around by the armpits and tossed me away like an empty beer crate.

'What was that for?' I said as I bounced.

'You know what it's for,' he said. 'F''hangin' around my daughter, that's what. I only ever tell anyone anythin' once, now git, go on.'

'I was bringin' your Tommy home,' I said. 'He's hurt himself.'

'It'll be nowt t'what I'll do t'him if I see him with you again, now clear off. I don't want you around here.'

'It's a free country,' I said after I'd backed away a few yards.

'It's a stinkin' country,' he said, 'that's what it is.

164

One rule f'everyone else an' another f'all those with the wrong coloured skins.'

'You didn't have t'come, did yer? Y'could have stayed where y'belonged, back in fuckin' Lagos!'

Don't worry, I didn't say that, I'm not mental, I hadn't had a kick on the head. It was Dole that said it but it saved me, at least. His dad pushed me down again, spilling my football boots on the floor and turned around in the middle of punching me and went back towards Dole.

'An' that's the last game of football you'll play, lad,' he said as he trapped Tommy at the corner of the privets and the gate. Tommy fell on the ground, covering his head and his futures while his dad punched and kicked and kneed him as Joanna screamed and bit and pulled at his hair, trying to get between them. They'd have still been there now if Dole's Mam hadn't come out of the house with the handle off the broom and my Mam wasn't passing the bottom of the road, just back from town with all her shopping.

It was when my Mam hit him with two pound of blackpudding that he stopped.

'None of your business, missus,' he said, wiping the grease off his forehead. 'Family matter this is.'

'An' that's part of my family sittin' there in the gutter,' she said.

'I told him t'keep away, I give him fair warnin'.'

'He's in the road, not in her bed, he's not doin' anythin'.'

'Keep him away from my family, you, woman.'

'If he's soft enough t'wanna know your family, that's his look-out. Anyone with you f'a father needs friends, an' don't you raise your hand t'me, I'll have you exported before y'know what's hit yer.'

'Come on, Ken,' his missus said, 'come in the house, the whole neighbourhood's watchin' us.'

All along the two rows of houses, windows had their curtains lifted, doors were half open, a couple of nosey faggots with no shame were standing at their gates, the bus queue'd missed two buses, and Mooey was peeping out from behind their privets with a bin lid over his head.

Her husband's shoulders sagged and his head went down; his big black boxer's frame seemed to shrivel up in front of us and he turned around and went in the house without another word, leaving us to pick up the pieces after the storm. Dole on the floor, nose bleeding, eyes wide open looking like two eggs in a bucket of brown sauce; Joanna crying on her Mam's shoulder, a little roly-poly of a woman, staring at the floor, my Mam helping me to me feet.

'I'm sorry,' Mrs Kew said.

'Couldn't be helped,' my Mam said, neither of them looking at each other. 'I would have left well alone if it hadn't been our Francis here.'

'I was helpin' Tommy home,' I said. 'That's all. He got a kick playin' football. On his head.'

'Shut up,' my Mam said.

'His dad's not well,' Mrs Kew said, 'he . . . he . . . well, lately, I don't know what's gone wrong . . . whatever we do, it's not enough t'please him . . . he didn't use t'be . . .' And then the tears overtook her and Dole got up and she buried her head into his chest, blood from his nose spread against her crinkled hair.

'I'll kill him, I will,' Dole said. 'I don't care, he can't go on like this, it's not right.'

'Ssh, ssh, pet, there now,' his Mam said, the pair of them trying to comfort each other and Joanna leading them down their garden path to the open door.

My Mam put her blackpudding back in her bag and we set off home. She never said anything all the way to our gate.

'Y'know,' she said as she lifted the gate up 'cos the bottom hinge was broken, 'I was on the bus comin' home an' when we got t'the baths this lovely girl about twenty or so got on. Proper cheerful smile she had, hair plastered down on her face; been swimmin'. Came an' sat by me with two of her mates. I didn't think nothin' of it at first, till I realized one of her friends was carryin' her costume an' towel for her. I didn't like t'look, y'know how it is, but when she got off the bus I saw what I'd just about guessed. She had no arms, just two little stumpy hands at the top of her shoulders. Thalidomide victim she'd be, poor little bugger, but she wasn't lettin' it get her down. Just think, Francis, she must have been in all that water, in front of everybody, flappin' about f'all she was worth, f'all the world t'see. Soft though it is, I was nearly in bloody tears when I got off that bus. An' then I gets meself mixed up in that little business. It makes y'realize what a mess the rest of the world's in, an' a bloody sight finer mess than we are, a lot of them. I can't help thinkin' about that girl walkin' around the baths with everyone else normal an' perfect an' her like that, an' facin' up to it, starin' life full in the face. Jesus, I don't know.'

We opened the door and our Tony came dancing towards us out of the back kitchen holding a cigar and a bottle of champagne perry. He ran up and hugged my Mam and turned to me, thought better of it and turned back to my Mam.

'Congratulate me, Mam,' he said. 'Go on, congratulate me!'

'Wha' for?' she said. 'Don't tell me y've gorra job.'

'Nah,' he said, 'this is good news, the best there is. I'm a daddy, you're a grandmother!'

'I've been one before, y'know,' she said.

'Arr but Hovis doesn't count.'

'He bloody well does t'me. Anyway, our Shirley's got three kids goin' t'school, y'not the first t'crack it an' y'won't be the last.'

'Come on, Mam, don't be a miseryhole, don't y'wanna know all about it 'ey? How it all happened. Y'should see it, dead spit of me, I'm not kiddin'.'

'The poor bastard,' she said. 'Its first words'll be a lie.'

'I knew it,' he said. 'I knew y'd be like this. Y'never give me any encouragement. An' here's me, hardly stopped in the alehouse so I could come home an' tell yis all about it. I come in here an' what happens? I told me dad an' he went upstairs without a word, our Arthur's at the Cubs an' Hovis doesn't understand. An' now you an' all.'

'Alright, alright,' my Mam said, taking her coat off and preparing herself, 'don't start feelin' sorry f'y'self, there'll be time enough f'that over the next twenty years. Just tell us – is it a boy or a girl?'

'Guess,' Tony said, going all coy and enjoying the attention.

'Sufferin' Christ,' my Mam said. 'I bet y'don't know y'bloody self.'

'It's a . . . boy!' he said. 'I've got a son an' heir!'

'Y'd better start findin' somethin' worthwhile t'leave him then,' I said, ' 'cos if y'kicked it now all he'd have is the rental on the telly, two pellet guns an' a broken moped.'

'I'm goin' back the pub,' he said. 'I've never been so insulted in me life. Y've got no appreciation of the finer qualities in life, that's what's wrong with you. Me an' Florrie's brought a little soul t'life all you can do is make fun. An' I'm goin' down the housin' first thing in the mornin' t'see about an exchange if that's goin' t'be y'attitude when Florrie comes home.'

'Was it an easy birth?' my Mam said, and he was away from the front door and back at her side, offering her the bottle.

168

'Easy?' he said, 'would anything' be hard f'my Florrie? Slipped out it did, Mam. She went into labour just like that.' He snapped his fingers and spilt the champagne all over his jacket. 'They took her down at half past nine, she had the pains at ten o'clock, they called me in at quarter past ten, by half past she was pushin' f'all she was worth, with the mask across her face an' the drip on her arm—'

'Did they let yer get that near, Tony?' I asked.

'Mam, tell him t'go away, will yer,' he said. 'This is me moment of triumph an' he's spoilin' it for me.'

'I'm goin',' I said. 'Y'don't have t'chase me. I don't wanna hear the bit where y'fainted into the nurse's arms anyway.'

'I didn't, see,' he said, 'so there, cleverclogs, I was fine, I didn't flicker an inch through it all, not even the afterlife.'

'Y'look as though y've seen a ghost.'

'Well, I never even felt like throwin' up, not once.'

'Is that a fact?' I said. 'Well, y've either got sick or y'breakfast all over y'pullover.'

'No I haven't,' he said, 'Y'can't trick me. I wiped it all off.'

I went into the back kitchen with Hovis who was helping himself to some dripping butties while the coast was clear.

'Our Tony's got a baby,' he said as the dripping dripped from between the bread and dropped on the table.

'I know,' I said, 'an' we'll never hear the last of it.'

'Have you ever got a baby, Franny?'

'Men don't have babies, only women.'

'But our Tony got one, he told me.'

'That's what I mean.'

'Has Goldilocks ever got a baby?'

'She might have by now, I expect. Dunno.'

169

'Make her got a baby, go on.'

'It's not up to me, our kid. Give us a bite of y'butty.'

'If you give Goldilocks a baby.'

'Okay, okay, Goldilocks gets a baby t'night. Who's gonna be the father? Have y'worked that one out yet?'

'Daddy Bear.'

'That'll get them talkin' at the maternity home. Wha're we goin' t'call this baby anyway?'

'*Me.* An' er . . . an'er,' he said, trying to think of all the words and put them in the right order, 'an' Goldilocks an' Daddy Bear live happily ever after with me in a big house in the woods, an' Daddy Bear plays games with me every day an' never never goes away.'

'That's a smart story y've got worked out there, Hovis. I tell yer what, you tell me the story t'night an' I'll suck me thumb an' go asleep 'cos I'm knackered.'

'I no want t'do that.'

'I didn' think y'would somehow.' I took a bite out of his butty and put the kettle on the stove.

'Tony told Nanna I no count,' Hovis said. 'I hear him.'

'Yeah, I know,' I said, 'he er . . . was talkin' about y'countin', y'know, one two three an' all that.'

'I can,' he said. 'I can count.'

'Go on then, count t'ten an' I'll fix yer up with Goldilocks as y'girl friend.'

'Er one, two . . . three . . . er an' anudder one an' anudder one an' . . .'

'Y'thick, you are,' I said. 'How old are yer now?'

'Old enough t'know better.'

'Take no notice t'me Mam, y'll be three next month, but when I was your age I was already four.'

'But I feel sick.'

'No bloody wonder; there's half a dozen pigs

170

gone into the drippin' on that butty alone.'

'An' . . . an' I've had these many,' he said, half chuffed and half going sickly yellow as he held up all the fingers on his left hand. I went to the dripping bowl and looked. It was almost empty.

'I know where I'll be tellin' you about Goldilocks t'night, Hovis,' I said. 'In the friggin' toilet.'

'I wanna go t'friggin' bed,' he said. 'I wanna go t'friggin' bed.'

'Come on then, I could do with a lie down.'

We went through the hallway. Tony'd got to the part where the matron was telling him that she'd been delivering babies for thirty years and she'd never seen anything like his before. The sucker, he thought it was a compliment.

I'd just got Hovis down after his fourth expedition to the bogs and managed to persuade him not to say 'friggin'' in front of everything when our Tony went off to visiting time singing 'My Blue Heaven'. My Mam took my Gran off to Bingo in the hope of putting some sense into her between houses, and I was settling down for a quiet night in watching *Top of the Pops* and David Attenborough up mountains again when there was a knock on the door and my dad's mates from the church plates came in.

My dad flew down from the bedroom where he seemed to spend most of his time these days, just lying there reading comics and murder magazines, and I got relegated to the back kitchen while they talked 'business'. I had a glass to the wall but it was like as if they were talking in church 'cos I couldn't hear nothing.

I'd even read the births, deaths and marriages in the *Echo* by half past nine and they were still at it in the other room and I'd missed the Thursday film on ITV as well. They didn't come out for a cup of tea neither so it must have been at least the Bank of England they were thinking about. I got fed up and walked down to the Dogs. I didn't really want to go there except to tell them about our brilliant recovery after they'd given us up for dead when the Apeman had scored those two goals, but there was nowhere else to go. They weren't in when I got there and it was just as well 'cos they wouldn't have believed me even if it'd been on *News at Ten*. I drifted around for a bit, doing nothing much except walking and meeting no-one I wanted to meet. I had no money with me so I couldn't go to town or something, even if I wanted to. Which I didn't, not on my own, not now I wasn't in the Odeon watching that film with Joanna, sharing popcorn or holding hands in the dark. Holding hands in the dark! I laughed to myself when I realized what I'd been thinking. If someone'd told me I'd be doing that six months ago I'd have started a fight there and then.

I saw the two platebearers dashing across the road by the Boundary for the last orders and so I headed back home just in time to meet our Tony at their door with a big bunch of flowers.

'Where d'y'get them?' I said. 'Been at the rose bushes in the park, have yer?'

'Gloria gave me them f'Mrs Barrett.'

'Arr, she still doesn't think she's y'mam, does she?'

''Course she does. Gloria thinks I'm great 'cos I care so much about her. Even said I'd make a lovely husband for some lucky girl. How about that f'droppin' hints 'ey?'

'You're evil, you are, Tony,' I said. 'D'y'know that? What's gonna happen when Mrs Barrett comes out of hospital?'

'I'm a bit worried about that meself,' he said. 'But I don't want t'pack Gloria up, I'll miss the money.'

'What money?'

'She draws her dole every Thursday now an'

172

gives it t'me. I told her I may as well have it as the soddin' government.'

'There is one thing y'could do,' I said. 'Y'could always tell Florrie that y'want one of them liberated marriages like y'read about in the *News of the World*, y'know, when everyone's swappin' partners like as if it's some big barn dance.'

'Oh, no,' he said, 'I'm not havin' that. I'm not lettin' my Florrie run around all over the estate, makin' herself cheap.'

'Y'a hypocrite, you are,' I said, remembering the Leighs the other night, 'that's what y'are, a hypocrite.'

'Don't you call me animal names,' he said, all injured. 'That's castin' a slur not just on me but on my child as well, I'll have you know. 'Ey, that reminds me, straight up, he smiled at me t'night, as God is me witness.'

'How old is he now?' I said.

'Eleven hours an' fifty-five minutes.'

'He'll be walkin' in the ward t'morrer at that rate.'

'Don't you know nothin' about kids?' he said as he put his key in the door. 'He won't be on two feet f'another three weeks at least yet. Oh an' by the way, if y'hear a motorbike in the night, don't worry, it'll only be Gloria.'

'I knew she reminded me of somethin',' I said.

He shut the door and whistled up the stairs, as happy as I've ever known him, but that was our Tony all over. He's never miserable for long 'cos he soon finds some soft little dream to wrap around himself, and he never has any nightmares either. Had a lot of jobs, our Tony, but none of them ever lasted longer than a fortnight, and yet there's one that he would have been perfect for – an astronaut. He wouldn't need a space ship to get up to the stars.

10

'Well, Francis, two weeks t'go t'Easter,' my dad
said when I came home from school for my dinner.
'Don't y'wish y'were taggin' along with us now?'

'No, dad.'

'Still time t'change y'mind, y'know.'

'No thanks. Anyway, I don't know how y'can
afford t'go y'selves, never mind addin' me on t'the
bill.'

'Where there's a will, there's a way,' he said,
giving me one of those winks that start at the
hairline and end at the chin. 'Don't f'get, y'know,
I've kept me hand in with a few odd jobs. Here an'
there.'

Like at one o'clock in the morning on Tuesday
night, I thought. Some painting and decorating job
that must have been. But I never said anything. I
didn't want him to know I'd been looking out of the
window, waiting for him to stop passing the plate
around and come home. I'd guessed by the fear in
his face when he'd gone out that night that he was
going on the rob. My Mam had too, for certain, but
she'd said nothing. The way things were, she'd
stopped caring where the money came from as
long as it came.

'I'm leavin' school the holiday after Easter,
anyway, dad.'

'Are yer? Jeez, it only seems like yesterday
y'started.'

'Yeah, so y'see, I'll be goin' out lookin' f'a job
that fortnight.'

'I'll pray for yer,' he said. 'If there's a church
next door t'the alehouse in Rhyl.'

174

'What would y'think about me goin' away, y'know, leavin' home, if I can't get a job around here?'

'Ask y'mother.'

'I thought y'might say that, somehow.'

'It's alright by me,' he said. 'Do what y'can t'better y'self, that's what I always say. Before it's too late.'

'Can I tell me Mam y'said that?'

'Well . . . I'd rather y'didn't.'

'I thought y'd say that an' all.'

'She's got high hopes in you, y'know, Francis, very high hopes. Always has had.'

'Must think I'm goin' t'live on a hill.'

'No, I'm bein' serious now, ever since y'was a little kid she's thought a lot of you.'

'Aye well, we all make mistakes.'

'I know she doesn't always show it,' he said, through a mouthful of beans, 'but she never was one t'show how she really felt, you know that, not until it was important, that is.'

'Whose is the plate under the grill, dad?'

'Hovis's. He's out in the back yard.'

'His bean's'll dry up.'

'Call him in then.'

'I've gorra go.'

'Why don't y'stay off this afternoon, give us a hand while y'mother's out?'

'Y'mean, mind Hovis while you go f'a pint?'

'It's funny y'should say that, the idea never crossed me mind, but . . .'

'No, I'm goin' in; Steve gives us trainin' every night now. For the final.'

'I'll come an' see that,' he said. 'When is it?'

'The day before we finish f'the Easter holidays. Up at the stadium.'

'Y'picture'll be in the *Reporter*.'

I pushed my plate away and stood up. My kit

175

was drying over the fire. Well, it would have been if my dad hadn't let the fire go out.

'What's the matter, son?' he said behind me as I shoved the stuff in a kit-bag.

'Nothin'. Me kit's not dry, that's all.'

'It's more than that, come on.'

'Is that the time? Jeez . . .'

'Y'mam says y'doin' a spot of courtin'.'

'Does she?'

'Is that what's worryin' yer?'

'Nothin' worryin' me, I'm alright.'

I put my coat on and walked to the front door while my dad followed me for a bit like a lame dog and then he went to call Hovis in and blow the flames out on the beans. I knew he wanted to talk to me some more but I got out of the house fast and walked back towards school. Someone had chalked 'SCULLY THE NIGGER LOVER LIVES HERE' at the bottom of the road during the dinner hour, but I pretended not to notice it and walked straight past.

I knew that if I threw a wobbler and wiped it all off, it'd be five foot high and multiplied by ten at tea-time. It's always the same. If we don't like a teacher in school and we put his name on the desks or the walls and he sees it and goes screwy, it only gives us a chance to do it more often. But if he takes no notice, we soon get fed up. I'd only put 'Les the Lesbian' on the woodwork door once and the Gaffer'd started a bigger search party than the one out looking for Lord Lucan.

Inside though, I wanted to shout and scream, there was no kidding myself about that. And to make matters worse, I didn't have a fucking clue who was doing it all. Whoever it was wasn't boasting about it, I could say that for certain, 'cos I hadn't heard a whisper and usually you know straight away when someone's done something 'cos they can't help but pose about it. I'm telling

176

yer, I was in such a state I was even beginning to suspect some of the teachers.

When I came around the corner by the youth centre and the parish club they were there waiting for me like they always are. The signs, painted white, big bloody letters, plastered on the wall like Guinness adverts. 'SCULLY THE SPADE DIGGER.' 'WHO LIKES BLACKCURRANT TARTS?' 'WHAT'S BLACK AND GOES OUT WITH A BIG HEAD?' 'GO HOME NIGGERS. GO WITH THEM NIGGER LOVERS.'

As I went past I could see out of the corner of my eye that everyone else walking back to school was watching me and wondering what I was going to do. No wonder the Dogs were always gone when I called for them. I hadn't even bothered the last few days. Yet, you know, the funny thing is that no-one had actually said anything to me, no-one'd come out with any crap to my face or anything like that. Even when I was out with Joanna, on the odd occasions we could escape from her dad's safety net, I'd walked right through the estate with her and seen piles of lads from school and they'd done nothing but look green or say 'Hello'. My stomach was in knots by the time I got into registration but no bastard on earth was going to know that. They weren't going to beat me, and even if they were I wasn't about to let them know it. Fuck that.

First lesson in the afternoon hadn't even begun to be boring when the teacher got a message to send me down to the headmaster's office. I walked along wondering what I'd done to get the stick this time, though, of course, you didn't need to have done anything to get the stick in our school. Maybe he'd had a chat with the school nurse and found out I didn't have piles after all.

I was the last one there 'cos I'd gone down the bogs and put half a toilet roll down me kecks just in case, and then I'd had a quick look round to see if anything more'd been written about me and Joanna since morning break. But I needn't have worried about the stick 'cos his room was full of the football team and our PE teacher, Samuels, in his best track suit with them go-faster stripes all over it. No jokes about niggers from him this afternoon, that was certain. The only time he'd taken us since we had a good team, he's come in the changing room and told Geoff Long to stop giving him black looks.

'The reason I have you all before me. this afternoon, gentlemen,' the headmaster said, 'is to thank you for your splendid achievements on the football field. Mr Samuels tells me that you have reached the under-sixteens cup final and I'm very pleased to hear it, very pleased indeed. The good name of the school depends on the pupils' performances outside the school gates just as much as their efforts behind a desk. Indeed, as I look around me now, I see one or two individuals who I am usually punishing instead of congratulating, and that is a most welcome change.' He looked over at me but I took no notice 'cos I was eyeing up his desk, and after that quick nose at me, that was all he did too: just stare at his blotting pad. 'And talking of thanking you, I think you should all join with me in thanking your PE teacher for all his hard work in producing such a fine team, don't you think?'

Well, Samuels thought so alright, but nobody else did. We all stood there with our mouths loose hinged, but there was worse to come.

'Indeed, Mr Samuels tells me that despite his occasionally having to miss some games due to business commitments, you have still managed to produce football of the highest standards; a tribute not just to you, I believe, but to the quality of Mr Samuels's skills as a coach.'

'Skills as a coach?' Jesus, Samuels knows nothing about football, nothing at all. His idea of a coach is the bus that takes us to away matches.

'And you can rest assured, boys,' Samuels said, smiling and suckholing at the same time, 'that from now until the final you will get my utmost attention. I'll have you at the full pitch of physical fitness.'

'Excellent,' the headmaster said. 'Excellent.'

What it meant though was that we'd have extra cross-countries in PE instead of games of pirates, that was all.

'But wha' about Steve?' Brian Bignall said, knowing full well that was what we were all wondering.

'Pardon?' the headmaster said. 'Who?'

'Mr Mason,' Samuels said. 'He's er very kindly taken the team once or twice in my absence.'

'Ah yes, Mr Mason.'

'F'the last four matches,' Brian said, 'an' he would have taken us f'more if he hadn't had a bad leg.'

'An' he's takin' us trainin' now,' Tommy said. 'Every night.'

'I didn't know that,' the headmaster said and stopped tearing strips off his blotting paper and looked over at Samuels who was weighing up whether he'd polished his shoes that morning. 'Well, I'm sure Mr Samuels can come to some arrangement with Mr Mason. After all, it is a team game when all's said an' done, isn't it?'

No-one said anything as the pair of them had a little titter for no reason that we could see. I was thinking of all the vultures suddenly appearing, ready and waiting for us, hanging about looking for a slice of something good. I suppose it always happens. The next thing we'd know, the Gaffer'd be down the workshop making us a special light-weight wooden football kit.

School dragged on through the afternoon until

four o'clock when we had training with Steve. We never had a chance to say anything to him about what'd happened in the headmaster's office 'cos, lo and behold, Samuels was stuck to his side like a sudden case of Siamese twins. He even tried to be one of the boys and join in when we finished off with a game of five-a-side, but nobody'd pass to him and Brian Bignall nearly knocked all his stripes off with one tackle so he give in and went for a smoke. It must have been a really weird feeling for him, still being in school at half past five at night. He only ever stays behind late when we put sugar in his petrol tank.

I met my Gran as I walked down past the church. She was just going into the parish priest's house with her feller 'cos she wanted a white wedding and they had to book their order.

'Is that you who's on the youth club wall?' she said.

'I don't think so,' I said. 'I could have sworn I was here talkin' t'you.'

'Don't be cheeky,' Steradent said. 'It's all writin' about you an' that coon.'

'Go an' see,' my Gran said, sounding just like him. She used to be a good old girl, my Gran, but since she met him she's been a different person. She wouldn't have been bothered once, she never said a thing when our Vera presented us with Hovis, but now she was marrying plastic gums, nothing was good enough.

'Disgustin', that's what it is,' her feller said, clicking his teeth together like castanets. 'Should be ashamed.'

'Who should?'

'Bringin' your family's good name into disrespect, that's what you're doin'.'

'No I'm not,' I said. 'It's me Gran who's doin' that, marryin' an old twat like you.'

'Take that back,' he said, 'take it back this minute.'

'I won't,' I said. 'It suits you better.'

'You wait till I get home,' me Gran said. 'Your mother'll hear about this, don't you worry.'

'Yeah, an' I know whose side she'll be on as well,' I said. 'It's none of your business what my business is. You're the last one t'talk, you are anyway, Gran; the state of him.'

'An' what d'y'mean by that?' her feller said, coming on all hard. He must have been reading about Kung Fu for pensioners. 'You say anythin' more about my future wife an' me, an' I'll knock shite out of you, young as y'are, d'y'hear me? Nothin' more than skin an' bones an' spunk, that's all you . . . oh, er, hello, Father O'Connell, I didn't see you there, er, just giving young Francis here a bit of advice, well, take that to heart, young man, a few words of wisdom from someone what's seen a lot more of life than you have never did no one any harm, that's right, isn't it, 'ey, Father?'

I didn't have to look at what was written on the youth club wall and I didn't even go past the youth club but climbed over the junior school fence and out through their gates. Our Arthur was in the playground with the Cubs, learning how to tie everyone in knots.

Life's full of surprises. When I got home, Henry was in the front room with a woman. Leastways, it looked like a woman, but they made train sets in all kinds of funny shapes and sizes these days.

I think he'd expected nobody to be in 'cos there isn't usually of a Friday tea-time. My Mam takes Hovis over to my aunty's in Dingle in the afternoon and they don't get back till late; my Gran's always out as soon as the clock strikes five and the parish club opens, my dad goes the dog racing and I usually go over to watch Tranmere Rovers under the floodlights, but I haven't been able to afford it lately, and anyway, it was too late now, what with training. I was taking Joanna out the next night as well, and needed the money 'cos she said she fancied going for a meal and even a Wimpy and chips'd stretch me.

'Er . . . er. Er, Francis, I'd like you t'meet Wendy,' he said, getting up a good head of steam and actually speaking a whole sentence without going off the track in the middle of it.

'Pleased t'meet yer, I'm sure,' I said. She looked like the back end of a goods wagon, but at least it was a start. I just hoped that if it got serious she wouldn't mind having her honeymoon stoking coal on the stopping train to Bradford.

'Are y'interested in trains, by any chance?' I asked as the toilet flushed upstairs and I wondered who could be up there.

'No. Why?'

'Oh just wonderin','' I said. Jeez, what would they have to talk about? Maybe she'd been in the Merchant Navy.

'An' Bugs Bunny an' all!' Mooey shouted as a cartoon came on the telly and he came bouncing down the stairs and through the doorway. 'This is my lucky day!'

'Wha're you doin' here?' I said.

'I've been here ages,' he said. 'Me Mam was watchin' Crossroads.' He fell onto the settee at the side of Wendy who tried to climb over the armpiece.

'Excuse me, Francis, can y'help me find the tea-caddy,' Henry said, winking and twitching and jerking his head towards the door.

'It's where it always is at the side of the tea-pot,' I said. I was a bit partial to Bugs Bunny and all.

'No it isn't. Me Mam must have moved it.' Wink, twitch, jerk.

'What's up, Doc,' Mooey said.

I followed our Henry out to the back kitchen and of course the first thing I saw was the frigging tea-caddy standing in its usual place.

'Arrey, Henry,' I said, 'there it—' I couldn't say anymore with his hand over me mouth.

'Help me,' he said, 'please help me.'

'Wha'?' I said as he took his hand away.

'It's him,' he said, biting his fingernails and shuffling about, 'y'mate, Mooey, can y'get rid of him? I've tried everythin'.'

'Y've gorra be brutal about these things, Henry,' I said. 'All's fair in love an' war. Just tell him t'fuck off, go on.'

'I don't like to.'

'I'll do it for yer, if y'want,' I said. 'If y'make it worth me while.'

'Will two quid get rid of him?' he said and reached into his back pocket.

'F'two quid y'won't even know he's been here, an' neither will he.'

'Ta, Francis,' he said and gave me the note. 'But don't tell him t'y'know, fuck off in front of We—'

'Don't close y'wallet yet, Henry.'

'But . . . but you said—'

'I know I did. That'll get rid of Mooey just great, but the question is, how much will it take t'get rid of me?'

'I thought a quid was too good to be true.'

'Dead right. I've got a promise as well t'morrer night an' another two quid'll take us t'one of them Chinese cafés instead of the Wimpy.'

'Here y'are then,' he said without a second's thought.

'Christ Almighty,' I said, 'you must have your promise in writin'.'

'I just don't want anyone around, that's all,' he said, and the way he said it made me guess that just like me but ten years older, he'd never had a woman. Maybe not even so much as kissed one. That train set blowing up could have been the best thing ever happened to him, though when he tells his mates in the Merch, I bet he won't talk about getting his hole. No chance. He'd tell everyone he got his tunnel.

183

'Right, Mooey,' I said as I went into the front room and left Henry t'make a cup of tea, 'we'll be off now, me and you. Y'haven't brought a coat with yer, have yer? Thought y'hadn't, come on now.'

'Er, er, no.'

'What was that?'

'Er, er, er, er, no.'

'Why the hell not?'

'It's Disneyland next,' he said. 'I always watch Disneyland.'

'We can see it down at the Dogs.'

'I'll miss the start, look here it is, see, it's startin' now. *The Wonderful World of Disney.* Oooh, look, it's about birds, I like it best when it's about birds, just look at that hawk. Innit ace 'ey? Isn't it, love? Wouldn't y'want t' have one of them?' He settled back for a good night's viewing while Henry came in with the tea-pot and two cups and saucers. He poured hers out and gave it to her and she put the saucer on her lap and smiled up at him and he smiled down at her and I saw the bulge in his trousers getting bigger and bigger. Good old Henry, found his middle leg at last.

'Look at how it flies through the air,' Mooey said. 'It's great how birds can do that, isn't it, Scull?'

'It's got somethin' t'do with their wings.'

'I know,' he said. 'I thought that as well. See that then! See what it did then? If I'd have been born a bird I'd wanna be a hawk.'

'D'y'think so?' our Henry said, still smiling at Wendy and slopping his tea into the saucer. 'I'd wanna be an eagle. Would you like t'be an eagle, Wendy?'

She did well. The smile hardly slipped off her face at all. 'Er, I haven't given it much consideration really,' she said.

'They're proud, them birds are,' Henry continued. 'Always have been the best bird, y'know, even in olden times.'

'Er, they might be smaller than eagles.' Mooey said, 'but size isn't everythin', that's what me Mam says.'

'Oh no,' Henry said. 'It's not just size. Eagles've got the lot. They're not frightened of nothin'.'

'Neither's a hawk.'

'I bet an eagle could fight a hawk,' Henry said, comin' over and sitting by Mooey on the couch.

'Y'wrong,' Mooey said.

'I'm not y'know,' Henry said. 'I know more about birds than you do.'

I had to laugh. Another ten minutes of this patter and him and Mooey'd be off down the woods in search of eagles and hawks and I'd be left to cop off with Henry's tart.

'If we run fast enough, we can get t'Mad Dog's durin' the first lot of adverts y'know, Mooey,' I said.

'Oh aye yeah,' Henry said. 'I forgot.'

'There's no adverts in this, it's the BBC,' Mooey said. 'An' anyway, your telly's better than theirs.' He could be a stubborn little sod when it suited him.

'Alright then,' I said, 'have it y'own way. I'm off down t'Chinsley Woods, in any case, after what I heard this afternoon in school. I'd much rather see the real thing than watch it on the box.'

'Course, Mooey never flickered, but Henry was all ears.

'Wha' is it, Frannie?' he said, almost into his mack ready to come with me.

'No, this wouldn't interest you, Henry,' I said. 'It's a hawk, not an eagle. A *hawk*, Henry, y'know, what Mooey likes best.'

'Did you say hawk then?' Mooey said.

'No, no, it doesn't matter, Mooey,' I said. 'I wouldn't wanna drag yer from y'favourite programme.'

185

'Alright,' he said and tried to move the couch a bit nearer the telly.

'But seein' as y'so interested in hawks,' I said as I pulled him back by his shirt, 'I wouldn't want yer to'miss somethin' y'might never see again. D'y'know what I was told in registration this afternoon, Mooey? I heard that the Great Green Mottled Elephant Hawk's been seen nestin' in Chinsley Woods!'

'The Great wha'?' he said. 'I've never heard of that.'

'I thought you were an expert on hawks, Mooey,' I said. 'You tell him, Henry, if y'don't believe me, Moo.'

'Oh yes, well,' Henry said, 'er, it's very rare, that bird is, very rare indeed.'

'Rare?' I said. 'Henry, y've just made the understatement of the year. Birds like that, Mooey, they don't grow on trees. I'm tellin' yer, if y'don't come an' see it now, y'in danger of missin' somethin' y'might not ever see again.'

'Y'kiddin' me.'

'Now, hey, Mooey, would I kid you, would I?'

'Yes.'

'Y've upset me, sayin' that, d'y'know? I thought y'knew me better than that. Don't y'realize I'm y'best mate? Remember? Y'told me y'self only the other day. Muckers don't kid each other over important things like birds.'

'What was it called again?'

'The er Great Green . . . somethin' or other. I don't know as much about birds as you do, Moo. I might just have it wrong, but they call it the Great Greenie in bird circles, so I've been told. An' d'y'know wha', it's so big, it has t'have the Corporation in t'build its nests.'

'Flippin' 'eck.'

'An' here's somethin' else I bet y'didn't know. It's the only bird in the world that's got landin' permission at Speke airport.'

As Mooey pulled me through the living room doorway I caught sight of Wendy's face. It was a picture. Her chin was on her tits and she was shaking her head as if she was trying to wake herself up in the middle of a mad dream. God alone knows what she was making of it all, and I doubted very much if Henry was capable of explaining it all to her.

I couldn't keep up with Mooey, running through the estate. He was charging ahead of me towards the woods, bawling, 'Come here, birdy, pretty birdy, come t'Mooey.'

When we climbed over the wall of the Chinsley estate we walked down the path leading to the big castle where the royal family have tea, bed and breakfast when they come to town but after a bit we slipped away through the trees to the centre of the woods where there's a little stream and all the pheasants hang out. I hadn't been there for years since I came with Henry and the times when I'd come over the wall with my dad and I'd stay 'lookout' and he'd go blasting at the pheasants with our Tony's pellet gun, and trying to tickle the fish in the stream. He's a ham-handed bugger at the best of times though, and never shot or tickled nothing except two sparrows and a frog one afternoon when he'd had ale in him.

We found a good speck and I broke a few branches off a tree and sat Mooey down with me in a dip.

'Here,' I said, 'hide behind them.'

He closed his eyes straight away. 'Shall I count up to fifty or a hundred?' he said. As soon as he got to ten he opened his eyes. 'Y'never hid,' he said.

'But you never counted up to fifty.'

'I can't count any more than ten.'

'Count up to ten five times.'

'Oh aye, I never thought of that.'

187

He had me in such a twist, when he started again I almost went off and hid.

I wanted to keep him there till eight o'clock at least, otherwise he'd be off back to Henry, catching him on the nest instead of this great whatsit we were supposed to be looking for. The only trouble was, every friggin bird or greenfly that flew near us, Mooey'd be out of hiding, grass and leaves dangling all over his face, howling, 'There it is, Scull, there it is, the great gozzie!'

'It's no good, Moo,' I said as I pulled him down for about the fifth time. 'The way y'goin' on, we'll have every bleedin' gamekeeper between here an' the African bush after us. Y've gorra be a bit subtle about it y'know, or we'll never see that bird, not with you messin' about like an Apache warrior.'

'I don't like cowboys an' indians any more,' he said, 'but I'll play soldiers if y'want.'

'No, listen, see that tree?'

'As long as I'm not the Nazi prisoner.'

'Look, Mooey, d'y'see that tree?'

'Is it I Spy? Is it? I like that even better than Hide an' Seek an' Soldiers.'

'No, this is much more fun than either of them. It's . . .'

'Postman's Knock?' he said, jumpin' up an' down with the thrill of it all. 'It is, isn't it? Smart! That's my favourite game of all time.'

'Look, Moo,' I said, 'd'y'wanna see this soddin' bird or not 'ey?'

'What bird?'

I had a hell of a hard time trying to get him to climb up that tree. He was so keen to find excuses not to go up there that he was near to the top before he asked me why he had to climb it anyway.

'Because,' I said, 'y're going' t'go up there an' whistle an' attract all the birds f'miles around. An' that big hawk'll come t'have a look at yer as well. Bound to, la'.'

The real reason was because he was driving me around the bend and I just wanted him out of the way for a bit while I recovered. He's great, Mooey, when there's a few others around to share the load, but when he's on his own with you there's no one to get him to destroy except yourself.

'Couldn't I whistle from down there?' he said. 'I er whistle much better with me feet on the floor.'

'No chance, Mooey,' I said. 'Every time y'open y'mouth down here, a thousand birds leave town.'

Give him his due, as soon as he reached the top he started whistling. But '76 Trombones' wasn't what I had in mind. I thought he was having me on till he got to the third verse of 'Colonel Bogey' and I had to break cover.

'No, Mooey,' I whispered up the tree, 'no songs, y'pillock. Pretend y'a bird. Make some bird noises.'

'Tweet. Tweet tweet.'

I was just about to race up there and strangle some sense into him when I heard someone thrashing through the trees and remembered that the gamewardens had no mercy if they caught you.

'Don't move or I'll knock y'head off.'

I turned around, but I'd already stopped wetting myself, 'cos it was only our Tony in his gumboots and parka, carrying his old pellet gun and thinking he was out of the cast of *Born Free*.

'Wha're you doin' here?' I said.

'Our Henry's just told me about this giant bird that's in here.'

'Oh yeah, well listen—'

'An' he said it's almost human, the things it can do.'

'That's what we're supposed t'be lookin' for an' all,' I said, 'but y'can—'

'Lookin'?' he said. 'Fuck that f'a lark. I'm gonna blast it out of the sky!'

'Wha' for?'

'Wha' for? Come on will yer. Worth money that

bird'll be,' he said. 'Stands t'reason. Stuffed, over the mantelpiece, charge fifty pence a look. The whole of Liverpool'll be queuein' up at me an' Florrie's front gate.'

'Well, I hate t'disapp—'

'Tweet. Tweet tweet.'

'What was that?' Tony said, spinning in all directions. 'Was that you?' he said, turning and pointing the gun straight at me. I wasn't going to hang about to explain with him so trigger happy and I dived behind a tree. No one was going to stuff me and put me over their mantelpiece. No chance.

'Tweet. Tweet tweet.'

'No, Tony, no!'

'Fuckin' hell, there it goes again, it is human,' he said, and let fly with half a pound of stale buckshot up the tree.

One thing he could be proud of, after the pain was gone, was that he fell good. You've got to hand it to Mooey. He skidded all the way down the tree, breaking branches and holding his bum, landed on his knees, took one look at our Tony standing there over him like Wyatt Earp in rubber gumboots, and he was off through the woods and over the wall.

You should have been there to see him move. No style or anything but everytime he looked over his shoulder and saw me and our Tony chasing after him, he gained another few yards on us. By the time we'd got to the East Lancs Road, he'd lost us completely.

Whatever kind of bird Mooey thought he was up that tree, it wasn't a homing pigeon. We waited in their road for him for ages but he never came back. I heard for a fact the following week that he ended up in this bird sanctuary in Ormskirk and his Mam had to go and fetch him the next day.

11

The night before the cup final, Dole killed his dad. Just like that. Took the carving knife and sliced him. The word was out all over the estate before the pubs were shut and so were the police. Isaiah could hardly believe his luck. One nigger less to worry about and another one to hunt down. Even better, they were both Catholics and all.

There were all kinds of stories about what happened. Some of them said it was 'cos his dad wouldn't let him play in the final, and others said Dole was trying to stop his dad from beating his Mam up. I even heard it was an accident, but of course there were those who said give a nigger a knife and what d'you expect?

My Mam locked the door on me that night and wouldn't let me out, but I went around there first thing in the morning on the way to school. There was still a crowd of gawpers hanging about and all the curtains were drawn, so I walked past. Needless to say, Joanna wasn't in school and when I knocked on the door at dinnertime there was no answer. One of the old biddies standing at her gate with sore eyes said they'd gone away during the morning, and another one further up the road told me they'd be at his Mam's brothers down the town, and if I wanted to see the body it might be at Craven's funeral parlour in the village.

When I went home the suitcases were out of the cockloft and my Mam was washing them down. She kept on finding little bits of plastic train passengers.

'Terrible isn't it?' she said as she took half an

arm out from between the leather straps. 'The poor woman.'

'Better off without him.'

'I know that,' she said, 'but it would have been much nicer if it'd been a car crash or somethin'. Her own son, an' on the run an' all.'

'He could have waited till t'night,' I said. 'We'll never win without him.'

'He'll miss more than one friggin' game where he's goin', when they catch him,' she said. 'There, that's better.' She got up off her knees and put the cases in the cupboard under the stairs. 'I polished y'boots as well, seein' as it's a big occasion, an' y'dinner's in the oven. It's y'favourite – steak an' kidney puddin'. Do us a favour before y'start an' go upstairs f'y' dad. I don't think he's out of bed yet.'

I had to shake my dad like a dirty carpet to get him awake. As he came around he started shouting, 'It wasn't me, I never did it,' and trying to crawl under the pillow. Not even the prospect of steak and kidney pudding could persuade him to face the world till I pulled all the bedclothes off him.

I let Hovis have most of my pie 'cos it'd be daft to overeat before the game, and anyway, I didn't feel like anything at all, especially suet and stodge. My Mam switched *News At One* on to see if Dole'd made the headlines and then she switched it straight back off 'cos it was all about unemployment and my dad gets in a right stew when he sees anything like that.

'I'm away,' I said.

'With a bit of luck, I might come up an' see yer,' my Mam said. 'If I can get the ironin' done in time.'

'Don't bother,' I said. 'Save y'self a walk f'nothin'.'

'Y'shouldn't be like that,' she said. 'Where's there's life there's hope.'

That was the trouble though. There wasn't much life in Dole's dad and all our hopes'd kicked it with him. But I didn't say that to my Mam, I could do without a lecture. Instead, I got my kit and went out the door as she tried to persuade my dad he'd be a dab hand with an iron after a bit of practice.

School was its usual thrill. We had the post-war depression in history with Lightning Fingers Faconfield and then double maths but he let us draw instead 'cos it was the last day but one and most of us wouldn't be coming back after Easter if we could help it. Anyway, after suffering five years of failing to get most of us past simple arithmetic, I don't suppose he fancied his chances of success in the final week. He was an old bore but at least he left us alone. Frigging Faconfield still thought there was a chance she'd see us one day on *University Challenge*.

At ten to four the message came for me to go down to the headmaster's office and with not having to go to the bogs for me armour, I was the first there. He was smiling. I looked around but there was only me in the doorway.

'Ah, Scully, yes, good, the great day has arrived.'

'Yes, sir.'

'How are you feeling? Confident, I hope?'

'Dead right, sir,' I said. Confident of losing about five-nil, I thought.

'Good, good. Fine.'

Silence. He walked around his desk, picked a pen up, put it down, lifted his trousers up and coughed, looked at his watch and ran his fingers through his hair.

'Er, yes, oh how are the piles these days?'

'Still bad, sir, but I give them a blast with the painkiller spray just before the match an' that seems t'do the trick.'

'Splendid,' he said without listening. I could

have told him our Arthur ties them up in reef knots for me and he wouldn't have noticed.

'Mmmm, most unfortunate having to make that late change, wasn't it? Who er is replacing Kew?'

'This new lad from the Dingle,' I said. Poor Mad Dog was almost in tears when he found out he wasn't picked. He'd been skiving off for a week till he heard about Dole and he'd galloped into school this morning expecting to be called to the rescue, but we had someone else. He was the same colour as Dole, but the resemblance ended as soon as he stood under a crossbar. Still, at least there was a possibility he might make the odd save and pay attention to the game, two qualities you couldn't always rely on Mad Dog for.

Another lap of his desk, a quick examination of the lace curtains, a study of his calendar and then face to face again. I stood there watching him trying to think of something to say that was of any interest to either of us, but short of asking me if I wanted to play with his desk, there was nothing. I could have stayed there all day embarrassing him; it wouldn't have bothered me at all 'cos I knew he hated it, but after a minute or so some more of the lads turned up and released him.

'Now, boys,' he said when everybody had arrived, and then he stopped and give us one of those slow sincere Cinerama looks where he starts at one end of the line and works his way to the other end, thinks he's done his duty and looks out of the window for the rest of the time. I can't even begin to tell you what he said, and I bet no one else could in that room either. All it sounded like to me was five minutes of non-stop gobshite. But that's it, isn't it? Give some people a bit of power and they think it gives them the automatic right to talk through their arses for hours on end. He was still talking past himself after the bell went but the phone rang and got us all off the hook. Another Cinerama look, and we were out of the door while he tried to calm down some parent whose son'd been severly chiselled by the Gaffer for sharpening his pencil on the electric saw.

We walked up to the stadium, hardly saying a word, carrying our kit-bags through the estate and across the main road, past the Boundary and the last dregs of the afternoon drinkers waiting for the doors to open again, ignoring cracks like 'They must be lookin' f'the Zambezi' and 'Since when have Nigeria been allowed in the Football League.' Some drunken old fart staggered up to Brian and me and said, 'Livingstone an' Stanley, I presume' as Brian knocked him into the traffic.

At one side of the hill, below the cemetery and the church, stands the stadium. The word 'stadium' is a joke around our way now, though it's not really funny at all. About five years ago the council made this big announcement in the local papers saying they were going to build the Stadium of the Seventies, the likes of which hadn't been seen nowhere before, and who knows, they said, we might even apply for the next Olympic Games. There was this drawing as well, and it made Wembley Stadium look like Tranmere Rovers ground after a bomb raid. The drawing had everythin': marble arches, big stands, a removable roof for when it doesn't rain, a running track all round the pitch, seats like cinema seats, an indoor gymnasium underneath the main stand, everything you could think of. Some of us were soft enough to believe that for once something was actually going to be done, especially as within days they had a load of excavators digging up the ground and flattening it and then some seed was sown and the runnin' track marked out.

About two weeks later, the fucking council ran

out of money and ever since then, that's all that's ever been done to the place, except for two wooden huts the size of sentry boxes, thrown up last year so you could get changed. No one's ever run on the track 'cos it's full of pot holes or tufts of wild grass, and the pitch isn't used much either 'cos you have to bring your own goalposts if you want a game.

When we got there a crowd was already forming on the running track and the Law was there, running about moving everyone back and then pounding on, while everyone sneaked forward again behind their backs. As we walked towards the changing rooms Isaiah came over and leant on the door, staring at us as we gathered around him.

'Now then, boys, anyone seen him?' he said.

'Who, officer?'

'You know who, Scully, an' no smart answers or you won't even see the game, never mind play in it. We're lookin' f'that Kew lad, y'don't think we've turned up t'watch you shower, do you? Superintendent seems t'think he'll be here, God knows why, but there y'are. If y'ask me, he'll be down the docks now, jumpin' the next boat back t'the jungle.'

'He was born in this country,' I said. 'Same as you.'

'We've all got our problems, now answer the question, has anyone seen him?'

'If y'really want t'know,' Brian said, 'he was in school yesterday.'

'Was he now?' Isaiah said, then realized that was no kind of clue at all. 'Okay, smartarse, but don't you worry, we'll catch him, an' Heaven help any of you if y'shieldin' him, that's all I can say.' And then he was off, racing back to shove some more juniors off the track and on to the mud-piles at the side. A big man, doing a big job.

The coach from Halewood was just arriving with

the other team at the gateway when I opened the door of our changing room and we all walked in. There, in the light from a little window at the side of the hut, we could see Dole sitting huddled up in the corner, trying to smile.

'Alright, boys,' he said while we slammed the door behind us and the heavy ones leant on it.

'What the fuck're you doin' here, Tommy?' I said. 'Are y'crazy?'

'There's dozens of coppers outside just lookin' f'you,' someone else said and we were all talking at once, all saying more or less the same thing.

'I'll have t'borrow someone's kit,' Dole said, all matter of fact as if he was at your door wanting a cup full of sugar.

'Y'can't . . . I mean, y'don't expect t'play, do yer?' Brian said.

'I'm not here f'the good of me health.'

'Y'll get caught,' Brian said. 'Y'bound to. Not even Isaiah's that soft.'

'What makes y'think he'll recognize me?' Dole said.

'Look, Tommy,' I said, 'it's an old joke an' I was there when Isaiah said it to yer, but it's different this time. They're not after yer f'breakin' shop windows or ridin' y'bike on the pavement. They mean business out there.'

'But who's t'know it's me?' he said.

'Oh Christ, the whole soddin' school.'

'They won't say anythin', you watch.'

'Steve'll recognize yer.'

'An' he won't say nothin' neither.'

'He will, he'll have to,' Brian said. 'That's the way it works f'teachers, even Steve. He might sympathize but he'll still shop yer.'

'Look,' Dole said, 'I'm here now, I'm going to'give meself up as soon as the game's over, I'm no fuckin' criminal, I haven't done nothin' no-one

197

else'd do in the same situation, so what difference does it make? I may as well play, it'll be alright, an' if it isn't, we've still got a substitute.'

'Let him play,' the lad said who was supposed to be in goal. 'I don't mind.'

'An' I'll disappear,' the substitute said. 'It's goin' t'look fuckin' funny if twelve players come in here an' thirteen go out.' Before we could argue he was at the door, peeping out and then off into the crowd.

'But why give y'self up?' I said. 'Don't give them a free gift, make the bastards fight f'everythin'.'

'The longer it goes on, the worse it'll be f'me,' Dole said. 'I've sat here all day since sun-up workin' it out. If I make a song an' dance about it, they'll build me up t'be another Black Panther. A friggin' real one this time.'

'It'd be great if he could get away with it, wouldn't it?' Geoff Long said.

'Dead right,' Brian said. 'That really would be workin' one up them.'

'There's someone tryin' t'get in,' one of the lads at the back said as they wrestled and shouldered the door and then Samuels shouted from the outside and banged on the wood.

'Alright,' Brian said, 'let's get changed,' and the four at the door moved away, letting Samuels charge through the doorway and go flat on his face over the kit-bags on the floor.

'Idiots,' he said, 'absolute idiots. What do you think you're at? Everyone should be changed by now. What's keeping you.'

'We're talkin' tactics,' I said, moving in front of Dole and knocking into half the team as they did the same.

'Tactics?' he laughed. 'What do you lot know about tactics? That's my department, you lot save y'energies for the game.'

198

'Where's Mr Mason?' Brian said. 'He usually tells us what t'do. He knows what he's talkin' about.'

'Are you being sarcastic, Bignall?' Samuels said, dusting the creases in his kecks, 'because if you are, it's still not too late to make changes. There's nothing I don't know about tactics, young man, I've got top qualifications.'

'Yeah, I know,' I said, 'but Mr Mason hasn't just read books, he's played as well.'

'By God, I'll deal with those remarks in the morning, you see if I don't. Have a lot to remember me by over Easter, you two will. Now get stripped and fast, the other team arrived after you and they're already changed. And if you must know, I asked Mr Mason to bring the goalposts up with the detention boys. He's with them now, the second crossbar's almost in place, everything's ready except for you shower. How you got this far with this kind of attitude beats me.'

'Is this a team talk?' Brian said as he pulled his red jersey over his head, 'because if it is, we aren't half gettin' inspired, aren't we, boys?'

'Take that shirt off, Bignall,' Samuels hissed, 'that is it, you're finished, your game's over. Get dressed and get out!'

'Down tools, lads,' I said.

One by one we all took our shirts off and threw them at Samuels's feet till they lay in a red heap covering his turn-ups and his shoes.

'You little bastards,' Samuels said, losing all control, 'I don't have t'be here, you know—'

'Don't let us keep yer,' I said.

'—I've given up my free time to be at this game and I'm not standing for impudence like this, I don't see why I should, get those shirts back on now, this minute, and you, Bignall, get out of this room, do you hear me, that's an order.'

Silence. Again. But this time all of us grouped there around Samuels, instead of just me with the headmaster and his dopey desk. And it wasn't embarrassment neither; it was sheer hatred from all sides.

Knock knock.

'May I come in?'

Talk of the devil; the headmaster in the doorway.

'Such peace and quiet, Mr Samuels, marvellous, you must tell me how you do it, but really, boys, now is not the time for meditation, the other team is at the door, the crowds are waiting, the posts are ready, the sun is shining, what are we waiting for?' His lips were moving but it was still his arse that was doing the talking. 'You, er, Langford, you're the captain, aren't you? Show an example, child, come on, here, here's a shirt, it doesn't matter about numbers now, might even confuse the opposition, get it on and get those boot laces tied up. Hurry, hurry, come on.'

And so we took our shirts back and climbed into them and hitched our shorts up, tied our laces and rubbed our legs while Samuels quietly choked and the headmaster walked around us like the general he obviously thought he was, throwing out ideas and advice he'd heard from Jimmy Hill on *Match of the Day*, the previous Saturday. Hardly a word was spoken by any of us, not even when Steve came in through the doorway, but least of all when the headmaster arrived at the corner where Tommy was sitting.

'Now look, son' he said, 'it's your first game for my school, I know that, but on behalf of everybody, I want you to know that we have every confidence in you. I can tell just by looking at you that here we have every inch a goalkeeper. In fact, and I think the rest of the team will back me up on this one, you look more like one than young Kew ever did, good though he was, I'm sure.'

'Thank you, sir,' Tommy said.

'Now just go out there and make every ball yours, and nothing can go wrong. You won't get better advice than that, young man. A fine display this evening and who knows where your future will take you. Right, Mr Mason? The team will run precisely the same, will it not?'

'Oh yes,' Steve said. 'In fact, I'm sure hardly anyone will be able to notice the difference between them. I know I can't.'

Samuels and the head were probably so full of themselves and thoughts of revenge or glory that they never even noticed when we all laughed and broke the silence, and they never saw Steve drifting over to me and Brian.

'What's he doing here?' he said, kneeling down in front of us and glancing over at Dole. 'Has he gone mad?'

'Just what we said an' all, Steve,' I whispered through me teeth, 'but he wouldn't take no f'an answer.'

'Tell him he has t'give himself up, for his own good.'

'*He* told *us* that,' Brian said, 'an' that's what he's doin' as soon as the match is over.'

'Best do it now,' Steve said. 'He won't last the game.'

'You try an' tell him,' I said. 'Go on, you talk to him. We don't even want him t'give up.'

But it was too late, the head was ordering us into line and giving us our marching orders and we were outside and across the tattered running track. Tommy stood near the halfway line instead of going towards goal and facin' the crowd, while me and Geoff Long took it in turns to flick a training ball at him. The ref was already on the pitch waiting when we came out so we hardly had two kicks when he was blowing for the two captains to toss up.

The worst thing about it, in the end, was that it was all my fault. No one else except mine and the heat of the moment. It was no good everyone telling me it could have been them two minutes later. It was me, it just had to fucking well be me.

The very first attack they make, a run down the left wing by their full back. Brian goes over and tackles him but the ball goes off his leg for a corner. Samuels and the headmaster already bored on the touchline, Isaiah, behind the goal, back turned to face the crowd, making the world a better place to live in by keeping the kids off the running track, ready for the next Olympics. Dole standing on his line, the whole stadium except a dozen bluebottles and teachers and their team, knowing who it really is between the sticks. An inswinging corner, their centre half goes up, beats everybody, heads the ball, first bounce for the corner of the net. Dole is down, crouched, hugging the ball. The crowd shout, Isaiah turns around, it's only another nigger on his knees, he turns back again. I run towards space on the right wing.

'*Tommy*,' I shout, '*Tommy!*'

At the top of me voice.

Like a foghorn on the Mersey.

Like the biggest prick since Errol Flynn.

'*To me*, give it *to me*,' I shout again, but even Samuels and the head can put two and two together and I see them scurrying around the touchline towards Isaiah as the ball comes towards me. I catch it in my arms and go running back towards the goalmouth, playing rugby for the first time in my life as the referee swallows his whistle and their team wonder when I was released.

'It's a mistake,' I say to Samuels and the head as they troop towards Isaiah. 'I'm so used t'sayin' it, I forgot, that's what it was, I got mixed up, it's not him at all, haven't y'got eyes. His hair's curlier,

202

he's left-handed, no stop, y've got the wrong—'

'Sergeant,' Samuels is saying to the back of Isaiah's helmet, 'Sergeant, this is important—'

'Look at them little hooligans, turn y'back an' they're all over—'

'Sergeant,' the headmaster says in his Napoleon voice, 'that boy in goal, that is the boy you are looking for. That's Thomas Kew.'

'What? Who? Where?' Isaiah is saying, turning all of a fluster as he lets kids run everywhere.

'The goalkeeper,' Samuels says, making sure he gets half of any reward money that's going, 'the one in the green jersey'. He whirls around and points towards the goal and nearly sticks his finger up Dole's nose as he stands by my side, his jersey already in his hand.

'Oh Jesus, I'm sorry, Tommy, honest I am,' I say. 'I could fuckin' kill meself.'

'Forget it.'

'Thomas Kew, I must warn you that anything you say—'

'I know,' Dole says. 'Y'not the only one who used to watch *The Sweeney*.'

The arm on his shoulder, all the juniors dancing on the running track, another copper running up, spit on both their backs as they take Tommy through the crowd with Samuels making a path for them, the referee taking the ball off me, Steve waving the new goalie on to the pitch, a free kick to them for hand ball, the game starts again, and after a bit, when Dole is no more than a black dot between two navy blue blobs in the distance, I join in as well.

I don't get ten yards on to the pitch and the referee is screeching at me to get off till he calls me back on. Don't I know the rules, he asks me. Fuck me sideways. Rules and fucking regulations, and those that make them, they make me fucking sick.

12

So we lost.

So what? That's what we said in the sentry box after the game.

We leave tomorrow, most of us, so who cares? We don't.

Here's the socks and here's the shorts, here's the shirt we won't ever wear again. Let someone else wash them, Steve.

Goodnight, Steve. Tara, Steve. Thanks, Steve.

Goodnight, lads. God bless.

You what? There is no God, Steve.

Along the path, down the hill, back across the main road, on to the estate. Going dark, the sun sinking beneath a block of flats further into town, shining on the windows of the flats behind us. We all took to the different streets in ones and twos and went back to our houses. No doubt we all got asked how we got on, and we all said we lost and sat around the table or in front of the telly and ate our teas without another word.

It was dark when I came back out of the house. My dad was gone already; part of the Holy Trinity off on another mission, our Henry was packing his bags ready to sail the next day, my Mam was behind a mountain of ironing that my dad'd messed up, and Hovis was crying for a story, but he wouldn't have liked the one I'd have told him, and why tell him now the whole world's a bundle of shit. So I let him cry, he'd find out soon enough.

Around the corner and into the Dogs' road, past the Kews' empty house, windows broken already. No one'd come out of that house and batter me again, and no one'd stand at the door and make me come in my pants neither. I'd asked everyone all day long and none of them knew where Joanna and her Mam was staying. Someone had to know, they just had to.

I almost thought twice about knocking at the Dogs' door. It was funny, but I hardly had anything to say to them anymore. What I had in mind for tonight though, it needed more than one to do it all.

'I heard y'got smashed,' Mad Dog said, not even trying to take the big smirk off his face.

'You heard right.'

'An' Dole got caught.'

'Right again. Two out of two. Wanna try f'the jackpot?'

'I'm glad I didn't go. I said y'd get beat.'

'Well anyway, come on, we're goin' out.'

'Celebratin'?' he said.

'Y'could say that. Celebreakin' more like.'

'Can I come too?' Snotty Dog said, coming to the door as well. 'There's nothin' on the telly.'

'Yeah, an' bring y'dad's saw an' that big tin of paint y'got from the wallpaper shop.'

'Y'what?'

'You heard.'

'I can't,' Mad Dog said. 'He flogged the saw last week.'

'An', he's painted all the bedrooms again as well,' Snotty Dog said. 'Y'know, he had nothin' t'do, like, with not havin' a job no more.'

'Er, er, boys, er where y'goin'? Seein' them hippies t'night? Can I come? I never saw them last time.' Mooey at my shoulder, game for anything, understanding nothing.

''Course y'can come, Mooey,' I said, 'but we've got some heavy liftin' t'do an' a lot of work ahead of us t'night.'

'As long as I don't have t'climb no trees,' he said. 'Me bum's still pebble-dashed from the other week.'

We were buggered when we finally sneaked back out of school through the same door we'd forced open earlier on so that we could get in. But it was worth it, we all knew that, especially Mooey who wasn't allowed to do woodwork in their school. And instead of being so tired we only wanted to go home, it made us feel like going on and doing a few more things while the taste was still with us. So we headed up past our house towards the lamp-post at the top of the road, facing the Leighs'.

There was a light on in the Leighs' front room, but they always leave that on when they go out. In case there are any burglars about. I left Mad Dog as look-out, kicking a tennis ball about in front of a couple of houses further down. It was Mooey's job once, but he used to get scared and run away all the time. It only had to be a noise and he'd be gone. Once, he ran away when a plane came over low. I think he thought it was the flying squad.

The Leighs' back garden looks out onto the edge of the waste land so we had no worry there. It was the end of the block and all, an' they had big privets at the back as well. There was only next door to think about and we could hear the start of the nine o'clock news blasting from their living room from where we were. They wouldn't have heard us if we'd used dynamite. We didn't though. We used Snotty Dog 'cos he's the drainpipe expert.

'Get goin',' I said, 'we've only got half an hour.'

He came racing down the stairs from their bedroom dribbling with excitement. ''Ey, y'll never guess what they've got up there in the bedroom,' he said. 'Y'won't. Go on, have a try.'

'An electric saw?' Mooey said.

'Nah, y'not even warm. They've got a portable telly!' he said as if it was the eighth wonder of the world. 'An' it works an' all, I switched it on. It's mine that is, I bagsed it first.'

It wasn't a bad house. You could tell they didn't have any kids. Everything was all neat and tidy and there was no scribbling on the walls or anything like that. They had a fridge as well, and after we'd dragged the big sack of balls out from under the stairs, we started making some butties out of the spam and tomatoes on the bottom of the fridge. I found a couple of bottles of lemonade too and Mooey tried to open a tin of fruit and cut himself on the lid. He stood there with blood dripping on the pineapple chunks till I took him over to the cold water tap and turned it on for him.

While the other two messed around like little kids I went into the front room and put the nine o'clock news on without the sound. Tranmere Rovers were playing and I wanted to know the score. Snotty Dog came in after me and threw his tomato butty at the telly and it hit Sue Lawley right in the face. We hadn't finished laughing when there was a knock on the door. Mooey stopped sucking his thumb and started to cry while Snotty Dog was at the back door pissing on their step before the knocking had stopped.

'Come back,' I said. 'It wouldn't be them now, would it? They wouldn't knock at their own front door, would they? Stupid.'

Mad Dog came racing through the privets and in the back door. 'It's a feller,' he said. 'Two fellers in a big car.'

'Oh shit, the Law,' Snotty Dog said and started to go again. 'Me Mam'll kill me.'

'I don't think it's coppers,' Mad Dog said.

'H ... how d'y'know?' Snotty Dog said, still stuck in a sprint position.

'Their car's fallin' apart an' one of them's got hair down t'his shoulders. But they've been up an' down twice. I watched them.'

207

"Ey, I bet they're on the rob as well,' I said.

'This is no time f'jokes, Scull,' Snotty Dog said. 'We're trapped in here, well we might be, they could have surrounded us already.'

'Come here,' I said.

We went back into the front room. Mooey was still there, crying in front of the telly, his finger bleeding on the carpet, and talking to Sue Lawley. 'I haven't done anythin',' he was saying. 'I haven't even took anythin' except these pineapple chunks. All I've had is a spam butty.'

Confessing already.

'Shut up,' I said as the knocker went again.

'One of us has t'fuckin' well go,' Mad Dog said.

'Go on then,' Snotty Dog said.

'If it's the paper boy I'll kick his brains in,' Mad Dog said and got to the living room door and then came back again. 'I tell y'wha', let's go out the back way 'ey?'

The others stood in the kitchen doorway ready to beat it if it was the Law as I walked into the hallway and switched on the light. The doorhandle was all old-fashioned and knobbly and daft.

'Me dad's not in,' I said before the stranger could speak. 'He's down the alehouse an' so's me Mam. Sorry.'

'I'm lookin' f'a feller by the name of John Hunter an" his missus,' he said. 'Carpet salesman, he is. D'y'happen t'know them, sonny. I could have sworn they lived here. Got a daughter about the same age as you. About fourteen, she'll be.'

'I'm nearly seventeen, mate,' I said.

'The daughter's name was er Janet.'

'Got blonde hair?'

'That's right.'

'Sometimes wears pigtails?'

'Yes, now y'come t'mention it, I think she used to.'

'Wears glasses an' a brace on her teeth?'

208

'By God, y'exactly right,' the feller said, looking as though he was genuinely surprised. 'Y'do know her.'

'Sorry, mister, never seen anyone around here that looks like that.'

'Er yes, er well, I'm sure they used t'live in this road. Still never mind, I'll try the next one up.'

'Yeah, you do that.'

I was right. He was on the rob; you could tell. He had all the patter and not only that, anyone else would have belted me for giving cheek.

'Tara then,' I said but the feller never answered. The others must have heard his footsteps moving away 'cos when I turned around they were all peeping from behind the door at different heights. When I looked back at the feller he was walking towards the car on the other side of the road.

"Ey, pal,' I said, 'd'y'mind shuttin' the gate after yer?'

Five minutes later, the way the Dogs were telling it to each other, they'd both been at the door with me and we'd formed a trio, telling the bloke to shut the gate, and I knew that by the time they'd let the whole estate in on the secret, I wouldn't even have been in on the raid. It suited me, especially when they started wanting to take everything that moved.

'F'fuck's sake, Mad Dog,' I said, 'what d'y'want with a picture of a green Chink an' three plaster ducks?'

'Me Mam's always wanted ducks on the wall an' me dad can sell that paintin' down the Boundary.'

'We didn't come t'strip the joint,' I said. 'All we want is the balls.'

'Y'kiddin'?' Snotty Dog said. 'Leave my portable telly behind?'

'Can't y'see?' I said. 'Crackers won't dare t'report the loss of a plastic bag full of balls, but she'll be scratchin' the soddin' ceiling if half her house has gone with them.'

'We won't take that much,' Mad Dog said.

'She won't hardly notice,' Snotty Dog said.

'Oh come on, will y'.'

'Sod off, Scully,' Snotty Dog said. 'Just 'cos you never saw it first.'

'That's right,' Mad Dog said.

'Can I take the rest of the spam?' Mooey said.

We hid the bag of balls on the waste land to collect the next day. And the others took what they wanted in the end. We'd still have been there arguing the toss when the Leighs got back if I hadn't given in. As if we hadn't done enough already that night, but it was like talking to the wall, talking to the Dogs. The last I saw of them as I walked down our road and they turned the corner of theirs, Snotty Dog was huffing and puffing with the telly, Mooey had just dropped one of the ducks and Mad Dog was hitting him with the painting.

When I got in our front room at home we had company. I knew that before I reached the door 'cos the telly was off, and there was that smell of incense and ciggies. It was Father O'Connell on the cadge on his collection round again, screwing a few more bob off us for prayer mats and candles and really vital things like that. I've got nothing against Father O'Connell apart from the fact he's a priest. He was always good to me in the Infants and Juniors when he wasn't getting shot at and losing his arm on safari, but I wish to God he was an electrician or a plumber or something.

'Good evenin', Francis,' he said, 'and how are we this fine night?' It's funny how the Irish never lose their accent isn't it? He's been in our parish since Jesus was left back for Israel but there's times when he still sounds as if he's just come off the boat with a bag of spuds and two pound of gelignite.

'I'm smashin', Father,' I said, 'cos when it comes down to it I always chicken out when it comes to priests. I can never really tell them how I feel. It must be all the confessions.

'Times're not too good f'many these days, indeed they're not,' he said. 'It's good t'hear you're doing well.'

'I wouldn't say that, Father, but I've had a good time t'night.'

'We were wonderin' actually, Father,' my Mam said, 'if you knew of any jobs that might be goin', you know, for Francis.'

'That I don't, I'm afraid, Mrs Scully, and you'll be the fourth mother t'ask me the selfsame question t'night.'

'I'm sorry,' she said, 'it's just that—'

'Of course, of course, nothing to be ashamed of at all. It's not you who should apologize for there being no jobs.'

'It just doesn't seem right,' my Mam said. 'Christ knows, I mean ... well, you know, Father.'

'A little blasphemy won't sent you packin' t'Hell, Mrs Scully.'

'It it does, there's a lot of people who've done us down I'd like t'meet there. We were brought up in the Depression, me an' his dad, an' then through the blitz an' bloody ration books, an' that joker with his 'y've never had it so good'; aye f'them what's always had it. An' then a few good years just t'trick yer into thinkin' things're goin' t'work out alright, before the world turns around an' hits y'kids in the face. It's never them at the top what suffer though, it's us down here what have t'go through it, as far as I can see. An' whatever the politicians say, it's always goin' t'be the same. It all comes back t'those that can least afford it.'

'I know,' he said, 'and all I can add is that

211

there're places even worse off than here, where there's nothing to fall back on; no state aid or benefits, just a few grass roots and swollen stomachs and children dead along the roadway.'

'But they've never seen any better have they, Father? I know you know more than me about it all, but it strikes me it's nature what does that t'them most of the time, not people.'

'Not always, I'm afraid.'

'Well, all we keep gettin' is promises an' nothin' else.'

'But a hundred years ago, Mrs Scully, all of us on this estate would have been peasants or industrial slave labour.'

'That's what I mean, Father,' my Mam said. 'Nothin's changed.'

'Er . . . mmmm,' he said and squirmed in his seat.

'D'y'want a cup of tea before y'go, Father?' I said.

'Thank you, my son, but it is gettin' late an' your good mother and I have already emptied a pot. It's the parish club an' a glass of Guinness for me.'

He stood up and tried to sweep the wrinkles from his shiny trousers and my Ma reached for her purse on the mantelpiece but he leant across the fireguard and put his only hand on top of hers.

'No, no,' he said, 'you mustn't. Not now. I couldn't take it. Put a little extra on the plate on Sunday.' He smiled, knowing full well my Mam doesn't go any more, but not knowing that even if she did, she wouldn't put money on any of the plates. No chance. It was then that we heard the noise of a car or something stopping outside, a quick burst of shouting and banging, the slamming of a door and then the noise of an engine revving up and away.

'"Carolina Moon, I'm pinin', pinin' f'the one who

waits f'me . . ."' It was my dad and no doubt with holes in the knees of his trousers from the sound of him. Father O'Connell continued smiling as though nothing was happening as my Mam took her hand away from under his and went into the hallway as my dad tried to turn the key in the front door and near strangled himself on the high notes.

'Jesus, Mary an' Joseph,' I heard my Mam say as she closed our door and opened the front one, while Father O'Connell pretended he'd never learnt that Commandment about taking the Lord's name in vain.

'"Carolina Moon",' he said. 'A lovely tune that. One of my favourites. A sister of mine has an old seventy-eight of Connie Francis singing it.'

'We've got that somewhere an' all,' I said. There was the sound of something being scraped along the lino in the hallway, but it didn't sound like my dad.

'Come out here a minute, will yer, Francis?' my Mam said, holding the door no more than an inch or two open. 'Sorry about this, Father,' she shouted through the gap.

'Can I lend a hand?' he said, and for the first time that I can remember, I heard my Mam sound not only frightened, but even worse – not in control of things.

'Oh no, no, y'mustn't,' she said. 'You just stay there, we can manage.'

My dad was clinging to the banisters like a survivor of a shipwreck and swaying about in the storm that must have been going on in his head. The smell of the priest had gone and in its place was the stench of whisky. What was left of an almost empty bottle in my dad's hands was slopping onto the floor and down the stairs, while at the doorway to the kitchen were six cartons of whisky and still stood in the front path was a crate of brown ale. In the front room I could hear Father O'Connell humming 'Carolina Moon'.

'Get them in the back-kitchen pantry, Francis,' my Mam said, 'an' hurry up, will yer.' I pushed the door open and began piling the cartons in among the brooms and mops and on top of the broken spin-drier.

'What have y'gone an' done this time?' my Mam half whispered, half screamed at my dad.

'I haven't done anyshin',' my dad breathed at her. 'Not a . . . sausage. I jusht minded the van, thash all, Bernadette.'

'An' those bastards went an' just dumped you outside the house like that? Fine friends they are, aren't they?'

'They wash angry at me,' he said, looking just like Hovis pretending to be ashamed when he'd pooed in his pants. 'Co . . . cosh the second one they knocked over, I drank shome of the firsht lot,' And then he giggled.

'You stupid sod.'

'I wash lonely.'

My Mam threw him back to the banisters and between us we got the crate out of the path and stuck that in the cupboard too, as my dad told us in passing that it was alright, the warehouse was insured, and slid down the wooden slats of the banister onto his knnes.

'Y'might well say y'prayers,' my Mam said as she picked him up, threw him over her shoulder and took him in the back kitchen. She propped him against the wall, put a chair under him and then knocked him down into it. 'Stay there an' don't movef'nothin',' she said, and then we both went back in to Father O'Connell, who'd moved onto 'Singin' in the Rain'.

'Well, Father, I don't know what t'—'

'Think nothin' of it,' he said. 'Nothin' at all.'

'Are y'sure y'won't take some money,' my Mam said.

'I am sure, an' I won't take it, now if you folk will excuse me, not even I can get a glass or two after closing time—'

'Of course, Father.'

Someone hit the front door with what seemed like a sledgehammer and my Mam nearly took off for the roof. I shot over to the curtains in time to see Isaiah at the front door, drawing his fist back again, the police car at the kerb, his mate leaning back in the driver's seat, lighting a ciggie.

'It's the law,' I said, and this time it really was.

'Oh shit an' derision,' she said and didn't even begin to apologize. Bang bang bang. My Mam over to the curtains, doing her bit banging back on the window. 'Wait y'bleedin' rush, will yer, I'm comin', aren't I' she shouted. 'Who d'y'think y'are, Kojak? She turned back to Father O'Connell. 'Er, listen, Father, d'y'think it might be better f'you if y'slipped out the back way? No point in you bein' involved is there? Just go through the fence an' down the Wainwrights' back entry an' y'almost in the parish club.'

'An' what would I be wantin' t'do that for?' he said, putting his hand in his jacket pocket. 'A sure sign of guilt that would be. Anyway, it might be better f'you if I stay here.'

My Mam nodded to me to get into the back kitchen and she went to the door. My plan of campaign was to turf my dad out into Hovis's long grass and Indian country but I needn't have bothered, as he wasn't there. The only sign of him was the whisky bottle and I threw that in the washing machine.

'Y'can't come in here,' my Mam said. 'Get out.'

'It's a bit late tellin' me that,' Isaiah said. 'I'm already in here.'

'Well turn around an' frig off, go on.'

'That's what I like about this estate, co-operation wherever y'go.'

'Y'might get a bit more co-operation if y'didn't act like the soddin' SS,' my Mam said, 'jackbootin' y'way into people's houses.'

'You invited me in, Mrs Scully,' Isaiah said. 'I could have sworn y'did. In fact, I will swear y'did.'

'No I didn't, an' I've got witnesses,' she said as he pushed past her.

'Y'son won't be much good t'yer, if that's what y'call a witness,' he said, pointing at me as I tried to block the back-kitchen doorway. 'He's goin' t'need all the witnesses he can lay his hands on, never mind bein' one himself.'

'Francis hasn't set foot outside of—' my Mam started and then stopped again as Father O'Connell came and stood by the other doorway.

'Sorry to interrupt, officer,' Father O'Connell said, 'but I can't recall Mrs Scully asking you to come in.'

'Y'wha?' Isaiah said. 'What're you doin' here?'

'My collection night,' Father O'Connell said.

'Well, isn't that remarkable,' Isaiah said, ''cos I've come collectin' an' all, but it's a portable telly I've come for.'

'Y've come the wrong house then,' my Mam said, shielding me as well as the contents of the pantry. 'My feller's out of work. Any money we get goes in their stomachs in here.'

'An' into the alehouse if my sense of smell doesn't deceive me,' Isaiah said. 'The house stinks of whisky.'

'You must have brought it in with yer then,' my Mam said, ''cos it wasn't here before.'

'Be that as it may, missus, now that I am here, you won't mind me lookin' around, will you?'

'Do you require a search warrant?' Father

O'Connell said, suddenly losing his accent and sounding like a barrister.

'Isn't that funny, Vicar?' Isaiah said. 'I can't f'the life of me remember whether I do or not. Gettin' terrible absentminded I am these days. Still, no harm in a little look over the place, is there, missus? Nothin' t'hide have yer, 'course y'haven't, move over will yer?'

'You cannot just walk into the privacy of people's houses without due cause or the necessary documents,' Father O'Connell persisted, joining us at the back-kitchen door.

'Is that a fact now?' Isaiah said. 'You seem t'know a lot more about the law than I do, Vicar.'

'Father.'

'Are yer now? Well, I'd keep that under y'hat if I were you.'

'I'll scratch y'eyes out if y'say anythin' like that again,' my Mam said.

'Put it this way, Vicar,' Isaiah continued, ignoring my Mam, which was almost his biggest mistake of the night, 'it appears t'me, not knowin' nothin' about these things, of course, only bein' a police sergeant meself, that if this delightful lady here has got somethin' t'hide, an' it happens t'be behind the door what you are now in front of, that you in fact are obstructin' a police officer in the course of his duty, an' f'a man in your position in this parish, that would be a very serious offence indeed; much worse than drinkin' after hours at the parish club. Correct me if I'm wrong, won't you, Vicar.'

'I have no certain knowledge of any wrongdoings in this house,' Father O'Connell said, still stuck to the door, 'and if I did have, I would inform the proper authorities. All I am saying is that your conduct and your attitude hardly encourage the development of respect for the Law and those who the rest of the lads, well, it's not that big an estate, I'd see them around. At the Social Security every Thursday morning.

Hovis insisted on wearing his swimming trunks going to bed that night and took his bucket and spade with him as well. He wanted me to tell him about Puff the Magic Dragon 'cos tit-end Tony'd told him he'd seen it in Rhyl, but he had to make do with Goldilocks and the Three Bears. I could have told him the football results backwards and he wouldn't have complained. He was already up to his neck in sand and ice-cream and the dragon's hot breath.

'—an' they all lived happily ever after, go asleep.'

'No.'

'Y'won't go t'morrer.'

'Shall.'

'Y'll go with a smacked bum then.'

'Shan't.'

'Right, I'll just go an' tell y'Gra—'

'I go asleep.'

'Lie down then, will yer,' I said. 'Y'jumpin' about like as if y've got worms.'

'I like worms,' he said. 'You cut them up an' they don't go dead. Cut them an' cut them an' cut them an' . . . an' it doesn't hurt them or make them cry, y'know.'

'Lucky old worms,' I said.

are supposed to enforce it.'

'Nice sermon that, I'll write t'Rome f'a translation,' Isaiah said as he bullied his way past Father O'Connell. 'Gorra proper way with words haven't yer? I only hope f'your sake y'hidin' nothin' in there, 'cos if y'are, just think, y'won't be a penguin anymore, y'll be a one-armed bandit.'

Father O'Connell didn't flinch or even say anything and neither did my Mam but she reached out at Isaiah and spun him sideways and spat in his face, a really good spray. 'You bastard,' she said, 'you evil Orange Lodge bastard!'

'Scum,' Isaiah said, wiping his face with his sleeve, 'nothin' but scum.' He kicked at the door and tore into the back kitchen, pulling at the cupboard on the wall, turning the chairs over, dragging the curtain away from underneath the sink, spinning like a bluebottle with a lung full of fly-killer. And then he came back to me and my Mam with our backs this time to the pantry door.

'What's in there then?'

'Mind y'own bloody business,' my Mam said.

'That's good enough f'me, that is,' Isaiah said and hauled us off the door and opened it. 'Well well well,' he said. 'I should be so lucky. Maybe I am Kojak after all, missus, or even Sherlock Holmes. Come f'a telly an' find a brewery. What's more, the owner seems t'be at home an' all.'

My dad was kneeling on the crate, his head jammed against the ceiling, blinking away at the sudden light, still rolling in the stormy sea and holding onto a sweeping brush to keep afloat.

'An' what're you doin' here, Mr Scully?' Isaiah said. 'It's a funny situation f'a brewery. Or maybe y'an off licence? A bit off the beaten track though, wouldn't y'say?'

'I've got plannin' permission off the council,' my dad said, doing his best and ready to go along with

218

anything for a bit of peace and quiet.

'Oh a joker,' Isaiah said, 'even better. Y'can come down the station an' entertain us, I'm goin' off duty soon.'

'Leave him alone or get it over with,' my Mam said.

'Right then, just you tell me what ya' doin' in there with all this stuff, an' if y'can satisfy my curiosity, I'll go away an' think nothin' more of it. I'm an easy-goin' feller.'

'I'm stock-takin',' my dad said as he gave up all hopes of rescue, rolled one last time against the brush handle and toppled towards Isaiah. Just before he got there, he brought up a lifetime's sick from his toe-nails up, streaming and splattering into Isaiah's ugly mis-fit face, drowning him with a gush of hot colour all over him as they fell onto the floor, wrapped arm in arm. I looked around. Father O'Connell had his eyes closed like as if he was praying. And I knew who needed his prayers and all.

13

They kept my dad in there all night, but about three o'clock in the morning, when my Mam'd started trying to phone High Court judges and all the papers, they let me and Mooey and the Dogs go. I never grassed on them or anything. Before Isaiah had even got me and my dad down to the police station, the Law had already got all kinds of reports of three lads walking down the Dogs' road looking like a furniture shop.

We never owned up, even though we knew we never had a chance 'cos the painting and the ducks were found in the Dogs' house, and anyway all our fingerprints and Mooey's blood were all over the Leighs'. What was worse, when the Dogs had arrived home that night, their dad took one look at the portable telly and he was off down the Boundary with it. Half an hour later he was running home with five quid between us and thirty for himself, only to be met by their Mam telling him we were all down the cop shop. She chased him back to the pub but the new owner must have slipped off to watch the midnight movie in bed.

Father O'Connell stayed in our house looking after Hovis and Arthur till one o'clock when my Gran came back from planning her elopement with Mr Plastic and our Henry returned from humping his coals on top of Wendy. He left a little note saying that if she needed anything just to let him know. My Mam had been as upset about Father O'Connell being there as almost anything else, and then having to ask him to stay with the kids. One thing for sure, none of the neighbours at the windows came to their doors and offered.

As I walked home with my Mam, I expected to get inside the house and have crap knocked out of me, 'cos I was well aware that it was all my fault again. Without the telly and the other rubbish there would have been no cause for Isaiah coming to our house in the first place and none of this would have happened. I knew that until just lately I could have stopped the others robbing that stuff. They would have moaned but they would have listened, but somehow I just couldn't be bothered. I didn't want to play games any more, and as far as I was concerned, all this farting around was finished. The others could grow up in their own time. Sod the lot of them.

My Mam pushed me into our pathway and slammed the gate behind her.

'Mrs Barrett could have done it,' she said, still going on about not having anyone to mind Hovis and Arthur. 'Why she had t'go off visitin' relatives this week of all weeks, I don't know. An' where's that brother of yours 'ey? That's what I want t'know.'

For the first time in his life, Tony's timing was perfect as he arrived at the bottom of the road, riding side-saddle on the back of Gloria's motorbike. Well, it was perfect for me, if not for him. As he walked backwards up the road blowing kisses and holding his heart, my Mam finally did hit the roof and then hit him all over the privets and into the house, holding onto his crash helmet for dear life and taking the beating that should have been mine. By the time my Mam'd finished with him, Gloria was a distant memory and I was upstairs in bed with the door locked.

Everyone was there in assembly the next morning.

They always are for the last day of term. Even the teachers. Usually, you can look out of the hall windows at five past nine and see them all strolling in late. The same bunch would be legging it down the car park at two seconds past four o'clock, but they never got the cane or told to go and pick the ciggie stumps up in the boys' bogs for detention.

The Dogs were further along the line from me and a gang of other lads were all around them, laughing and joking. Snotty Dog had time to give me a quick thumbs-up and jerk his head towards the headmaster's room, and then he was back to telling them what it was like to be Billy the Kid. They didn't see the police car slide into the driveway and two coppers get out.

It all went quiet when the bell went for the start of assembly. We were in our class lines with the first years at the front and the sixth form at the back. The girls were on one side and we were on the other. Mrs Faconfield was standing at the piano flexing her fingers and looking nervous. Someone said the hymn was going to be 'Mary Had a Little Lamb' 'cos that was the only one she knew right through without messing up. I wish I had a quid for every time she'd played a different tune to what the choir sang. The choir! That's another misprint. Next door's moggy sings better after I've hit it with half an house brick. But nothing can compare with Faconfield. Sometimes she strings together a whole row of bum notes and you can see all the men teachers on the stage laughing their cocks off behind their hymn books.

The Gaffer was walking around at the side of the piano, with a steel ruler in his hand, pretending he was getting the first years into line but really showing off his new movable stairs that he'd done for the headmaster for the front of the stage. They were on rollers and he must have worked on them day and night so they could be ready for the last day. He'd even painted them the same colour as the curtains – lavatory green.

There was the thump of heavy shoes on the wooden floor as the headmaster appeared through the swing doors at the back of the hall. He marched, head down, towards the front, looking as though he'd lost a bollock or his best friend, but then again, I'm not surprised. The Gaffer wasn't exactly overjoyed with life neither, but he got a bit happier, the poor unsuspecting tit-end, as the headmaster got nearer.

It was dead quiet as he started up the steps, with the Gaffer standing alongside them like a doorman at the Odean. The only sound you could hear was the binmen outside the dinner canteen taking yesterday's swill back to the pigs. But nobody took any notice of that, not when the headmaster reached the top of the steps where they were supposed to join the edge of the stage. 'Cos it was then that he tripped and the stairs rolled neatly away from under him, all over the Gaffer's toes.

The only fault was that it didn't go on long enough. He should have been on top of Snowdon when it happened and made a good job of it. First of all he stumbled for a bit and put his hands up to stop himself from falling. Then his hymn book shot up in the air and hit Samuels on the head and woke him up, as the head ran forward with his arms out as though he was going to take off in his cape and fly back into the wall. Instead, he butted the lectern in the centre of the stage and sat down with his back to us. It even beat the time last year when Fatty Arbuckle, the old headmistress, leant against the hall door and it gave away on her.

Only, no one laughed. Not then anyway. Mrs Faconfield, standing up for a better view, put her hands on the piano and played a few notes that were better than usual, while the Gaffer stood by the steps and wondered if there was any good woodwork jobs going in New Zealand or South America. Finally, our deputy head gave the headmaster a hanky and a hand up.

When he turned around he nodded over to Mrs Faconfield and she just nodded back and smiled all sympathetic, like. After all, she must have known exactly how he felt. That kind of thing was always happening to her of a Saturday night.

'The hymn please, Mrs Faconfield,' he said after they'd bobbed heads at each other another couple of times. He had a nose bleed right through the 'Ave Maria' and Mrs Faconfield was in great form and slipped in a chorus of 'May is the Month of Mary' as a special treat. He tried to sing along for a bit, but most of the time he had his head back and his deputy's hanky across his face.

When Faconfield finished off with a flourish, beating the choir to the end by a verse and a half, the headmaster slowly brought his nose down to the usual level and did the old trick of waiting for silence, but then his nose started gushing again, so he had to look back at the ceiling. That was how he ended up talking to us, as if we were flies on the rafters.

'This, I know, is for some of you your last sniff sniff Easter at St Malachy's. Some, I am certain, will consider it their very last day and fail to return after the holidays. Some, again, will say goodbye to their schooldays not with regret or even pleasure, but with sniff sniff hatred. Not many, but a few, and it is a sad reflection on the level of present-day society that these sniff sniff few, and their wanton acts of destruction, are considered by the more feeble-minded amongst us as heroes. Such an act took place in this school last night. Nothing was sniff sniff taken, theft was probably not even contemplated. Instead, the only aim was seemingly to destroy. The amount of effort used would have been highly commendable if used properly, but instead, all these sniff sniff swallow sniff sniff idiots have to show for their hard work is my ... my ... my new oakwood writing desk, lying sawn in half in the woodwork room. Sniff.'

It was a bit suspicious, to say the least, when about 700 heads swivelled around and looked straight at me and the Dogs. I could have burst the pair of them there and then as the whole school turned jury on us and gave their verdict without having to speak. They've got mouths like the Mersey Tunnel, the Dogs. They don't seem to realize that the pleasure's in doing the fucking thing, not in telling the world that you've done it.

'The police have been informed, and I do not hesitate in warning those involved that I will sniff sniff press for the heaviest penalties. This kind of thing has to stop, and if the culprits are, as I suspect, from this school, I can warn them now that their chances of employment are, as from last night, nil, if my reference is to be any guideline.'

Our school gets broken into every week, right? Regular as clockwork. And books're ripped and the piano jumped on and the art room left swimming in powdered paint, but nothing'd ever been done or even talked about as far as I knew – until now. I don't mind telling you I sort of regretted doing it when I'd woken up, but now, after that, I wish we'd burnt the whole fucking dump down.

He stepped off the stage after one last sniff and the teachers in the front row all leant forward hoping for a second house, but he got down alright and began the walk towards the back, looking for lost pound notes. When he got towards the fifth forms he lifted his head to wipe the blood from his nose, and accidentally, I think, happened to look straight at me. No doubt he'd probably been thinking of me as one of the likely candidates, and he faltered a bit and almost stopped. I stood there and met his stare with the biggest widest cheesiest grin I could stretch my mouth around, and held it like a straitjacket until his stride picked up and he went past. What could he do? He could do nothing. Nothing to hurt me anyway, however many times he caned me.

We spent the rest of the morning down the police station, 'helpin'' them with their 'enquiries'. The book that Isaiah had been promising to throw at us since we were in the Juniors was finally lobbed in our direction. The way they were talking, I could imagine the police carpenter building the scaffolds in the police car park, but after they charged us with breaking and entering the school and the Leighs' burglary and a bit of vandalism, they ran out of things to threaten us with, so they let us go.

My Mam was screaming the waiting room down as we came out of the interview room and so I stayed behind for her. There was no point in going back to school, even if we weren't already suspended or expelled by now, though as the others went off and left me, I heard Mad Dog complaining 'cos he had a dinner ticket.

I don't think Isaiah had been off duty since the night before, although he'd done himself the favour of changing his uniform. He was even more thrilled to bits when my Mam had calmed down and told him she wanted to confess on behalf of my dad and told him about the two plate-bearers. He wouldn't have done that to save his life, but she knew, like we all did in our family, that without other people pushing him, my dad'd be more immaculate than the Virgin Mary.

They didn't release my dad though, even after

Isaiah sent a big squad car around the plate-bearers' house. I mean, my Mam didn't expect him to get a medal or anything but she was at least counting on bail 'cos they were going on holiday the next day. When my Mam started screaming again and got Isaiah trapped in the corner farthest away from the door, a plainclothes CID bloke came in and told her my dad was going in front of the magistrates in the afternoon and according to Isaiah they believed there was about ten years' unsolved crimes in the area that they could get him for. Everything from raping a lolly-pop lady to holding a black Mass in the sports centre.

As for Dole, he'd gone and all. Down to Risley remand centre the other side of Warrington, but not before the Law'd had some fun with him. One of the bastards showed us what he said was Dole's bloodstains on the wall when we wouldn't talk about robbing the Leighs. 'Look,' he said, 'see, they've gone brown, must be his.'

Most other people would have found the gas oven already, I suppose, but when I came home with my Mam the only thing she put in the oven was my dinner. I was still expecting a thumping any minute but it still hadn't happened, though our Tony was nicely puffed up around the eyes.

As I picked at my pastie my Mam set to work, packing the kids' things away in the suitcase, while Hovis danced around the house with a bucket and spade that had once been mine, singing, 'We're All Goin' on a Summer Holiday'. All three of them, my Mam, him and our Arthur. And it was Easter time and pissing down outside.

'D'y'really want t'go, Mam?' I said.

'What kind of a stupid question is that?' she said. 'Of course I don't flamin' well want t'go, but everythin's booked, I've got the bus tickets, the kids'll break their hearts, what else can I do? It's

227

goin' t'be bad enough gettin' the money back f'me Mam an' y'dad.'

'But can y'still afford t'go?'

'Just about. Jeez, I can just see us turnin' up at that boardin' house t'morrer an' me sayin', I'm sorry but me mother's eloped an' me husband's in jail.'

'I've got t'report t'the cop shop every day, Monday t'Friday, y'know.'

'Serves yer soddin' well right. It's you should have got that hidin', not our Tony. Thought y'had more sense than that. Bloody great it'll be if y'father gets sent down an' you follow him. What're we goin' to do then 'ey? Vera'll have t'have Hovis back, that's f'certain. I'll be workin' again I will, if I can get a job.'

'It'll be alright, Mam.'

'I'm glad someone thinks so, now eat y'dinner instead of lookin' at it, there's some stuff for yer t'take down the bagwash. I want everythin' neat an' tidy before we go.'

When I got back from the launderette our Henry was up and being told the bits of news he didn't know by my Gran who was also packing, hell for leather, but wasn't going on holiday.

'I've always known he was weak, that father of yours,' she was saying to Henry as she knelt on her old trunk and trapped a pair of buckled shoes between the lid and the lock. 'No backbone, that's his trouble. I said it often enough when they was courtin', God knows I did, but it was just a waste of breath. Thirty years of misery your mother's had due t'him, thirty bloody years. I hope he gets the same, I do. Give y'mother some peace for a change.'

'You goin'll give her some more an' all, won't it, Gran,' Henry said. I nearly tripped over my bagwash with the shock.

'I'll be buggered,' my Gran said and climbed off her trunk to have a closer look at our Henry and it sprang open and all her girdles bounced on the floor alongside her squashed shoes. 'I never thought I'd live t'see the day when you give me cheek, young Henry. What in Christ's name's got into you?'

'That's what I was goin' t'ask you, Gran,' he said as evenly as before, but it was still anyone else's equivalent of calling her a randy old bugger.

'I'm gettin' a taxi,' she said, 'right this minute. If I had any doubts about leavin' a sinkin' ship before, I haven't got any now.' She put her coat on back to front and started struggling with her shoes. 'An' another thing, there'll be nothin' down f'you when I kick it, Henry Scully, that's f'certain. You were the only one I was thinkin' of, an' that was only out of pity. Y'don't have t'spell it out t'me what y'meant then.'

'If the label fits, Gran—'

'My God, y'even doin' it on purpose, the whole world's turned upside down.'

'Y'trunk'll be at the door when y'come back, Gran,' he said and she give a little yelp like as if Mooey Morgan had just changed into Magnus Magnusson before her very eyes.

'What has got into yer, Henry?' I said after she'd limped off and I was helping him throw her things into the trunk.

'Wha'd'y'mean?'

'Y've changed overnight. Somethin' must have happened.'

'It's nothin' t'the changes I've seen this house go through since the last time I was home on leave.'

'It's a right time f'packin' up an' leavin' though, isn't it?' I said. 'You go t'morrer an' all. It's like a friggin' evacuation.'

'But I'll only be gone a few weeks this time.'

229

'That just means y'll have a short leave.'

'Will it?'

'I dunno, you're the sailor, but I thought—'

'I've about had me whack of the sea,' he said. 'Last time f'me this'll be. I'll be comin' home f'good then I reckon.'

'But what'll y'do?'

'A couple of mates I went away with started on the buses last Christmas. Ships on wheels. It's about the only job that seems to be going these days.'

'When did y'work all this out?'

'Oh, last night, more or less.' He smiled at me and then bounced all over my Gran's trunk till it was shut.

There you are, eh? Despite everything else that'd happened, at least one of us was alright. There was a light shining at the end of Henry's track.

'What's the matter?' he said.

'Oh nothin',' I said. 'Cracked it though, haven't yer? 'Ey? Y'have, haven't yer?'

'I don't know what y'mean,' he said, blushing up and fidgeting. He hadn't altered *that* much.

'What time did you get home last night then? Miss the last bus did yer? Y'll be alright though when y'drivin' one. It can't go without yer then.'

'Give us a hand with me Gran's trunk,' he said, 'an' just shut up, I haven't told me Mam yet.'

'About Wendy?'

'About anythin', an' don't you jump t'no conclusions about her, I'm stayin' home f'more reasons than her now.'

'Y'should never have been a sailor anyway, should yer, Henry? Our Tony reckons y'get seasick in the bath.'

Getting chased through the house by your elder brother may not seem like that much fun, or even unusual, but when it was someone who you'd secretly given up hope on, who you thought was sheets to the wind, it could be pretty smart, even when he catches hold of your arm and twists it up your back. Anyway, it took my mind off a lot of things I didn't even want to begin to think about and when I backheeled him in the balls and dived under his bed, it was his turn to howl. Henry was just about to drop the bed on my head when the taxi-driver knocked on the door and my Mam came racing up the stairs, clobbered the both of us and made us carry the trunk to the taxi.

My Gran stayed in the taxi and wouldn't speak to us, except to tell us to frig off when we pulled faces at her through the window, but her and my Mam forgave and forgot and hugged each other. My Gran said it was her one last chance to have a good time, sod the white wedding, you're only old once, and we'll be in the Labour Club the Saturday you come home, don't forget now, you deserve a medal for what you've had to put up with. They'd still have been there at midnight going through the good old days, day by day, if the taxi-driver hadn't started his clock.

I stood at the window at ten past four and watched everyone streaming past from school, running in the road and swinging around the lamp-posts, having a quick drag before they got into their own street and then swear blind to their Mams that they haven't been smoking, it was the others. Three weeks off and all. And six weeks in the summer. The holidays were worth something at least. I'd miss them alright. If I ever got a job. But I wouldn't miss much else except Steve and I could always stop him in the street and thank him for what he did for me despite all the others. One event I wouldn't regret letting slip was going down the bogs for a shit. There'd be no more muck about me on the walls now. I'd soon be forgotten. As for

14

I was glad to be on my own. I never had been before, and never wanted to, but it couldn't have come at a better time. It was kind of smart to be boss of the house, buying food, paying the milk and making all the decisions, even if I was only making them for meself. The days shot over after the Saturday morning when Henry went through the doorway and my Mam and the kids followed.

My Mam even went off half happy, knowing that Henry was coming back for good, though every morning for the first few days I kept expecting her back, carrying Hovis and dragging Arthur and bursting me 'cos the house was a mess. I became proper neat and tidy and washed the dishes and put the rubbish in the bin and even emptied the ash trays, but on the Thursday I got a postcard saying she was having a nice time and the boarding house was nice and the weather was keeping nice and Arthur wrote a PS about the ace fairground, so I threw the Hoover away.

Once or twice I went up the field for a game of footie and I got the bus over to Dingle to see my aunty on Easter Monday but she was out. Most days though I just got up about eleven, reported to the police station, went to see my dad and then queued at the chippy for my dinner. It was in the chippy that I saw Geoff Long and Stanner for the first time since the final.

'Any news about Tommy?' I said.

'Risley,' Geoff said.

'I knew that. Don't y'know any more than that?'

'That's all there is t'know. We can't afford t'get

up there, even if they'd let us in,' Geoff said.

'They'd let you in though from what I've heard, Scull,' Stanner said.

'I was framed.'

'So was that picture y'robbed an' all, wasn't it?'

'We're collectin' t'send somethin' t'Tommy, by the way,' Geoff said, holding out his hand.

'I thought this was a chippy, not a church,' I said. 'I hope it gets to him.'

'It will.'

'How're y'gettin' it there then?'

'When we've got enough we're goin' down t'see his Mam.'

'Y'mean y'know where they're livin' then?' I said.

'Yeah, next door but one t'where we used t'live,' Geoff said. 'With Tommy's uncle.'

'Frig me, I've been tryin' t'find that out since it all happened. I asked the both of you then.'

'We didn't know then, did we?'

'Well, come on.'

'Funny enough,' Geoff said, 'but we might just have had a memory lapse about the number of the house.'

'An' the name of the street.'

'After all, we fancy her as well, y'know,' Geoff said.

'Arr come on will yer, play the white man.'

'We don't like that game,' Stanner said.

'There's a queue waitin' behind you lads, d'y'realize?' the woman serving at the counter said. 'Hurry up, wha'd'y'want?'

'Portion of chips please an' a fish,' I said.

'Same f'us as well,' Geoff said. 'He's payin'.'

'Who is?' I said. 'Not me, brother, on y'way.'

'Alright then,' Stanner said, 'we'll just have t'wait till we get some more money f'Tommy's present, instead of goin' down there t'night.'

234

'An' it'll be your fault,' Geoff said to me.

'Why me?'

''Cos the money we'd have saved if you'd have bought us our dinner would, by a strange co-incidence—'

'Er . . . y'sure y'don't want any peas with them, lads?' I said. 'How about a cake from Cousins?'

I started getting ready about two o'clock, as soon as I'd eaten my chips. Prepared doesn't do justice to what I was by the time seven o'clock came and Stanner and Geoff called for me. I'd even written her a little note in case she was out, telling her I wanted to see her again, and that my Mam was away till the end of the week. I didn't quite put it like that, not the two together, but there was no harm in wishful thinking.

Two hours later I was back at home, and reckoning that was all I'd ever be doing – thinking about it and wishing it would happen – 'cos when we got down there, only her Mam was in. The minute I arrived I wanted to go, not because it was some darky's flat or nothing, but just because everything looked as though it was pissed on again. Not only was Joanna at a disco in some youth club down there called the Blackie, she'd gone with her uncle. Safe enough, you might think, unless you were Marie Morgan, but I saw this feller's photograph on the mantelpiece with him looking no older than Tommy and like Stevie Wonder with twenty-twenty vision. Some fucking uncle he was turning out to be.

I give her Mam the note, signed a petition about Tommy, had a cup of tea, read Tommy's letters and started pining for our house. As soon as I could manage it without upsetting anyone, I suddenly realized I'd promised to baby sit for our Tony, and I was standing at the bus stop looking like I'd escaped from a tailor's window, with even the

235

few white kids knocking about staring at me strange.

By a quarter to ten I was in bed, having a wank, fighting the feeling that I wanted to have a good cry for meself, and hearing our Tony through the wall as he made coochie-coo noises one minute and then screamed the house down the next when it brought its bottle up all over him.

'Course, after that, by the Friday of the second week I'd let the whole house fall apart. Dust and dishes and chip paper were everywhere and I'd run out of money. Even the tin of asparagus soup our Arthur had brought home once instead of oxtail, got opened up and eaten. The only clean place in the house was the sink 'cos I hadn't used it for anything. The bus from Rhyl wouldn't get in till about one o'clock the next day, so I was going to get up early and at least make it look as though I'd made an attempt.

That is until eight o'clock on the Friday night, when I'd just decided on *The A-Team*, a film with sub titles that might have some tits in it, and bed. I'd found some silver down the side of my dad's armchair and got a bag of chips and a fish cake from the chippy, but I was still hungry so I was putting some straw-berry jam on some Farley rusks out of the bottom of the cupboard when there was a knock on the door. They could fuck off if it was anyone wanted money off us.

'Hello, Franny.'

Joanna.

A Farley's rusk behind my back, jam dripping on the floor, my socks humming loud and strong, the first thought I have is to close the door. Come back later, bring some food and a deodorant spray.

'Come in, Joanna, er the place is a bit of a mess like, y'know, I was just about t'—'

'Let me help yer,' she said, and so for the first hour of the night I'd been waiting for since the

236

second I saw her, I'm down on me knees with a scrubbing brush full of friggin 1001 and she's collecting chip paper and empty bean cans like as if they were the silver paper that we used to bring into the Infants to help buy a blind dog.

They were bathing the baby in the front room when I sneaked in the back way to our Tony's and borrowed a quarter of tea, a bottle of milk and two pound of sugar. While our Tony was there clapping and cheering and shouting, 'Look, Florrie, look, he's swimmin', see that breaststroke, look see, oh shite, quick, he's swallowed some,' I nipped to their pantry and grabbed a jar of coffee. Miserable sods, they had no biscuits.

'I got your letter,' she said as she sat down on the couch and I turned the telly off.

'The post must be slow around your way,' I said. 'Took nearly a week t'get t'yer,' but she took no notice and soon we were using up about a fifth of the space on the couch.

There were lots of things I wanted to tell her, but not many that I could actually open my mouth and come out with. I wanted to say the kind of thing you'd laugh at people saying on the telly or down the picture house in those soft films with the soft colours and soft actors and a hundred-piece orchestra all playing the violin. And nothing on earth, not even her, was going to make me say that.

'When d'y'think y'll be movin' back?' I said when we came up for air.

'I don't think we will be comin' back here.'

'I didn't mean in the same house, y'know.'

'I know, it's just me Mam doesn't want t'go anywhere where she's been before.'

'Start again, like?'

She nodded and turned away from me to face the blank screen of the telly.

'Can I come with yer?' I said, joking. 'Y'know, start again as well?' I put my arm around her and felt her seem to move away from me. 'Well, what about the council?' I said. 'They can put y' elsewhere. Y'don't even have t'be on this estate, y'could go the one behind the village, by the railway station. Some nice flats up there.'

'It's not up to me.'

'Y'must have some say in the matter.'

'I think . . . well, I know she wants t'go further than that, out of Liverpool altogether. Everywhere she goes, she says she just feels that she's been there before, you know, with me dad.'

'Alright, that's easily solved; how about Kirkby? Miles from here, miles from town, not in Liverpool at all when y'think about it, couldn't be better. Got a great market, Kirkby has. Me Mam's always talkin' about it. D'y'know wha', she got a dress from there once, an'—'

'She loved me dad, believe it or not—'

Shit shit shit, it's all going wrong, I know it is.

'Maybe y'Mam did, Joanna, I don't know, but from what I—'

'We all did, Tommy more than any of us in a way. We never stopped lovin' him y'know, the memory of him an' the laughter an' the way he'd hug me Mam when he came home from work, before—'

'But, but listen, girl, memories're no good to yer, not now. I've got them an' all, I remember things an' think t'meself, "Jeez, we had a smashin' time there, me an' me dad, I was happy then." But it makes no soddin' difference t'*now*. Memories the last things y'want t'remember when y've got y'whole life ahead of her. Y'only have the one life y'know. Y'can't be wearin' widow's weeds f'y'dad when y'the same age as y'Mam. Come on, love, listen. Don't y'see that?'

'There's more to it than that,' she said and stared at the telly. It was getting more attention now when it wasn't on, than it had ever had before. I edged away from her on the couch and stuck out my bottom lip and had a good sulk, not 'cos I wanted to, or to get me own way, but just because I knew that whatever I did or said, she'd made up her mind, or had it made up for her.

'I'll make a cup of tea,' she said.

'Before y'go,' I said and took hold of her hands as she stood up.

'I don't have t'go yet.'

'But y'are goin' aren't yer? I mean, you an' y'Mam. An' y'uncle too, as far as I know.'

'I tried t'tell you that, just now.'

'I heard yer.'

'As soon as we find out about Tommy, but it might be ages before we know that.'

'But where? Where y'goin'?'

'Me married sister lives in Wolverhampton.'

'The Black Country.'

'Very funny,' she said and pulled her hands away from mine.

'It wasn't meant t'be,' I shouted as she went into the back kitchen. ''Cos it's not funny at all.'

'I didn't have t'come t'night,' she said as she ran the water to wash the cups.

'That's great that is,' I said as I banged the door behind me and came up to her. 'Flamin' great. What y'trying t'say is that y'didn't have t'come up here t'give me the privilege of personally tellin' me t'screw off, that y'could have written me a letter or just gone the disco again an' had a good laugh with y'uncle an' all y'new nig-nog friends. That's what it is, isn't it?'

'All my *old* nig-nog friends,' she said, rubbing the patterns off the cups, 'I knew them a long time before I ever met you, an' that didn't stop me goin' with you then, did it?'

'But what about y'uncle?' I said. 'How long has he been y'uncle?'

'Don't, Franny, just stop it, will yer!'

'Alright, but answer me this; was he y'uncle before he was y'friend? Was he?'

She turned around at me, wide and wild-eyed, and the words came splintering out. 'My uncle *is* my uncle an' he's twenty-two years old an' he goes t'Liverpool University – it is allowed y'know, nignogs can go there – an' his girl friend's in her final year at Bristol, an' y'd really like her, Franny, she's lovely an' pure an' clean an' *white!*'

The cup broke on the floor and I trod on the bloody thing in my stocking feet as I took hold of her and I didn't know whether to scream and shout 'shit' or say I was sorry. When I ended up hopping around the room on one foot, nobody could be that angry or hurt that they wouldn't laugh. Anyway, I knew that we both knew it wasn't anger at the stupid things I'd said, but at the way things'd turned out for us. Against us, more like.

That cup of tea never got made, not then anyway. I'd cut myself between the toes, but the state I was in it was if I'd tried to kill meself, there was so much blood. She helped me up the stairs and took me to the bathroom, but chickened out of taking my sock off. I sat on the edge of the bath and ran cold water over my foot, and the great gaping wound I thought would need stitches was only a little nick. I found some of my dad's Styptic and the bleeding soon stopped.

There wasn't another clean pair of socks in my cupboard, but it was a good excuse to go in my Mam and dad's room to see if he'd left any behind. Would you believe, the pain was so bad she had to support me all the way over to the wardrobe by the double bed?

'I'm beginnin' t'think you stepped on that cup on purpose, Francis Scully,' she said as she sat on the bed and I tried to find a pair with no holes in. As I sat with her, examining my dad's socks, I realized that I had her where I'd always wanted her. What I wanted next was a few words to say, something to cover my arm going around her shoulder for a quick submission, but for a change I was at a loss for words.

'I've never been on a bed with anyone before,' she said. It wasn't brilliant and it was as old as the hills, but it was a start. I put my hand on her shoulder and said, 'Neither have I,' and she said, 'Who d'you think y'kiddin'?' And there we were, lying flat, with our heads on the pillows by the headboard.

I'd like to tell you it was off with the drawers and on with the job but I wouldn't even be kidding you, never mind myself. I'd been seeing her long enough to know that getting past kissing her was difficult enough.

But being on a bed was much better than a park bench or a back entry on a dark night, forever keeping one eye open for peeping Toms and bluebottles and little kids. We were relaxed and natural with each other, and above all hidden. The world was like a shop closed down for the night, troubles forgotten, the past locked away, and the next day could take care of itself.

All was fine till she said 'No' and stopped me as I put my hand on the zip of her jeans.

'I won't hurt,' I said. 'We'll not go no further if y'don't want to.'

'How much further can you go than that?'

'I just want to hold you there.'

'Not me,' she said. 'You.' Her hand was on my stomach, nervous, the palms wet with sweat.

'Not me without you,' I said.

'You'll have to help me first. I don't know what t'do.'

'Neither do I with you.'

She fumbled and found me, her hand shaking, her eyes shut tight. I took her hand away and found the switch to turn the lights out and then I put her hand back and put my hand over hers and slowly started the rhythm I'd practised on myself so many times before as I thought about her, and now she was here. She took my hand between her legs, then back to her zip. As she lifted herself up I took her jeans down and then her body moved and her legs opened until my finger found the space, wet and warm and we started together.

It didn't take long. As her hand beat between my legs and I did what I could for her, we came nearer and nearer to each other until those final last gasp jerks when I was above her, and my hand was gone from underneath her, and she was screaming and holding me down towards where my hand had been, and I poured all I had to give her over and around her. But nowhere near being in her. And as I lay with my head on her breast, I felt the most awful stupid sort of sadness; the death of someone, or something.

'Are you alright?' I asked.

'Yes, just wet.'

'I'm sorry.'

'It wasn't only you.'

'I wish I could have—'

'I know,' she said. 'So do I.'

'The next time.'

'Yes,' she said, a long time later. 'The next time.'

That's right, I thought, the first long-distance screw. All the way down the M6 to Wolverhampton. Maybe we could find a way of fucking by phone. 'I'm trying to connect you—'

'Don't go, Joanna, not . . . I mean, not t'night, I

know y've got t'go t'night, but I mean always. Find a way of stayin', friggin' hell, *please*.'

I took myself off her and we lay facing the ceiling, not looking at each other, just the cracks and my dad's pathetic attempts at covering them over.

'What I did t'night, f'you . . . an' f'me, don't y'see, Franny, I'll never do it again, not f'a long time, not with you or anyone; can't you see, can't you understand it was my way of sayin', "I love you."'

'It was also the best bum's rush I've ever had.'

'You know it was more than than.'

'Yeah, but it still boils down t'the same thing, doesn't it? Whatever I feel about yer, I can't say t'you what you just said t'me, 'cos I know y'going t'get off this bed an' go home an' sooner or later y'goin' t'be where I'll never see yer again.'

'You don't know that. Nothin's definite, nothin's as planned as you make it sound. I don't want it t'happen but I can't just walk away from me Mam.'

'But y'can just walk away from me.'

'Y'actin' stupid again,' she said.

'That's alright,' I said. 'I am stupid.'

'Self-pity's no pity at all.'

'D'y'know what, Joanna, I couldn't believe it when y'first said y'd go out with me. I never thought of yer as bein' black or nothin' like that. I just thought of yer as bein' better, more than I deserve, too good f'me.'

'You are stupid then.'

'But I'm not,' I said, ''cos, y'see, although I knew all those things, an' I know well enough what some people around here think of me, it didn't make no difference, 'cos I know one other thing that they don't know – I'm not goin' t'be stuck here on this estate all me flamin' life, knockin' off portable tellies an' doin' demolition jobs on desks, collectin' Social Security, gettin' bored an' gettin' a beer gut.

No chance. I'm goin' t'do somethin' with meself, I am.'

'An' what is it y'goin' to'do?' she said. I could tell she wasn't taking the piss, but she was smiling and I knew she didn't really believe me.

'Well, I don't know, not proper, I don't know what it is, an' y'can laugh about it later, tell all y'mates, I don't care, it's just that ever since I was a little kid, I've known, like y'know—'

It all seemed daft. I was going to tell her something I wouldn't even tell my own Mam, but somehow it was so important that I had to tell her.

'—Y'see, I always thought I was goin' t'be famous. That I was goin' t'be a star; see, I said y'd laugh, but when I was a kid – about six or seven I suppose – me Mam an' dad used t'take me an' our Vera an' Tony an' Henry on the bus every so often t'see me Aunty Lil in Oldham. It was about the nearest we ever got t'a holiday, an' t'spend the time on the way there an' back, I used t'look at all the people on the bus an' walkin' past us in the street an' I'd say t'meself – only meself – "They don't know it, but they've just been looked at by the future captain of Liverpool an' England", an' I'd dream of scorin' the winnin' goal in the World Cup an' bein' made a knight, like. Just like Alf Ramsey an' Matt Busby an' anyone what sails around the world. "Arise, Sir Francis Scully.' 'Ta, Queen."'

She was still laughing alright, but it wasn't Marie Morgan's type of laugh or my Mam's or anyone else's I've ever heard. She was laughing 'cos I'd told her something secret and soft and it was alright. She rolled over and hugged me like a little kid.

'Listen,' she said, 'tell me this, what're you goin' to be a star at, so I'll know when people ask me.'

'Whatever it is, it's goin' t'be somethin'. I'm not goin' t'grow old an' grey an' turn into dung an'

244

dust an' friggin daisies. Not without doin' some-thin' first.'

'That sounds just like poetry,' she said. 'Maybe y'could become a poet.'

'I know what I could do,' I said. 'I could go on the clubs.'

'An act?'

'No, an hat check-girl. Listen, I could do it easy, y'don't need no qualifications t'make people laugh, an' when I want to—'

'It's not as easy as y'think, y'know, I've gorran uncle—'

'Another one?'

'Yes, an' he's real as well, but he's in a steel band an' it's all sweat an' guts.'

'Of course it is, I'm not kiddin' meself on that score, but I don't mind doin' that if it's f'somethin' worthwhile - like meself. Just look at all the comedians what've come out of Liverpool: Jimmy Tarbuck, Tom O'Connor, all the Everton football team, Mickey Finn and all the old ones before our time - they're all just ordinary fellers, I bet, with a bit of magic, a talent f'makin' people laugh. That Tom O'Connor even used t'be a soddin' school-teacher an' if he can be as brilliant as he is, I'm sure I can do it.'

'Any black jokes an' I'll leave you.'

'Well, y'see, there was this big black buck nigger . . .'

We had that cup of tea then and I was about as happy as I'd been in all my lousy frigging life, and I talked myself hoarse, releasing things I never even knew I'd thought, planning the future like I was reading the tea leaves, trying to keep us away from the moment when she'd say again what she'd said before, what she'd come all the way over to tell me. I always thought in real life people just said 'Fuck you, I'm goin',' and slammed the door. I never thought it could be as slow and painful as this. One second I'd be on top of the world and the next I'd sense that her silence was just a way of getting ready for the final reminder, and so I'd start talking again.

I'd got her to the bus stop with a fascinating description of the time I got run over coming out of the ice rink and ended up in the old people's ward of Newsham General and every time I woke up someone was dead. If the bus had been on time I could have said, 'See yer tomorrer, I'll meet you at yours,' and thrown her on the bottom deck, but the bus wasn't on time.

'Look Franny,' she said, cutting short the start of the highlights of my football career, 'about t'night, you were right, I had come up t'tell you it was no good goin' on, I can't say it now 'cos, even more than I did before, I don't want t'stop seein' you, if that makes sense, but there doesn't seem any sort of way that we can keep goin' on with you here . . . an' me down there.'

'An' how far's Bristol?' I said. 'Twice as bloody far as Wolverhampton. If y'uncle can do it, I don't see why we can't.'

If there'd been a telly in the road, she'd have looked at it.

'That was a lie,' she said. 'He hasn't got a girl friend anywhere, black or white or purple an' green. I only said it so you'd stop bein' jealous of someone there's no need t'be jealous about.'

'What *do* y'want 'ey.' I said. 'Just tell me that.'

'I want t'do what's right. I want t'make me Mam happy.'

'Alright, alright,' I said. 'I can understand that, go on, clear off, don't come back, never even think about it, an' if y'can't remember me name next week, that's fine, but f'Christ's sake, girl, let's stop all this fartin' around; y'know where I live, y'know

246

what I feel about yer, I'm not goin' t'beg no more t'night, I've had enough.'

I turned away from her and walked off. She wouldn't have long to wait. Two buses were creeping around the roundabouts and heading down the hill, one of them had to be hers. Every step I took there was this love-sick loony in my earhole, whining and whimpering, 'Go on, go back an' beg, get down on y'knees an' plead,' but I kept going. I wasn't going back, I knew enough, I'd be good on stage, always leave them wanting more, and as sure as I was walking away and the moaning was getting fainter, I knew that what'd happened tonight was because she did care for me, 'cos she wasn't lying when she said she loved me. She didn't do all that what she did 'cos there was nothing else she could do to keep me, 'cos getting my old man out from down my pants was what was expected of her, 'cos she wanted to keep me, have someone to support her, like a crutch or a wheelchair.

But I could think of someone who was in that list somewhere, who did favours 'cos otherwise no-one'd do her one. There on the corner, swinging her handbag and looking bored, flicking her ciggie down the grid, first time, perfect shot, was Marie Morgan.

Joanna's bus went past me I looked up at the top deck without seeing her, and then watched and waited till she was safely gone, till she never got off the bus at the next stop and came crying into me arms. And then I walked across the road.

''Ey, Marie, come here.'

I was so aggressive I even frightened myself, but she came over to me alright.

'Fancy a cup of tea?' I said. 'The pot's still warm.'

'Don't mind if I do.'

We settled for Hovis's single bed and Mickey

Mouse on the wall. I wasn't going to have her on my bed, the state it was in, and I didn't want to use my Mam and Dad's, so that was all there was apart from the couch and the cockloft. I'd lain on Hovis's bed so many times anyway, it felt like mine. When she sat down to take her shoes off I almost started telling her about Goldilocks lost in the woods.

'Y'hurtin' me,' she said.

'Well, it's hard.'

'I bloody well hope so.'

'I mean gettin' it in. Y'need radar.'

'Most people I know manage.'

'Okay, okay, just don't start gigglin'.'

'I can't help it. Ooh, ow! Right a bit will yer.'

'Your right or mine?'

'Er, mine. I think.'

'Am I gettin' warm?'

'Oh honest t'God, Franny Scully, y'should be wearin' short trousers an' ankle socks. Down a bit, no not *that* far, up a bit, a bit more.'

'Soddin' hell, it's like the Golden Shot.'

'That's it,' she said, 'push, Franny, push, come on, ooooh, that's nice, go on, go on, don't stop.'

15

I was the captain of this banana boat three days out of Jamaica, full of rum and adventure and singing 'Daydelight an' I Wanna Go Home'. The wind was in my hair and my suntan was so good I'd nearly been sold as a slave the last time I was in port. I stood there ready to haul the Jolly Roger up at the first sight of Spanish gold and a boat smaller than ours, and I was laughing away to myself 'cos I'd left Mooey and the Dogs still working on the Birkenhead ferry. Then, all of a sudden, I saw a sailing ship coming toward us, straight from the African coast, with Joanna chained to the top deck and this prick dressed like the cast of *Mutiny on The Bounty* whipping her. I ordered our Henry to stop being sick and get full speed ahead and we were alongside in no time at all. All that their crew could do was throw stones and shout, but stones were no good against me, they just hit the window and fell into the water. I was working out why they were hitting the window 'cos glass hadn't been invented yet, when a stone cracked one of the panes and I stood up with the top sheet of the bed around me, and looked out of the window.

There, below me, standing in the path, were Mad Dog, Snotty Dog and Mooey, carrying suitcases. Well, the Dogs were carrying suitcases. Mooey, was holding a plastic bag with Tesco written on it.

'What the fuck're you doin'?' I said through the broken pane.

'Sorry about that,' Mad Dog said. 'We didn't

expect Mooey t'even hit the house, but we've been tryin' f'ages.'

'Where're y'goin'?'

'The Shetland isles,' Snotty Dog said.

'Y'wha'?'

'We're doin' a Ronald Biggs, Scully!' Mad Dog said.

'He went t'Brazil, not the north of friggin' Scotland.'

'But once we make some fast money, we can go anywhere we want as well, an' no one t'stop us,' Snotty Dog said.

'No one need know who we are,' Mad Dog said.

'Or what we've done.'

'Get a flat,' Mad Dog said.

'A luxury one,' Snotty Dog said, 'an' a couple of birds.'

'I've gone off birds,' Mooey said.

'Y'cracked,' I said. 'Y'll never make it, an' even if y'do, there'll be nothin' down for yer.'

'But anythin'll be better than bein' stuck in this dump waitin' round like pillocks f'our case t'come up,' Mad Dog said.

'Y'll be missed straight away.'

'No we won't,' Mad Dog said. 'I've got it planned. It's Saturday t'day, right? The Law won't even know we've gone till Monday when we're supposed t'report. They might not even bother doin' anythin' till Tuesday.'

'I don't know,' I said.

'Chicken,' Snotty Dog said.

'An' donkeys,' Mooey said. 'There's donkeys up there an' all, Scull.'

'Ponies,' I said, 'an' anyway, I haven't got any money.'

'We've got enough t'get up there,' Snotty Dog said. 'Pay us when y'get y'first week's wages. Y'won't miss it out of three hundred quid.'

'Me Mam's comin' home t'day.'

'Y'are chicken,' Snotty Dog said. 'I told Mooey it was a waste of time comin' around here.'

'I haven't got any clean clothes,' I shouted down.

'It's pathetic, isn't it 'ey?' Snotty Dog said. 'Have y'ever heard the like. I suppose y've got t'make the beds as well. Just think, we all used t'look up t'you once.'

'Y'don't have t'come,' Mad Dog said. 'I can always buy a map on the motorway.'

I looked around at what I was leaving. Marie was snoring away, curled up, back turned, lost in her own dreams of banana boats or cemetery walls, Arthur could have the room to himself, my Mam would go mad for an hour or so before realizing it was one less mouth to feed, and Hovis would miss Goldilocks.

'Wait in the entry,' I said.

Clothes everywhere, under my bed, behind the couch, at the side of the bath, all thrown into two kit-bags and then thrown out again when I discover an old holdall of our Tony's sticking out the back of the wardrobe. I've got to the front door before I remember Marie. Up the stairs again, bounce into the room, turn sick at the smell of old socks and sex, give her a shake and hold my nose.

'Marie, come on, love, time t'get up an' go home.'

'Urrrgh.'

'Yeah, I know but come on.'

'Sod off, Mam.'

'Marie!'

Nothing but a good head of steam. Shake shake, slap slap.

'Ten more minutes, that's all, Mam, honest.'

'Have you got someone up there with you?' Mad Dog at the letterbox.

'Who me? 'Course not, I'm comin' now.'

Halfway down the stairs and back again, tidy

my Mam's sheets, think about last night, give
Marie another shaking, but not a sign of stirring.
That's it then, to hell with her. If she's still here
when my Mam comes back she only has to say she
got lost and my Mam'll believe her. It could just as
easily have been Mooey in there. And Hovis'll be
thrilled t'bits. Three years of asking 'Who's Been
Sleepin' in My Bed?' and he comes home to find a
real live Goldilocks. With black hair and a disease
of the gums. So much for fairy stories.

We got the workers' bus to the East Lancs road,
the top deck almost empty and the few men that
were there talking of short time and redundancies,
and the first bit of overtime since before Christmas,
but wasn't that always a sign, one of them said, for
a firm closing down? A quick stockpile and then
thank you very much; what can I do now at my
age, that's what I want to know, fucking manage-
ment and government, it's all their fault.

The first lift a good one, a chara on the way to
Bolton to pick up a load of spastic kids; a seat each,
and a driver not bothered if we never talked as
long as we didn't put our feet on the seats.

Out and thanks a lot at the lights at Haydock,
the M6 ahead of us on both sides. I stop the others
taking the southbound approach road, and we sit
on our cases by the sign that says, 'The North,
Carlisle and Scotland'. And wait. Well and truly
morning now, the sun up over some woods to the
east but lost behind the smoke and haze of
Manchester.

An hour gone and the Dogs still skipping and
whistling and smiling, saying, 'Isn't it great 'ey,
bein' free like this,' and 'It won't be long, the next
lorry, you watch.' About a hundred next lorries
later one stops and we go running towards the tail
lights.

The fact that the driver's Scottish is enough for

the Dogs and they start piling in as soon as he opens his mouth.

"Eh, hang on, lads, where y'goin'?'

'Y'know,' Mad Dog said, 'the Shetlands, where the oil is.'

'Arr, I'm no' much good t'yer then. Glasgow's as far as I'm goin', an' no further.'

'That's alright, mister, we'll go an' see Celtic play.'

'But, sonny, the Shetlands're a long way away from Glasgow.'

'Are they?' Mad Dog said. 'Oh, still, it doesn't matter, there's no panic is there, boys? We don't have t'go scoutin' f'a job till the Monday, come 'head.' Him and Snotty Dog piled in and I went to give Mooey a leg up.

'Only two of y', son, that's all I can take.'

'Er, well, er, Scull,' Snotty Dog said from the window of the driver's cabin, trying hard not to look chuffed but still closing the door at the same time, 'there's not enough room f'you an' Mooey, but don't worry, y'll soon catch us up on the road, we'll wait for yer in Glasgow, alright?'

'Deffo, Snotty,' I said. 'See yer there, at the match.'

'Last one stinks,' Mooey said as the lorry blew diesel fumes all over us and rolled down the approach road.

'Er, wha'y'wavin' two fingers at that lorry for, Scull?' Mooey says as it disappears onto the motorway.

'Nothin' Moo. Just a message f'the Dogs, that's all.'

'Oh, I see. It's just that er someone told me in school that like er, an' I'm only repeatin' what they said—' He's close to my ear, whispering, looking around, making sure no-one else can hear him, '— that er two fingers means "Fuck off".' He put his

253

hand over his mouth and looked shocked that he'd actually said it, just to cover up in case God was watching.

'That's right, Mooey, it does.'

'Aren't we friends with them no more.'

'Y'could say that, la'.'

'What happened? Did we have a fight?'

'Not so that y'd notice.'

'An' er y'sure y'not friends with them no more?'

'We haven't really been friends f'a long time, Mooey.'

'I know.'

'So, why're y'askin'?'

'I er just want t'make sure.'

'Make sure of what?'

'That y'not friends with them no more.'

'Fuckin' hell, Mooey.'

'So that y'wont hit me when I tell y' what they said about yer behind y'back.'

'Oh aye?'

'They didn't want y' t'come with us t'see them donkeys, y'know; they almost made me go without yer, but they er, like—'

'Didn't know how t'get there without me?'

'Well er, I think so.'

'Any more bits of gossip, Mooey, while y'at it?'

'No,' he said and looked into my eyes and then down at his feet.

'Come on, y'may as well tell me, I won't get upset.'

'Y'certain y'not friends with them?'

'Jesus Christ!'

'Well, er there was the paint, Scull.'

'What friggin' paint?'

'That paint they er robbed from the wallpaper shop.'

'So wha'?'

'It was them what wrote all those dirty things

about yer on the walls, 'ey no, gerroff, it's me only pullover.'

'Who told you? Come on, who told yer? How d'y'know?'

'I er helped them, Scull.'

I didn't hit him, didn't even get near to it. Even let go of him straight away, pushed him from me, watched him fall over and cover himself up in case I kicked him. He stayed down there for a long time just in case I didn't want to hit anyone when they were down and then he got up and tried to see what it was I was looking at in the distance.

'Wait till I see them,' I said finally.

'We'll see them t'morrer.'

'Will we?'

'Er, don't get me muddled, Scull, I thought we were meetin' them in Glasgow, like, y'know. Y'wont tell them it was me will yer?'

'Let me ask y'this, Moo. How much money y'got on yer?'

'I haven't got any money on me, Scull.'

'There y'are then. I haven't got any neither.'

'But . . . but they said y'didn't have t'pay f'y'donkey rides up there. They said it's free an' y'can get pullovers cheap an' all.'

I got hold of his hand just as he was ready to thumb another lorry and I picked up our Tony's holdall and lifted up his Tesco bag for him. A pair of undies and his football kit, poor sod. I turned him around and put his bag over his wrist and let it slide down to his elbow and we walked back towards the East Lancs Road. On the other side of the lights was a sign saying 'M6, Wolverhampton and the South'. I made my mind up I'd be standing there one day, and once I'd done that, I decided to give her till Tuesday and then, fuck it, I'd go and see her. Nothing as good as that was going to slip through my hands. Not without a fight. No chance.

'They made me do it y'know,' Mooey said.

'It's alright—'

'I didn't want to, but they said—'

'Forget it, Mooey. Just get a move on, will you.'

'Er, like, where we going?'

'Home.'

'I thought y'wanted to see the Dogs?'

'Knowin' them, I'll see them soon enough.'

'But er . . . wha' about the donkey islands?'

'Y'don't really want t'go there, Mooey.'

'Don't I?'

'No.'

'Oh, okay. But er why're we goin' home?'

'We're goin' home t'face the music, Moo.'

'Arrey, do we have to?' he said. 'I don't like dancin'.'

THE END